DATE DUE

| | | | |
|---|---|---|---|
| MAY 18 1996 | MAY 27 1997 | | |
| July 8, 1996 | | | |
| | JUL 31 1997 | | |
| SEP 13 1996 | NOV 10 1998 | | |
| OCT 15 1996 | MAY 09 2002 | | |
| NOV 07 1996 | MAY 26 2015 ILL | | |
| DEC 03 1996 | | | |
| DEC 18 1996 | | | |
| FEB 04 1997 | | | |
| FEB 19 1997 | | | |
| APR 23 1997 | | | |

894 Dix
562-1527
781-3390

# A Perfect Silence

Alba Ambert



Arte Público Press
Houston, Texas
1995

This volume is made possible through grants from the National Endowment for the Arts (a federal agency), the Lila Wallace-Reader's Digest Fund, and the Andrew W. Mellon Foundation.

*Recovering the past, creating the future*

Arte Público Press
University of Houston
Houston, Texas 77204-2090

Cover design by Kathryn Vosburg-Seretti
Original art "La Tormenta" by GRONK

Ambert, Alba
A perfect silence / by Alba Ambert.
p. cm.
ISBN 1-55885-125-9
I. Title.
PS3551.M23P47 1995
813'.54—dc20 94-29360
CIP

The paper used in this publication meets the requirements of the American National Standard for Permanence of Paper for Printed Library Materials Z39.48-1984. ♾



Sections of this book have been published as "Dusks" in *The Americas Review*, Vol. 17, No. 2, 1989, and "Losses" in *The Americas Review*, Vol. 21, Nos. 3 & 4, 1993.

Also by the author

The Mirror Is Always There (poetry)
Habito tu nombre (poetry)
The Fifth Sun (poetry)
Porque hay silencio (novel)
Every Greek Has a Story (oral history)
Gotas sobre el columpio (poetry)

To my mother Isabel,
who perished in the shantytown,
and to Yanira, who escaped.

*Desde adentro.*
*Desde el fondo de todo lo inevitable.*
*Desde el sollozo en espiral de espadas.*
*Desde la rama trágica*
*de un silencio perfecto.*

Julia de Burgos

# A Perfect Silence

# 1

Convinced that death is darkness, I want to be sure. Black and still all memories sponged clean. I swallow the pills one by one. I gulp and pause holding the heaves down. Gulp, gag, pause. Ten of the forty lie on my lap, and my stomach shrinks like a fist. Thick bubbles clog my throat, so I wait a moment. When I take the last one, my tongue is chalky and my mouth floods with thin saliva. It strikes me then that, like Kafka's night, darkness is not dark enough. So I creep into bed and slip a black sleeping mask over my eyes. I shiver under the blanket and curl toward the wall. Darkness slips into me.

The ambulance howled as it breasted through the haze of solitary Cambridge streets. Plunged in a dark dream, I knew nothing of the battle that strangers in white waged to make me live when I wanted to die.

Just before dawn, I swim out of the dream with the bitter taste of charcoal deep in my throat. I lift my sluggish head and see a room stuffed with smoky shadows. A wire fastens my chest to a small beeping machine. I scan the room slowly, trying to make sense of the white sheet, the IV plugged into a vein, the trim night stand with a thermometer and a plastic bed pan.

I am still alive.

I sigh, and my head falls back, heavy and inert. But why? I had been so careful to make it work this time. Even had a chunk of Italian bread and some whole milk before, though I was not hungry. Why am I alive then? Unless Dante was mistaken and there is a fourth circle with beeping monitors. I try to get up and run, somewhere, anywhere. Instead, nausea creeps up my throat. I shudder and feel a scratchiness in my teeth. I poke dark waters and feebly drift away. Gossamer threads stitch my eyelids tight with sleep.

When I wake up, misty shadows gather heavily in the folds of the room. I am here. Where have I come from? My throat, dry as sun-drenched paper, crackles when I swallow. Something is burning in my chest. A thought crushes my head like a vise. *Time is but a...*I lose the thought then pick it up again—*a...a...slowly slowly falling heavy with sleep darkness...*—but lose it once more. What is it, the taunting blur, the hint of thought that fleetingly lights up and then vanishes before I can hold on to it? A haunting, hollow glimpse, an understanding that cannot be remembered.

My mind moves on. Then I remember. I try to move again, but in a surprising act of insubordination, my arm refuses to obey. I stare at the arm in dismay as it lies dead on my abdomen. I wait and sleep and sleep and wait and forget that I wait. A nurse brushes against the bed, takes my pulse and temperature. After checking the IV drip, she leaves quietly.

The thermometer gleams. I grasp the hard thin glass and snap it in half on the edge of the night stand. Mercury drips from the slender stem as I dig deeply into my wrist. I have no further strength to repeat the act and drop the thermometer on the floor. The monitor beeps steadily. I see the blood spilling in a hot dark circle on the sheet. The room swallows its outrage.

A dog's bark whips through the air. In the background, the melody of a distant piano drips notes of quiet sadness. The distant bark echoes in my weary temples. I search and search in my mind, but cannot recognize the relentless barking. Shadows hang on my eyelashes like fronds of cobwebs, and in a blind fragment of the brain, a memory beckons with enticing fingers. The memory is not clear, but reeks of an atavistic sadness, passive for centuries. The piano notes tremble nostalgically. I bend my head to the distant tune with the faraway awareness I have when I trace the steady drip of water spilling from eaves, or when soreness aches in my breasts every month. I am uneasy, restless. I find no word to name this anxiety. The piano grieves. The dog barks. I flick away the tears.

External voices bear deep down into my consciousness like rusty nails. Words crush together, voices tightly knit. A roar races through my head and I hear my name mentioned.

"Where's Blanca?" someone asks.

"Saw her in her room a while ago," the other voice says.

I lie still. Quiet. Small. Like a still quiet sparrow watching a hawk rake the sullen sky. Studiously examining the gray topography of the ceiling, I try to still the dissonant voices in the hall, the squeak of the medicine trolley, the din of automobiles outside, and the solitary dog barking arcane warnings. I dive under the pillow. In the darkness, the voice of my own mind offers no peace.

"What're you doing lying there? You've got an appointment, you know." The tall nurse stands arms akimbo, sternly scrutinizing the room for possible infractions to the rules of the institution.

"I'm not seeing anyone," I respond tendentiously.

"Come on, up you go. Can't lie in bed all day. It's not therapeutic. If you cooperate with us, we'll cooperate with you."

I do not appreciate the veiled threat. Imagining the thick dossier they keep, neatly annotated by staff and doctors, I decide to attend the scheduled session with the psychiatrist. If I don't cooperate, they could hold me in the hospital beyond the prescribed confinement period. I feel a clutch of fear and get out of bed.

As the nurse escorts me down the east wing, I glance into the other rooms. They are all the same, permeated by the singular odor of sick flesh. It reminds me of the scent of dead flowers mingled with sweat, semen, wet soil. The intense odor of disappointment. Did I smell too? The thought strikes abruptly, and with sudden concern, I stick my nose in an armpit and sniff.

Nose under armpit, I nearly bump into Nina, an old woman who bellows in the hall brandishing a cane against imaginary provocations. As soon as Nina arrived at the hospital, she staked out her claims. On the first day, she appropriated the chair at the head of the dining room table. If some unsuspecting patient sat in Nina's place, a merciless shower of blows from the cane fell on the victim's back. On the second day, the old woman claimed one of the shower stalls. Although she often forgot what it was she had claimed, by the end of the first week, everyone was tiptoeing around her. Now, she protects her bit of the corridor, just outside her room, with vehemence.

"What the hell are you people doing here? Out! Out, I say!" she yells.

I quickly measure the space required to squeeze by Nina's territory without encountering the calamities of her cane. The nurse quickens her step, and without a word, points a finger at Nina. Fear flickers in Nina's eyes for a second and she drops the cane to her side. I sidle past Nina and glance over my shoulder apprehensively.

The nurse presses my arm.

"Wait here while I bring this file to the office, Blanca."

I drift past the nurses' station and catch a glimpse of Ursula curled up in the narrow bed of her gloomy room. A private nurse reads a newspaper under a spot of light coming in from the window. The room has a faint smell of chemicals and urine. Ursula stirs, and the nurse flashes a cautious glance in her direction. Ursula sits up suddenly, tossing her blankets away as though they were on fire. Her face is contorted with fear and rage as she stammers incoherently. She leaps out of bed, clutching at her nightgown and kneels before the statue of the Virgin Mary by her nightstand. Her hands are clasped tightly together.

"Forgive me, Virgin Mary, please forgive my acts of despicable vileness. Oh, please, I beg of you."

Shaking uncontrollably, Ursula sobs and puts her hands to her face. The private nurse tries to pull her up from the floor, and Ursula turns to her, full of hostility.

"Leave me alone, you traitor. I know the tales you've been telling my husband. And...and God, about me. Why're you on his side? Tell me that! Don't you know he's a two-timing liar?"

"Your husband's a two-timer?" The nurse asks distractedly while she prompts Ursula to get into bed.

"Yes, God is. I married him because I trusted him. I believed all his promises, but he did evil things to me."

"Who did?"

"My husband, God. He promised me daffodils. Lots of them. Even in the winter."

The private nurse expertly swings Ursula to face the wall, raises her nightgown and jabs her with a tranquilizer.

"I'm from Siberia and he doesn't believe it." Ursula crosses herself many times, mumbling Hail Marys.

The private nurse turns away from Ursula's bed. A flicker of distaste crosses her face when she sees me. She shuts the door. I press my forehead to the door and feel a hand on my shoulder. The nurse has returned with several folders under an arm and nudges me across the common room to another long corridor.

At the door to the psychiatrist's office, I brush my forehead and eyelids with the tips of my fingers. Sluggishness settles deeply in my eyes. The nurse looks at me with indifference. "I'll pick you up when you're finished," she says crisply and walks away.

I enter a spacious office with two cushioned armchairs. The desk is at a right angle to a leather couch. Several abstract paintings spill vibrant colors on the white walls. Books cram the shelves. Dr. Hackson sits in his usual armchair near the desk and greets me with a slight inclination of the head. He is a man of few words, I have discovered. I cross the expanse of blue carpet and sit in the armchair near the window. I am glad the drapes are not drawn. I face the window and examine the gray sky beyond its barless clarity.

"How're you today?" Dr. Hackson asks as he scrawls in his notebook.

I tip my head back and look at the freshly painted ceiling. It does not offer the interesting topography of cracks and peeling paint I can leisurely explore in my room. I read the book titles lined behind the doctor's chair.

I try to say something, but cough instead. I construct words in my mind and attempt to attach them to the voice that clamors in my darkness. I hear the man say something. What was it? What did he say? What am I going to respond? Well, it depends on what he said. But what did he say? What did he say? Desperately, I blurt the first thought I can attach to words.

"Everything that is, is, either in itself, or in something else." Jesus, I hadn't read Spinoza since Philosophy 101. Where did that come from?

Dr. Hackson looks at me and says, "Oh?"

"Well," I plunge on, what else could I do? "I'm not sure that what is, is. And how can I know what is without looking at what was." I fidget and try to arrange my face into soft lines that will hide my anxiety.

"I'm not explaining it right. I'll try again. I think that maybe by going back, way back, to the beginning, and then working my way from there to the present, to what is, maybe I'll find a way of understanding who I am and maybe why I am."

"What comes to mind when you think about that?"

"Think about what?"

"What you were just saying."

"What did I say?" I eye him suspiciously.

"You said you want to understand who you are and why you are, as you put it."

I look out the window again. Where am I going with all of this? I'm not very coherent today. Will he consider it a sign of madness? My heart thumps like a drum. I can feel myself become agitated. The room is quiet and serene. I breathe it in to calm myself and slowly exhale.

"I've always tried not to remember things. To move on without looking back. It was the only way to survive, I thought. But then, here I am, not doing too well despite the slate I tried so hard to erase."

I gaze at the elm tree beyond the window.

It all served a purpose, I suppose. If I had looked back, even once, I would have failed to see where I wanted to go. I had to stifle memories so there would be room to hope. I needed to see clearly ahead in order to believe that there really was a path leading me away from my labyrinth of hurt. A path leading to something better. And I did it. I became the someone I thought I wanted to be. Then, just as I was beginning to accomplish things, I was overwhelmed by a sense of loss. Little things started getting to me. When people asked me about my parents, about the past I had tried to obliterate, I realized that I could not really live without a past. That memory is important after all.

I slide to the edge of the chair.

"Maybe it's time to go back to the beginning and everything that came afterwards. Try to make some sense of my past, reconstruct it so I can deal with it somehow. Try to understand my world instead of erasing it."

The psychiatrist bends over his notebook. Was he taking notes or composing letters? Who knows? I gaze at the gray sky again.

Patterns repeat themselves over and over in the life of a person. Episodes of betrayal, loss, madness, cruelty, death, seem to recur, again and again, like themes in a symphony. I am flooded by the power of these patterns and forget the sequence of events that make the patterns not only possible, but the essence of my life.

I try hard to remember, and heavy with memories of what I never saw and of what I saw but had forgotten, I hold a balled fist to my mouth and reel back, far back, into the bent curve of time.

# 2

She was born in El Fanguito, in an *arrabal*, a shantytown, in San Juan. *Fanguito* is the diminutive of mud. That was where she was born: in the mud, not even a full-fledged mud, mind you, a diminished one. So she was a shantytowner, an *arrabalera*. Or she still is. She did not know whether she could ever peel herself from the circumstances of birth. She thought she was still an *arrabalera*, though she was not sure. She wished it were as romantic as it sounded in tangos. She had taken great pains to don the accouterments of normalcy. She did not dress like a shantytowner, but she was. She could not scrub it off. It was not easy to escape the accident of birth. But she tried. Even got an education. She had trekked long and hard to escape El Fanguito.

Blanca reconstructed her mother's life like a puzzle, from overheard conversations, things people told her. Her mother's name was Isabel. She was a shantytown-dwelling seamstress. Another *arrabalera*. Blanca's father, Ramón, was a milkman and a skirt chaser. He was not a good provider, so Isabel worked in the shirt factory across from the bus stop, at Parada 20. Every morning she crossed the fetid mud channels, climbing hills, threading through familiar alleys. On Fernández Juncos Avenue, she bought a penny's worth of bread for lunch. Her long black braid swept from side to side like a pendulum, and she entered with the factory whistle to melt into the production line. In the evenings she returned to the crate-and-carton boarded shack, her back split with pain, carrying in her handbag bread crumbs and an envelope of sweat. But her envelope was quickly assaulted by the grasping hands of the shopkeeper, the loan shark, the spiritualist. After feeding the exploiting hands, she sat in her caned rocking chair and felt the vigorous kicks of the infant swelling inside her. While she waited for Ramón, a rancid candle scrawled her shadow on the walls of the squalid shack. In the hardscrabble barrio, he strutted into other women's beds, swollen with conceit like a pigeon's chest, while she waited.

Life and death tangled among the dwellers of the pestilent shantytown. Darkness teetered suspiciously over the spindly-legged huts. The shacks were like old women hiking their skirts as they stood in mud, stiff with muck. Shadows sagged into scruffy silhouettes. A solitary boy ran barefoot, hopping from board to board, careful not to fall in the mud. A dog barked, hoarse from years of chasing ghosts.

While Isabel waited for her husband, an angry harpoon dug into her deepest bower. The pain, white as steel, kicked up into her chest. She could hardly breathe. Her chest was blue with hurt, her cough red with blood. She called the boy who hopped in the shadows and sent him to fetch Doña Luz, the shantytown midwife. Isabel did not scream when the pain stabbed her center with the anger of a vengeful god. She bit her lips when she pushed, but she did not scream.

Doña Luz, a slight middle-aged woman with a yellow kerchief wrapped around her head, rushed into the shack. She washed her hands in a tin basin and folded a sheet over Isabel's knees. When she concluded the examination, she wiped perspiration from her brow and frowned.

"We've got to take you to the hospital, the kid's coming buttocks first."

"No," Isabel gasped. "Never!"

"Why not? Listen to me, Isabel. You're a small woman; this child'll rip you apart. It's coming the wrong way. I tell you, I can't do this."

"My enemies, my enemies are listening," Isabel moaned.

"What're you talking about? Enemies, enemies, what silliness has gotten into you?"

"The spiritualist told me that they put a curse on me. I won't give them the pleasure of seeing me like this. Never! Do you hear me? If you won't help me, as God is my witness, I'll do it alone."

"All right, all right, don't get excited. I'll do what I can. Try to relax. It'll be a while still." She dabbed the pain- battered woman with a wet rag.

Time dragged on. The implacable pain hacked Isabel's flesh. She begged under her breath, lying in a puddle of sweat, to God, the saints, the Blessed Virgin. They remained deaf and immutable witnesses. She arched like a cat and plunged her chest into her back, tore her throat pushing pushing pushing, oh, God almighty, so hard, so very hard, but still she could not push the infant out. She fell back on her pillow, dead tired, lathered in sweat, but flames lapped at her insides. Her uterus writhed and punched, forcing her into more tortuous pushing. Again and again. She pushed harder and harder, her eyes white as foam. Pain whorled through her insides. She had never known such agony. She pushed for a whole day and the eternity of a dark night. Her bloodless fists wrung the edges of the sheet. Doña Luz nudged a rolled rag between her teeth. A groan, thick and spongy and wet, choked her taut throat when, ripping her vagina like a veil, Blanca was thrust out, buttocks first, back turned to the world, not wanting to see what she had so insistently tried to avoid.

Isabel named the child in honor of her favorite singer who sang romantic, hypnotic melodies that deadened her awareness of reality. Blanca had later heard the plaintive songs of

Blanca Rosa Gil many times. She understood they had helped Isabel ease the pain of the shantytown, her hovel, her unfaithful husband, the ache clutching at her ribs. With the songs in her mind, Isabel ignored the rale in her chest when she walked or sat or lay down. She forgot the tightness in her lungs, her cough-ridden insomnia. She forgot to remember the scarlet spit that stained her white handkerchief.

When Ramón saw Blanca for the first time, his only comment before walking out was that she looked like a tadpole. After giving birth, Isabel was too weak to work, so he gave her money every week for the sustenance of the child he preferred not to see. Isabel never complained, never visited a doctor, only the shantytown spiritualist, the physician of the poor, who prepared medicinal droughts to root out the spell that everyone said had been cast on her.

I notice a change in Dr. Hackson's breathing. He slips into a stupor and, abruptly, his chin drops to his chest. He jerks his head up, looks at me sheepishly and coughs weakly. I look out the window again. The day is hard as flint.

The same aroma of patchouli that haunts me in the mornings wafts in from somewhere in the past and rouses a distinct landscape in my dark memory. I can hear myself, baby-voiced, wailing in the night.

Ma-mi-ta. Ma-miiiiii-ta. Ma-miiiiiiii-ta. The child's cries punctured the night. On all fours, she rocked to the rhythm of her own voice, eyes and fists clenched tightly. She missed the sweet scent of bread on her mother's fingers, the pillowy warmth of her breasts, her soft voice humming her to sleep. Her brain could not understand the absence of a being that was part of her being. It was like the absence of air, of arms. Without her, how could she see the world? How could she gallop over alleys or listen to the beat of life in her chest? How could she crawl under her mother's skin to see the universe through her eyes? It was an incomprehensible disappearance. Her thoughts formulated questions when she registered the absence, the want, the need. Questions without words. Turbulent emotions uprooted her soul. Silence and loneliness roared like an empty shell. The absence was raw pain.

Then voices settled in her, piercing, intruding. "Your mother's with God now," they said in their black dresses, and the child knew that they lied. The sun was sharp that day. It could have been any month in the endless summer of Puerto Rico. The child ran into every nook and crawled under the dusty haze of her mother's cot. Where could she be? How could she breathe or talk or eat if not with her? How could she see without her eyes? She had only known herself through her. How could she breathe or talk or eat if she was gone? Eyes stitched like wounds, the child cried until they took her away in a black bundle.

Maybe she witnessed her mother's death and that is why she will always wonder about silence. Who knows? Aunty Andrea took her in. She was Isabel's aunt and very old.

Blanca sat in Aunty Andrea's lap in the afternoons when the sun was too hot to play outside and dust lay dry as dead bones and just as quiet. Sometimes a dog barked or a confused cock sprung a weary crow. She felt content in the woman's big lap. Aunty Andrea licked her middle finger and turned the pages of her Bible as she mumbled the lines slowly. At times she lifted a page and, with her thumbs, divided it in two. Miraculous, Blanca wondered, how she could create new pages this way. Blanca slept to her mumbles until heavy feet slapped against the bare wooden floor and she ran and squatted under the shack with the chickens until the pounding feet were heard on the creaky wooden steps and dust rose on the road. It was Aunty Andrea's son. Blanca has since forgotten his name. Later, Aunty Andrea would call Blanca, Blanquita, and she knew there would be peace.

At night he staggered into the shack. When he did not see the girl, he did not remember her. But if he returned early or rose from his bed before she escaped, he would have his sport. Aunty Andrea was afraid of him, too. She would wait until he left or slept to pull out a wooden crate she hid under her bed. In it she stored tiny tins of unguents, a eucalyptus alcohol she concocted herself, a framed Saint Jude and her Bible. Every night before they climbed into bed, she mumbled to the picture and crossed herself many times. On a bad day, she would pry a tin open and anoint Blanca's bruises. The cigarette burns required more extensive treatment, so she combed the fields at dawn for black calabash leaves, and after crushing them, she patted them on the girl's blistered skin while mumbling prayers and warnings.

The Arecibo village shone in the noon heat when a rare automobile lifted its gravel-filled voice on the dirt road and crunched to a stop. Shoeless, bare-buttocked children gathered round the long dusty car. A big man sprung from the dust. Squatting under the shack with the chickens, Blanca saw his heavy shoes approach. Many feet pounded above her, some with the sharp edge of shoes, others muted. Then she heard Aunty Andrea call "Blanca, Blanquita."

The man looked vaguely familiar. He slurped black coffee from the only glass cup in their possession. It was white with pink flowers. Aunty Andrea drank from a tin can. Her son sat on his cot and smoked. "So this is the girl. She's getting big," the man said. "What's the matter, don't you recognize your own father?" Years later he told Blanca this story many times with some degree of resentment. Why he would resent her lack of recognition, she would never understand, but for some reason he thought she owed him her life. He said he would take her for a ride in the long, dusty car. Liar, liar. Blanca loved cars, their speed, their deep rumblings, the hot wind blowing her hair back, the acrid smell of gasoline. She kissed Aunty Andrea hastily not knowing she would never see her again.

She cried that night for her and cried for days and many nights afterwards. "Where are we going?" she asked her father and he responded cryptically. She wondered what a new york was.

Aunty Andrea would certainly know. She knew many things. She knew the mysteries of the full moon and the evil eye, and she could interpret the neat marks in a book. She would look up at the sky, eyes squinting, and say a storm is brewing, and the thick air would roll away. The sky would darken, mumbling louder than Aunty Andrea, and the wild winds would climb the steps and rush into the shack through wooden boards, jostling the kerosene lamps. The rain would clatter on the zinc roof and spill through the rafters like an angry mob. Aunty Andrea would scurry about with the buckets and pans and rags she had prepared. Because she knew.

That was a long time ago, another life. I have lived so many lives since then I sometimes feel trapped between mirrors. I look down at my hands and squeeze my fingers.

"It's time," Dr. Hackson says briskly. Now that he's fully awake, he says something else. Some kind of advice. I get up with some uncertainty. Having traveled so far back unloosening my neatly tied past, I feel bewildered when brought back to a place that is now alien to me. The doctor's words swirl in my head. I look out the window to escape what he says.

I hear a dry rap at the door. The doctor says something else as I walk out. Some kind of advice. I wave his words away with a long sweep of my hand.

# 3

Morning shadows drape the hospital common room in gray. A streak of light slices the darkness into slivers. A figure stands in a corner. I recognize the crest of Miguel's spiky hair. His bright eyes sink into the darkness of his black shirt as he dips his head forward and I know he has not slept. The dull morning light grazes him, and he staggers to another dark corner, and another, until none are left and he stands awkwardly stark, blinking in the light.

Miguel spots me and walks over, holding a set of earphones in his fist, a portable tape player clipped to his belt.

"How ya doin', Blanca?"

"Hello, Miguel. Everything okay?"

"Not bad, not bad. Didn't know you were an artista."

"I'm not, but sitting around doing nothing is not therapeutic."

"Yeah," he smiles. Then he glances around the room and lowers his voice conspiratorially. "You know why we're in here, don't you?"

"What do you mean?"

"It's the man. He wants to keep us locked up one way or another. We're suspicious of shrinks and stay away from them when we can. It kinda helps not to speak English. Makes them stay away from us, too. But when they catch us, they lock us up for a real brain-burning. That's the way it is, you know?"

Miguel glances over his shoulder.

"It's part of the game, man. You know, less than white is bad for you. And we fall for it. You know, I met a Puerto Rican guy once who had a Confederate flag sticker on his windshield. Jesus! But, I tell you, we're lucky not to be in the state mental hospital, that's really the pits. It's where they put most of us. I was there when my father wouldn't let me use his health insurance to come to a private clinic. Wanted to teach me a lesson. But I went real crazy. They treated us bad. Man, these people treat their dogs better. A bro' found a rusty can in the yard and cut his wrists open one night. That's when I freaked out, man."

"Why were you in?"

"Alcohol, drugs, a lotta drugs. Then, I don't know what got into me, some kinda bad feeling, and I tried to kill myself." He pauses and starts fumbling with his earphones, pretending to be distracted. "Couldn't sleep last night either. Don't know how much longer I can hold out. These jerks won't give me a sleeping pill. You give 'em to everyone else, I says. They wanna clean my system, they says. Man, but I can't sleep."

With this, Miguel plugs in his earphones and sets off to pace across the common room. He nods constantly, affirming the beat of the music with his pineapple-spiked head. My Uncle Liberato had hair like that and also spent a life nodding, not to music as Miguel did, but to a world that went on only in his head.

Madness: one of the patterns in Blanca's life. She met her great uncle Liberato on her return to Puerto Rico at the age of 12. Every first of the month she boarded the bus to Ponce de León Avenue and Parada 19. From there she walked down to El Fanguito carrying a grocery bag brimming with country eggs, a pound of coffee, yucca, avocados and other fruit and vegetables, and ten dollars in her pocket for Mamá Paula, Blanca's paternal great grandmother.

Mamá Paula was 97 and lived in a rented shack with her son Liberato. He could not bear the sight of shoes or belts, so he was always barefoot and secured his trousers with twine. He spent his days squatting on the floor drawing angles with his tall thin frame while he cursed the woman responsible for his insanity with all the vile words in his repertoire. Everyone said the woman he cursed had cast a spell on him. Except for his curses, Liberato was calm.

On the only occasion when he was possessed by a paroxysm of anger and distress, he was young and strong. Ignited by the fury of whatever passion lurked in him, he stomped outside and rocked the shack where he lived with Mamá Paula again and again, like a hurricane. Mamá Paula screamed and ran out of the rocking shack as he proffered strings of colorful obscenities. Neighborhood men subdued him and dragged him to a mental institution. The insane asylum was so crowded, Liberato escaped without anyone noticing his absence. He returned home to Mamá Paula. Humiliated by the horrors he suffered at the institution, he was tame for the rest of his life.

When Blanca visited, Liberato always asked her the same question:

"You're Ramón's girl, aren't you?"

Blanca nodded, and Liberato smiled, satisfied by the affirmation of what he remembered and, except for his cursing, remained silent for the rest of the visit.

Mamá Paula brewed coffee with a thick cone-shaped sock hung from a circular wire which extended out into a long handle. She stirred the dark aromatic coffee grains in the water that boiled on a table-top kerosene stove. When a thick brown foam floated to the surface, she poured the mixture through the conical sock into a large tin can. The smell was sweet and strong, like honey. She boiled milk and sifted it through a small wire strainer to remove the thick seamed skin that collected on the surface. She served Blanca in a pink plastic cup reserved for visitors.

When not squatting on the floor hurling obscenities, Liberato vigorously engaged in cleaning the shack. He wet a large rag in a metallic barrel they kept outside to collect rainwater, and wiped the floor boards. Then he rinsed the rag several times, making sure all the dust was removed, and wrung it with his long skinny hands. Finally, he wiped the floor dry. Once the floor was dry to his satisfaction, he repeated his actions until the voices in his head became louder and louder and he was forced to squat on the floor and resume his cursing.

Blanca loved Liberato. A mad man with a turbulent past, entangled in shadows only he could discern, he had escaped the harshness of the poor man's never-ending and meaningless life of work. There was something romantic, Blanca mused, in the fulfillment of his destiny, something tender in his remembrance of the mysterious woman he cursed constantly. A woman who remained alive in his hate, which was probably the other side of love.

I can still hear a dog barking in the distance and I shudder. I sit in a corner of the common room, away from the other patients, and start to draw with colored pencils, biting my lower lip. I sketch quickly. Figures hiding in the branches of a despondent willow, bloody members dripping on purple blades of grass. I need time to think. But I have no use for the thoughts that appear suddenly, without my wanting them, and subject me to their dissonance. I want to capture those thoughts without meaning, words, names, phrases and by taming them, make them mine.

"Lunch time." Miguel's voice startles me. "Saved you a chair away from the old lady," he says.

Patients have their meals at a long table. All except Ursula, who is usually heavily drugged and rarely eats with the others. Nina sits at the head of the table, the position she has claimed, and pounds the floor with her cane.

"What kinda junk is this?" she bellows, the loose skin in her upper arm trembling.

Her full-blown bluster pours from a tiny mouth sunk like a hole in her face. Forever mourning losses, she only wears widow's weeds. A conch comb holds a bun at the nape of her thin neck. She grabs the arm of a white-clad orderly.

"I don't wanna eat this junk, do you hear me? Whatta you think I am, a cow? Feeding me grass like this?" Nina sweeps a hand over the table, and her plate shatters on the floor. Lettuce sodden with French dressing clings to the orderly's white uniform. Two male nurses rush from the office and drag Nina away.

When Nina's last bellow echoes and dies, the dining room slumps into silence. The patients look intently at their trays and earnestly spread butter on their bread rolls, slice the grayish meat of indistinct identity, and chew and swallow deliberately. Debra stares at the skeins of noodles on her plate in evident distress. When Silvia starts stirring her coffee frantically, making ringing sounds as the spoon hits the cup, only Miguel does not look up. He avoids at all costs contact with the eyes of others. I understand his reluctance. In the wounded eyes of others, he sees his own pain duplicated.

In this thin wedge of existence, a scalable barrier exists between madness and sanity. Some remain straddled between the two. Others make periodic incursions to the alienated world, returning sporadically to breathe the air of normal people, which before long repulses them and sends them back to the refuge of their private worlds. Some, like me, remain at the edge of madness, tempted constantly by its promises of forgetfulness and relief. Many navigate to the edenic and infernal land forever, their minds swept clean of their most painful memories, yet their brains cluttered with odds and ends like a century-old attic.

Miguel wolfs his food down with singularity of purpose. He stares at his empty plate and rubs his fingertips together to remove some bread crumbs. I pick at the food and finally pass my plate to Miguel who gratefully eats the leftovers. When he finishes, I put the tray on the counter and hurry out of the dining room before Castule, the resident pyromaniac, begins pushing his dentures out with his tongue as he does after every meal, rhythmically clacking them in and out.

Back in the common room, I find that sketching surrealistic figures is not at all soothing, so I try to construct words. I spin thoughts in my head but cannot name them. For many nights now I wake up at midnight with the echoes of words ringing in my mind. Later, when the day is heavy with ennui, the words hide in a distant fold of the brain. I stare at the blank sheet of paper and suck on the ballpoint pen. Thoughts anchor me once more in the present. I am not crazy all the time. Only when I want to escape. Only when its perfection and silence draw me inexorably into the calm waters of madness or the definitive peace of death.

# 4

One could say that a big word precipitated Blanca's suicide attempt. Though, of course, it was nothing as trivial as that. Despondency had been corroding her slowly, almost imperceptibly. She kept the chill in her heart a secret that was never to be revealed. She appeared to be content, calm. Women are adept at everything that is hidden. She locked herself in her bedroom for her episodes of weeping and wringing of the hands and went through the days feeling outside of herself, like a ghostly spectator of her own life.

Then one night, the immensity of all her losses crushed her, and all she saw was a trail of loss. She could walk back along that trail and retrace the life she had lived through all her losses. They hovered like ghosts, insubstantial, in a void. Their absence an eloquent reminder of what lay behind her as she moved on, faster and faster, stretching the distance between her past and what might have been a future. She had no present as she raced through the spectrum of days and weeks and months and years, rushing to days without tomorrows.

The powdery sands of her island slipped away like a dream. Somewhere along the way, she lost the sweetness of ripe plantains on her tongue and the snap of tin roofs settling in the hot sun. Because she lost her mother there, her first and most devastating loss, she had lived a life of exile in gray cities of unforgiving geometries. Because no degree of triumph could ever compensate for that loss, she always managed to turn success into hurt and accomplishments into burdens.

Then she lost her childhood. That seemed to be the way with her. One loss led to another. And another. At some point it became a habit and she started losing things, important things like the ring someone gave her as a token of love. The engraved pen her friends presented her with at a celebration dinner when she got her graduate degree. The skirt purchased with her first paycheck and worn like a talisman whenever she ventured into potentially hostile territory. Her biography was written with a chain of lost objects.

And she lost memories. Dark gaps punctured like flesh wounds, holes gaping at what she could not possibly remember. Entire years were wiped out like a wrong answer on a slate. And she would never know the right answer. Then, having climbed the wall of exile, unable to turn back, she ceased to own the recognizable, and was lost to herself.

When she finally understood this, the realization was not sudden. It came with time, after the losses were heaped up like bones in a common grave. After the guilt and the rage. Until she finally longed for the ultimate loss, the loss that would end all losses. Nothing mattered then, but the overpowering wish to die. Her young daughter, her students, the life she had made for herself. Nothing existed but her unbearable pain and her need to end it.

The day had started as usual with the public radio newscaster chirping at six on the dot. As always. And as always, Blanca woke up heart pounding in her throat. Waking up was discovering a stranger in her bed. Then she realized it was she who was the stranger, and she felt an odd sense of relief, for a while at least. That morning she hauled her stiff body out of bed, eyes clotted with sleep. She spat the gluey taste of nightmares into the bathroom sink and pointedly avoided her reflection in the mirror. Mirrors should always be ignored early in the morning, she thought, certainly before the first cup of coffee. She stood at the kitchen window like a sunflower in search of light. A familiar smell she could not recognize awoke a smoky landscape in her memory: An elusive warren of pebbled roads crowded with jerry-built shacks teetering in a thick marsh. The air redolent of sewage, haze, head-clinging kerosene, and kidney beans simmering in coriander and tomato sauce. It was the texture of silent smells that she remembered, for she remembered no sounds. Not even words.

The soft tick of the kitchen clock nudged her back. It was time to wake up Taína and make sure she was ready for school before the bus came. Then she had to go to work.

The high school where she worked as a bilingual teacher was a massive brick structure, a thick blot of indistinct architecture. Squatting on a barren hill, it stared sullenly at the pale Boston neighborhood in the muted light. The term bilingual teacher was a misnomer. She taught history and civics in Spanish to students who had recently arrived from Puerto Rico, the Dominican Republic, and Central America. The school was defined by misnomers. Black, Latino, and Asian students were bused in for integration purposes. So many white students had fled, though, it was just another segregated school. The bilingual teachers' office was really a large closet in the basement used to store textbooks and school supplies. There were no desks or chairs. Every morning the four bilinguals, as they were called, huddled under the bare bulb while the bilingual coordinator gave them the day's directives.

When Blanca walked into the first-period classroom—bilingual teachers had no permanently assigned rooms; they used whatever rooms were free—she could feel a migraine coming. She remembered dreaming that she swallowed cat fur and felt a lump in her stomach. She took a couple of Fiorinal and said *buenos días* to the students as they walked in. José fell asleep during a discussion of the doctrine of Manifest Destiny. Blanca hoped it was not a comment on her teaching.

"José," she said and tapped his shoulder. The class started giggling, delighted for the respite.

"Sorry, Miss Amaro, but I didn't get much sleep last night," he said sheepishly.

"Try to stay awake, José, and take a rest before you go to work tonight."

"Okay, but I was hearing everything you said, like in a dream. It's like those tapes you buy to learn things while you're sleeping. A person's mind never rests, you know."

"I'm certainly relieved to hear that. We were discussing the assigned reading for today that starts on page 136," Blanca continued, mustering as much enthusiasm as her migraine would allow.

The day's thick humid air pervaded everyone's mood. During Latin American History, Iris was engaged in serious woolgathering when Blanca asked her about Bolívar's dream. Iris recovered enough to comment that she would not be in school long enough to find out. Once when the students were asked to write a composition on what they wanted to be when they finished school, Iris had responded, in handwriting that was large, bold, and squiggly, like her earrings, "When I finish school I want to be nothing." Blanca made a mental note to talk to her later.

After third period, Moisés, one of the school's most promising students, came up to Blanca's desk. He was short and slender, with a wispy beard he cultivated caringly. Moisés was the only Latino in the state of Massachusetts enrolled in Calculus. This occurred after the complaints his crusading father lodged with an advocacy group bore fruit. Moisés lolled about the desk while Blanca collected her books and notes. When she looked up, he asked, "Miss Amaro, can I talk to you?"

"What's on your mind?"

"Mrs. Retamal said we would read Cervantes for Spanish lit. I got real excited, but then she gave us this baby book. I'm ashamed to be seen with it!"

He dug into his back pocket and produced a slender paperback. Blanca leafed through it, glanced at the many illustrations and the simplified Spanish and handed it back.

Moisés continued. "They think we're stupid. I don't want to read any baby book. I'm sixteen! Just because I don't speak English well doesn't mean I'm stupid." He looked mutinous.

"How are you doing in the rest of your classes?"

"I'm working hard. My father checks the backs of my thighs to see if I've been studying hard enough, you know."

"What do you mean?"

"If I have no hairs there it means I've been sitting and studying for a lot of hours. Believe me, the backs of my thighs are bald by now. But I'll never learn anything important if they don't give us harder books. This is stupid. All my life I wanted to read *Don Quixote*." His voice trailed away. "And Mrs. Retamal is always saying Puerto Ricans can't speak Spanish. Man, that makes me furious. She says the right word for orange is *naranja*, not *china*. Is *china* wrong?" he asked anxiously.

"Of course not. It's just that some people don't understand how words develop—the origin of words—called etymology. In Puerto Rico we call an orange *china* instead of *naranja*, because the orange was called *la fruta de la China* by the Spaniards. In Puerto Rico the fruit was called that for a while, but eventually the description was dropped and it was simply called *china*. So, it's all quite logical. By the way, the word *naranja* is of Arabic origin."

"Wow, that's great! Wait till I tell Mrs. Retamal. She's gonna flip."

"Borrow a genuine *Don Quixote* from the library. There's a Spanish literature section at the Jamaica Plain branch in your neighborhood. I'm not a literature expert, but we can discuss it together if you like."

"Yeah, I want to learn the big words, like you. What was that word you used, the one that means where words come from?"

"*Etimología*. Write it down, so you don't forget." She printed it on the chalk board.

"*Etimología*," he enunciated carefully as he copied. "Now that's a big word! I'm gonna try it on Mrs. Retamal, too. Hey, won't this get you in trouble with her?" he asked slyly. "You know, reading the real *Don Quixote* and helping me out with it?"

"Let me worry about that."

Moisés gave her a thumbs up and rushed to his next class.

Blanca massaged her temples gingerly and wondered what she was getting into. Not only was she engaging in pedagogical sabotage, but probably what was more daunting, she was grappling with the Knight of the Sorrowful Countenance, Don Quixote himself. It was hard enough to keep up with U.S. History, Latin American History, World History and Civics for her daily classes. But she had always been somewhat of a rebel. She ascribed it to an adolescence of dancing with doorknobs. Men had later accused her of leading when they danced, unable to grant her this modicum of control. But that was another story.

The day limped on sadly. The fourth was her free period. Free was another misnomer with all the grading, photocopying, and paperwork to be done. Free meant without teaching. Freedom was not having to teach. Now, that's an idea, she thought. During hall duty before Blanca's free period, she ran into Carmen Sánchez, the bilingual math teacher. The principal, Dr. McLaughlin, rushed by waving a minatory finger and yelled, "speak English, speak English," which succeeded in leaving them bereft of any speech.

"The English-only Gestapo strikes again," Carmen laughed when she recovered all her faculties. Blanca could not even roll her eyes to the ceiling on account of the migraine. "So much for free speech," she managed to say wearily.

She dragged a chair to the basement where she sat in the bilingual office. Wedged in the sarcophagus between shelves of science books and pencils, she graded the U.S. History quiz she gave every Friday.

She had detention duty, something she dreaded. Students she had never seen before—it was a big school—showed up with their detention slips and glowered at her before sitting down sullenly. The afternoon settled heavily, and through the frosted windows, she could see the first flutters of snow.

A fight broke out between a Vietnamese and a Puerto Rican. With great display of purpose so as not to be misinterpreted, Tran grazed Miguel's shoulder when he walked by his desk. Miguel shoved him, and before Blanca could intervene, they were rolling on the floor in a tight clinch. Students were always fighting over girls or because someone gave someone else a bad look. That was the excuse, but the squabbles were really territorial. Very little territory was left at the bottom of the heap, and everyone fought for it. There was no other choice. Falling out of the bottom was falling into oblivion. It was a crucial struggle.

Blanca kept this view to herself when she called Mr. Grody, the physical education teacher in charge of discipline problems. A former linebacker with a small head, ham-thick neck and fiercely overextended shoulders, he really was a cliché, the poor man. He also taught science to monolinguals, and his teaching method consisted of playing tape recordings on the functions of the heart or the structure of molecules, and having students copy while they listened. Exams were then based on the contents of the tapes, duly transcribed, correctly or incorrectly, by the students. Mr. Grody dragged Tran and Miguel off to the office for suspension proceedings. Blanca settled in her chair again—still had some of those U.S. History quizzes to grade—and surveyed the four taciturn boys sprawled in front of her. Legs splayed like dropped scissors, they defined their territory and drummed on their desks or stared at the ceiling.

On the way home, Blanca checked out a copy of *Don Quixote* at the library. On the train, she slid her handbag under an arm, held onto the swaying strap, and shoved her free hand in a pocket. One could never predict when a purse snatcher would strike. It was best to be alert. With her scant dollars neatly folded in a wallet, she would not make it easy for anyone to deprive her of her earnings. She could still remember her indigent student days when she survived on popcorn and strong black coffee. On special occasions she would splurge on a package of macaroni and cheese, only 53 cents a serving.

She slogged through the slush on the sidewalk. She felt threatened by the blanched sky, heavy with snow. Cars splashed and tore into the vault of mist that hung over the city. It was dark when she reached the apartment. Taína had left a note. She was at a neighbor's until dinner time.

Blanca flicked the light on, looked into the hallway mirror and realized that what was left was right and what was right was left. She was lost in the mirror's reversibility. Alice's wonderland mirror had depth; Blanca's was flat as boredom. Her features stared back starkly like a photograph under a spiteful klieg light. A shadow cut a line diagonally across one eye and climbed into darkness. When her eyes stared back, she knew that she would never again see the second glimpsed before it was devoured by that moment. She stepped back. A creepy intimacy lurked in the shadows. A painful spasm jabbed her neck and established its predominance like an insolent despot. She tried to shake it off and turned on the stereo. Brahms always soothed her with hints of melancholic rain over landscapes dappled with sheep. But not that evening. She sank into the cadence of pain. Fear drenched her. Nothingness seeped into her pores, eye sockets, nostrils, the slash between her legs. It entered her, corroded her blood, ravished her flesh, and she was left an empty shell. She felt nothing. She was nothing.

After dinner, Taína went into her room to talk on the phone. At twelve, she displayed the bold independence of children brought up by single working mothers. Blanca, who had sat at the dinner table just to keep Taína company, took more medication for her migraine and went straight to bed.

By midnight, Blanca was wide awake, feeling a terrible sense of foreboding. She stared into the darkness beyond the window. It seemed calmer out there where trees stirred idly in their beds of stone. Snow was falling briskly, softly. Feathery petals of white. The color of absolute silence.

Don Quixote waited on her night stand. She picked it up and spread it open. She could not see anything in the dark. But she did not have the energy to get up. It was hard to open a book and refrain from reading, though. Even when a book was in a foreign language, there seemed to be an intellectual imperative to read, to make sense out of symbols. That deep-rooted need to interpret symbols vanquished her inertia. She went to the living room and turned on the light. It glowed softly on the amber pages. She closed the book and examined its proud spine. Her fingers glided over the gilt-encrusted title. She examined the library flap glued to the inside of the back cover. The book had not been checked out in six years. It was a long time to wait. *Don Quixote*, the first modern novel, stranded like a beached boat. She moistened her lips and dipped into it, parting its petals gently, inhaling its fragrance of bruised oaks. She read the indomitable knight's lament,

> *So many strange things have befallen me in this castle that I dare not give any positive answer to any question asked me concerning anything in it. Perhaps you will be able to judge of the affairs of this castle as they really and truly are, and not as they appear to me.*

A gaunt Don Quixote muttering to himself, fearing a reality that unraveled reluctantly. He lost his truth to the truth of others. Blanca wondered what Moisés would think about the relative nature of reality. The ambiguity of all that is. Adolescents believe in absolutes, in the unerring reliability of the senses. Only during adolescence are people so certain of their beliefs, of the rightness of their perspectives. Adolescents know with the certainty worthy of a pope what is right and what is wrong. Black and white. Good and bad. Batman and Godzilla. The right strut, the wrong hairdo. The ability to find answers to all questions. Adolescents know, adults doubt. Could she possibly convey to Moisés the relativity of reality? How could she relate it to Moisés' circumstances, though? Of what relevance was Don Quixote to ghetto existence? Cervantes wrote about sorrow and the clash of conflicting ideals. The ghetto was sorrow and clash and conflict. She might be able to find the link, or more accurately, the threads that coil through diverse experiences and make them one. Was there a way of attaching meaning, a meaning Moisés could accept, to a fake knight's misadventures? Could she bear the burden of teaching Moisés the big words?

Inexplicably, an overwhelming sense of loss washed over her. She felt thrust into a deep, dark, pitch-black cave. Moisés, Taína, her friends, her work, her life, everything and everyone faded into oblivion. The endless night was a hole on the earth, and she fell into it. She was bitterly aware of existing, deep in the hole. I'm here. Where have I come from? she thought desperately. Tears never came, they stopped somewhere right behind her eyes, despite the most inconceivable pain.

She reached for the pills.

# 5

I sit across from Dr. Hackson. When life dies, I wonder, does death live? Does death live when life dies? I pull myself out of this train of thought that is leading me nowhere. And I think of something innocuous to say.

"Had another migraine yesterday."

"Why do you suppose that is?" Dr. Hackson asks.

"I don't know. Maybe I'm eating too much sugar."

"What do you really think about these frequent migraines?"

"I can't stand them anymore. I'm getting them every week now. The let's-go-to-the-hospital-for-a-Demerol-shot kind. But I'm already in a hospital, aren't I? Well, all they gave me was Tylenol. It won't even touch it. But...I don't know why I'm getting migraines."

"You may remember what you said to me the other day." He paused, weighing his words. "You said you felt shattered. Maybe your migraines are an indication of this feeling of being split apart."

I glance at him skeptically and proceed to study the palms of my hands. I am quiet for a while.

"I've been split apart many times. Passed around from hand to hand too often. So many people walked in and out of my life; it's difficult to remember a lot of my childhood. I have gaps...events and people seem like shadows in my mind. I can't bring them to the surface." I pause. "Others I remember well..."

I remember my arrival in New York vividly and lose myself in reminiscence.

When her father took Blanca away, she cried for Aunty Andrea that first night in New York, and she cried even more the next day when her father's mother said she would be living with her now and Aunty Andrea was far, far away.

New York, hateful New York. It was a dark, dirty place, stuffed with tall houses with many windows and many doors. The doors were always locked. When Blanca peeked out the window, there was no brilliant sun that made her eyes squint or her skin lie still and quiet, drinking its heat. No one smelled of sunshine in New York. It was dingy, the colors muted like a curtain faded by the sun.

What she hated most, though, was the old woman who claimed she was her mother now. She had her father's blue eyes and his curly hair, and she never read or sat Blanca in her lap. She spanked her when she cried and made her call her Mami. It was so hard, because Blanca's real Mami was fresh in her memory. She could still smell the sweet aroma of warm milk on her mother's skin and feel her soft breath on her face when she picked her up. Blanca had sat for hours, face buried in the cleave of her round breasts while she hummed in her rocker. The old woman had skin Blanca did not want to touch. Her rough hands scoured her skin when she bathed her, and Blanca turned her face from her sour breath whenever she spoke.

Day in day out, the fabric of the South Bronx spread, and its threads tamped its texture into her forever. Forever seemed like a terrible thing. Blanca thought she would always be trapped in the dark and drab and damp of that gutted, rat-swollen basement. Everyone, rats and humans, scurrying about, nostrils flaring, day in day out.

On 138th Street, men of the barrio, bandannas tied around their foreheads, roll dice. Empty-faced spectators hover on stoop steps, pulling hard on cigarettes and warm cans of beer. Someone flips a joke. Lethargic laughter rattles up to the sweaty women bent over window sills, arms crossed on folded towels. The women sniff the camphor air and watch the action on the stoops. They keep an eye on the ash-soaked boys pitching pennies at brick walls.

The heat is thick. Bongos and conga drums pulsate in the buckled air. The heat awakens atavistic yearnings for faraway suns. Heat drenches the South Bronx skies with sweat. Desolation. Alienation. Hunger. Apathy. A wick drenched in wrath ready to blaze violence.

Everyone waits—the dropouts, the laid-off, the janitors, bellhops, dishwashers—men and women who live with the insults that are constantly thrown at their feet, so they must look down. Weary of scrubbing toilets and scavenging trashcans, they wait out the long hours it takes to live through a day.

They flock to the streets seeking relief from the windowless, lightless, cheerless scorch of cold-water tenements. They bunch up in street corners shrinking from the cockroaches, the crying infants, the shrieking radios in their rooms. They skirt the garbage in the yards, the stench of urine clinging to stairwells, the harsh smell of smog. The street pushes its wares. Heroine and rum. Men snuffle and spit and squint under the hazy sun. They stare through the women who walk by, skirts hot as broth. A scuffle breaks out in the heat. A switchblade glints. A man gambles his life. It is worth so little.

At a distance, the mournful voice of Felipe Rodríguez, *La Voz*, makes an unusual appeal for wine: "Bartender, pour my wine in a broken glass. I want to bleed drop by drop the poison of her treacherous kiss." For even kisses kindle pain in the barrio. The jukebox bellows songs of agony and wrath. There is little hope embroidered in the notes that weave indolently through the days and the nights.

On his first day in the South Bronx, Ramón faced the sky, hoping to catch a bit of sunlight through the soot-sodden haze. The flight from San Juan had given him time to think. On the four-engine airplane, while the little girl slept by his side, Ramón wondered about his mother, Paquita, who now offered to help him, his mother who had given him away like a changeling when he was only ten. He roamed through life propelled by events without considering that there could be alternatives to the path in front of him. There were no choices in his world of poverty, so he accepted destiny as it presented itself. The thought of breaking paths where none existed never occurred to him. So when his mother offered to raise his child and find him a job in New York, he never gave it a second thought.

Ramón was a young man of twenty-eight. He slipped into his past effortlessly. It was a past his mother dominated despite her absence, because Ramón mulled over the grievances against his mother again and again in spite of himself.

He wondered why she worried about him now after abandoning him to his fate so many years before. People said it was never too late, but he went through hell when she abandoned Ramón, his brother Tomás, and their sisters, Consuelo and Evangelina. Paquita kept Pedro, the youngest, with her because he was asthmatic and needed her more than the others. That's what she said. Ramón wasn't fooled, though. He knew Pedro was her favorite. The rest of her children were healthy, Paquita said, and they could withstand whatever happened. She gave them away like old clothing to different families, and Ramón never saw his brothers and sisters again until they were all grown up.

Ramón was taken in by his *padrinos*, his godparents. He never went past the second grade, so there was not much he could do except farm work. He slept on a straw mat in the storage shed. When the cocks crowed, Ramón was already out in the tobacco fields where he worked until sunset. Ramón's godmother gave him leftover slop after she fed the pigs. Sometimes she sat on the wooden steps that led to the *batey* while she ate a boiled yam. Ramón would stare at her because he had nothing to eat all day. After eating the meaty insides, she would spit the skin into her palm and throw it at him. She laughed through her black toothless gums when he gobbled up the skin soaked in saliva, taking care that none dropped to the ground. And she had TB, too. That's how it was in those days.

Ramón's godfather beat him with a cane rod to make him work harder, like a burro. At fourteen, he escaped into the brambles one night when his godfather went after him with a machete because he caught Ramón necking with his youngest daughter. His godfather swore he'd make minced meat out of him. Ramón ended up at an aunt's house in Santurce. He did any odd job he could find to make a living. After a few years he started delivering milk for *Tres Monjitas*. Then he married Isabel.

Ramón never felt that Paquita was his true mother. He called her *Mamá* out of respect. But she was never a mother to him. Then she married a very young man who, Ramón thought, must make good money because she sent him the plane tickets. Just like that, without asking whether Ramón wanted to go to New York or not. Well, he had nothing better to do in Puerto Rico anyhow. Paquita demanded that he bring the child with him to New York. So he did, even though the child was fine at Andrea's.

Ramón was surprised to see how big the girl was. Last time he had seen her, she looked like a tadpole. She didn't even recognize him when he picked her up. She cried so hard when he took her away, Ramón had to spank her so she would shut up. At least Paquita took her off his hands so he could have some peace.

# 6

Extremes occur cyclically in a universe propelled by laws of birth and destruction. Like the five suns of Aztec lore that preside over the multiple beginnings and extinctions of the world, like the death star called Nemesis that every six million years floods the earth with the frost of darkness and extinguishes all but the staunchest life forms. Yet, despite the havoc and annihilation, the floods and ice and utter darkness, despite the five suns and the mighty death star, fresh species manage to spring to life among the ruins, adapting to the new worlds.

Blanca's universe contained its own Nemesis, a fifth sun that threatened to erase the uniqueness of every member of her family: her grandmother. Paquita had an insatiable need to destroy. She was unable to accept the distinctive features of others, least of all in her own family. The blood they shared was an indissoluble bond that made them one, like a tribe or a web. She not only required their physical presence in her life, she demanded their minds and souls. Paquita pronounced herself the force ruling this unity and was willing to destroy whoever threatened her rule. The question remained whether she was mighty enough for the absolute destruction of renegades or whether the objects of her wrath could succeed in rising from the ashes of a world beyond her realm.

Everyone said Paquita had been a beauty as a young woman, but the tenacious pull of years weighted down by disillusionment tugged at a grim face that set stubbornly in implacable judgment. Her hard voice, frequently mocking, divulged her disdain for the weaknesses of others. Her opinions were inalterable and unquestionable precepts. To count Paquita as an enemy was worse than confronting death itself. She always said: "I forgive but I never forget," while emphasizing the pronouncement with a blow to her chest. It was true. She never forgot a transgression. She never forgave either.

Because Paquita never forgave, her youngest daughter Evangelina exacted retribution in a silent act of rebellion.

It happened many years before, but Paquita's grown children never forgot how it happened nor why. They were all scattered about the Puerto Rican countryside in those days, living here and there with one family or another. Working the fields from dawn to dusk. Always hungry. Always tired. Evangelina had been taken in at a very young age by an aunt and her husband.

One morning Evangelina awoke with a start. Her heart raced and her eyes searched in the darkness. It was that dream again. She dreamed the moon was dead and the night filled with darkness, a darkness so great it struck her heart with fear. It was a heavy, suffocating darkness, a black so dense it swallowed her with sucking contractions. It was a bad omen, she knew. She must see the spiritualist as soon as she finished her chores.

Her aunt Carmela stirred. Evangelina focused on the dark figure lying on the floor covered with a thin blanket. Diomedes, her aunt's husband, snored in his wide cotton mesh hammock. He wrapped the sides around him so that his lean figure hung like a body in a shroud.

Dawn was climbing slowly. Evangelina pulled back the faded cotton scrap nailed to the entrance of the shack and looked out at the fields. Everyone said she was pretty, with her olive skin, long black braids, and sparkling brown eyes wide as a child's. She had a tender face, oval and smooth.

She had only left the village twice, and on both occasions she proudly wore a pair of borrowed shoes. Her cousin had an extra pair that she had found hidden in the brush. The shoes were black and had large square buckles on the sides. They were small for the cousin, but she refused to part with them permanently. After all, she could now truthfully say she was the owner of two pairs of shoes. Evangelina stuffed them with bits of rag and walked several kilometers to her godmother's wake. It had been a sad occasion. But the Feast of San Felipe Apóstol was the happiest of her life. She had danced all night with a young cane cutter, and now they were planning to live together as soon as he put aside some money to build a small house.

"Evangelina, are you daydreaming again, girl?" Carmela's voice startled her. "Get some kindling to start the coffee," she said wearily as the dark bundles on the floor came to life.

Evangelina brought a heap of firewood and set it on the black iron grill. "I dreamed the moon was dead again, Aunty," she whispered anxiously. Carmela scooped water from a wooden barrel with a gourd cup and poured it into a black kettle.

"Maybe I should see a priest, huh?" Evangelina insisted.

"A lot of good that'll do!" humphed Carmela. "The priest will tell you to say your Hail Marys and Our Fathers and order you to Mass on Sundays. What's that gonna do?"

"What should I do, then?"

"Get yourself settled with that young man of yours so he'll feed you," Diomedes said as he picked up a gourd of steaming coffee and slurped. "How old are you now?" he asked.

"Fifteen, Uncle."

"You wanna be an old maid, is that what you want? I can't feed and dress you anymore; it's time you went off on your own." He looked at Carmela's bulging abdomen. "We got another mouth to feed soon."

"But who'll help Aunty with the chores and the children if I go?"

"Elisa. She's about ten now, a big girl. She'll be ripe for a man soon, too."

Carmela worked silently at the stove. Evangelina was a grown woman, and her young man was a good catch. But she loved her like her own daughter, and it would hurt to see her go. It was women's fate, though. Nothing she could do.

Diomedes put on his straw hat, took his machete, and headed toward the fields. It was the *tiempo muerto* or dead season when the sugar cane fields were littered with stubble after the harvest. Though the cane cutting season was over, he had a lot of work to do. He was charged with burning and clearing the fields of trash and termites, spreading new seeds, and digging irrigation ditches.

Evangelina drank some black coffee, and, carrying a bundle of dirty clothes and tallow soap, retreated to the river, her favorite place. Climbing the hill quickly and weaving through the prickly bramble that lay low on the ground, she clambered down the other side of the hill slope pounding hard on the matted earth. She heard footsteps and stopped at a small dell. She put the sack of soiled clothes under a low canopy of stunted trees and noiselessly approached a thicket hedge. She parted the branches aside and saw Paquita, face gleaming with perspiration, marching up the path that led to the plantation houses.

Evangelina stepped out shyly. She had not seen her mother in several years, but she would recognize that angry face anywhere.

"What's this business about running off with a field hand?" Paquita screeched without preamble. "How come he didn't come ask for my permission? Who does he think I am, trash like him? And you better not have a turkey in the oven, young lady."

Before Evangelina could step back, Paquita grabbed her by the hair and slapped her face, her shoulders, her chest. When her strength was spent, she let go, and Evangelina crumbled on the ground.

"Let this be a lesson to you. Don't think that because I live all the way in Santurce, I don't know what you're up to, you little slut. I know everything that goes on around here. Everything! I'm going to Carmela's right now to give her a piece of my mind. And you can forget about this peasant of yours. If he didn't have the respect to talk to me, your own mother, about any plans he had with you, he's out of the picture."

The next morning, Evangelina was found in the tobacco shed hanging from the rafters. For the rest of her life Paquita would matter-of-factly dismiss her daughter's death by saying that there had been an epidemic of suicides in Manatí that year, as though Evangelina had been claimed by cholera or yellow fever.

Paquita took her granddaughter in, but warned Ramón about his monetary responsibility towards the child. She expected a weekly sum for Blanca's sustenance, or else he would have to deal with her. To avoid confrontations with Paquita, Ramón paid the stipulated weekly sum, and every once in a while, perhaps goaded by his conscience, he provided a few extra dollars for luxury items such as a little taffeta dress for Christmas. Relieved of countless obligations beyond the monetary one, Ramón gladly delivered Blanca to his mother.

Blanca slept on a cot that she unfolded every night in the living room of the small apartment. Lying there before the lights were turned off, she would stare at the bleeding Sacred Heart of Jesus hanging on the wall. Then Paquita's husband Salvador, the man Blanca called Papá, would give her his blessing and turn off the light before going into the bedroom.

Every night as Blanca lay in the dark, she counted her fingers to convince herself that she was still there. She feared that once she fell asleep, she would drown under the sheets.

Darkness felt vast and wide as an ocean.

Blanca heard the story many times. Her grandmother launched into frequent soliloquies about her life in Puerto Rico and New York when callers dropped in for a cup of strong Puerto Rican coffee.

One afternoon, a little boy drowned in the mud and the shantytown yammered noisily. Salvador stood hesitantly looking into the shack where Paquita lived with her son Pedro.

"Doña Paquita," he called, craning his neck so his voice would carry over the rickety board and into the four-legged shack.

"What is it?" she said, turning her back to the hot kerosene stove, perspiration dripping down her flushed face. She approached the open door.

"Good afternoon." He gave a slight bow and tapped the rim of his hat. "Could you come out a minute, please? I would like to talk to you."

It was the tacit moral code. A decent woman never received male callers in her home while she was alone and her son Pedro was too small to be considered a suitable chaperon. Paquita went out as she wiped her hands on the faded housedress she wore when she came home from work. Salvador glanced at her sideways. She crossed the creaking board that straddled the mud canal between the shack and the dirt road.

It was dinner time in the shantytown and the crusty odor of cod fritters sizzling in white-hot lard mingled with the sharp smell of sewage. For months now, Salvador had gazed at her wistfully when she returned from Miramar where she washed and ironed for a rich family. The young man swallowed the vision of her wide hips quavering under her flowery print dresses, but he had not mustered the courage to address her directly until that moment.

On steady ground, they faced each other.

"Good afternoon," he repeated and twirled his straw hat nervously between his hands.

"Good afternoon."

"Um, I've wanted to say something to you for a while now. I spoke to your brother Chebo, and he said it was fine with him, if you agree."

"What in the devil's name are you talking about? What plots are you and Chebo hatching?"

"No, no, it's not a plot; it's just that I'm a bachelor, you see. I live alone and need a companion. You understand? I know you're a hard-working woman, always in your home, and I'd like, if you allow me, to visit you in Chebo's house on Sunday afternoons. That is, if you allow me."

She smirked. "You must be joking, Salvador. I'm old enough to be your mother."

"That's nothing. I'm almost 20 and I'm a hard worker." He spoke rapidly, trying to say all he had come to say before she turned away. "I don't like the young ladies of today. All they want is to look pretty and waste their time talking nonsense."

"You're crazy. And I'm warning Chebo not to stick his nose into my business. Forget it." She swiped the air as though shooing a mosquito and shook her head from side-to-side. She crossed the wooden board to her shack without a backward glance.

But Salvador did not surrender. He liked this mature woman with strong character. He was dazzled by her blue eyes and pink cheeks. He knew she was almost forty and had four children somewhere in the hills of Manatí. But they were all grown by now and the youngest one, Pedro, liked him. He won him over by carving little wooden horses for him to play with.

Flattered by the constant attentions of the young man and egged on by her brother Chebo, Paquita relented. They lived together and from their meager wages saved enough money for Salvador's immigration to New York where he would seek, in the streets paved with gold, a better life for his new family.

While Salvador was in New York, Paquita wove through the maze of shantytown alleys looking for the rare person who could read the letters she received from him, and what was more difficult, someone who could write her responses.

There were nights when bats flapped on the corrugated tin roof and frightened Paquita. She would turn the knob of an oil lantern and it would cast its sputtering glow over her as she maintained her tireless vigil with her asthmatic boy, who struggled ferociously for each breath of air.

On one of those nights of vigil, she lay down on her cot, dead tired after a long day of hard work. Startled by a noise outside, she rose, opened the door, and found another small door. She opened it and walked through to a circular stone stairway curling into darkness. Hesitantly, she went down the stairs, smelling the musky air of shadows and listening to the rhythmic lap of water. When she reached the bottom, she could see a tiny white boat rocking on a glassy lake. She clambered into the boat, sat on the plank that crossed the beam, and the boat glided toward a disc of light. The disc became larger and larger, and suddenly she found herself in a wide blue rippling river, bobbing to a shore that was green and lush with bamboo and fern. She felt the cool air of thick vegetation on her skin and racing through her hair. She drifted to shore, got off the boat, and headed toward a rustling soursop tree rooted in a bed of sand. The bright sun drove her under its enormous shade. Then she poked her head behind the smooth bark, and the gleam of a distant forest struck her. She was inexplicably drawn to it. A narrow stone path led into the forest. She penetrated the thickness of its vegetation, and as she entered farther, it grew darker. The trees were so tall that they blanketed the sky. Here and there shafts of light penetrated like milky beams and warmed her skin. She could feel the rustling of leaves under her feet. When she came to a clearing, a plume of smoke drifted through the green forest. An archangel rose from a thick white cloud. He was identical to the Gabriel posing on the promotional calendar of Mueblería Cimarrón that hung on her wall. With a voice that seemed to emerge from the depths of the soil, the archangel spoke. His voice was unintelligible, yet somehow the swirling sound attached itself to her mind and she understood that he was telling her how to cure her asthmatic son Pedro.

The sky was tinted pink and orange by the early morning light when Paquita woke up and rushed to a *botánica*, the local herbalist shop. She banged on the owner's door.

"What the hell is all this racket?" A scowling barefoot woman opened the door.

"I need some iodine."

"What?"

"Iodine, I need iodine."

"Jesus, Mary and Joseph, can't you wait until decent people are up?"

"No, no, I dreamed of Archangel Gabriel, and I can't wait."

"You're crazy," the woman mumbled under her breath and turned around.

Paquita clutched at her cotton night shift, ready to tear it off.

"Ok, ok, I'll sell it to you. Is a peseta's worth enough?"

Paquita's shadow faded in the dawn and the *botánica* owner shook her head.

"May it poison your insides, you whore," she cursed.

Once back home, Paquita pulled a jar of honey from a wooden tub, poured some into an old tomato sauce tin used for drinking water, and since the Archangel had not volunteered the necessary proportions, she put a few drops of iodine into the heavy golden honey. She held her breath and stirred the mixture carefully. With a gourd strip, she stuffed the celestial remedy into Pedro's reluctant mouth. She feared the iodine might poison the child, but she believed in the infallibility of visions. She fed the boy the potion three times a day. Three seemed like a good honest number with magical endowments.

The miraculous disappearance of Pedro's bronchial asthma provided Paquita with a favorite topic of conversation for many years.

The day Paquita had been waiting for finally arrived. Pesky flies whirred in black swarms, not respecting the impatient slaps of the slum dwellers. A hot noon sun beat on the tin roofs of the *arrabal*, beaming heat in all directions and stirring the muck-moist odor of sewage that rose from the mud. Paquita hurried past the gambling parlor, stomping on a few bright purple weeds which sprouted from under dusty stones. Distractedly she kicked a dead mouse aside, and a swarm of red ants scrambled in confused circles. She walked around the scurrying ants and stood at the open door of a jerrybuilt shack. She knocked on the door jamb.

"*Buenos días*," she called into the shack.

A teenage girl peeked out timidly. She wore a pale blue shift. A thin naked toddler was perched on her hip.

"Mariana, a letter from New York." Paquita held out the white envelope rimmed with blue and red stripes. It had two rows of letters over a pair of wings. "It's Salvador," she said as though he were waiting breathlessly inside the folded sheet of paper. "Read it to me, please."

"Come in, Doña Paquita, and sit down if you like. I'll put the baby down so she doesn't bother us. Sorry I don't offer you anything. You know Severo's out of work," She shrugged resignedly and held out a bony hand for the letter. Curlicued veins threaded under the skin of her pale, almost transparent palm.

Mariana stood by the door under a shaft of dusty light that helped her see better. She rested a bare foot over the other and leaned against the door jamb. She peered at the envelope closely and read haltingly, "Ah-eer mah-eel, *correo aéreo*. That means it came on an airplane, not a ship."

Paquita looked up admiringly. How did this slip of a child know so much? As though reading her mind, Mariana said:

"I went to school for a long time, you know. Years. Finished the fourth grade even." She looked past Paquita's shoulder at the child sitting on the floor quietly sucking her thumb. "Then I got in trouble." Mariana turned crimson and lowered her eyes. "I could've been someone," she mumbled under her breath as she unfolded the lined paper, smoothing it with her fingertips before she started reading.

Paquita cocked an ear toward the girl and concentrated on Salvador's words. When the girl finished, Paquita thanked her and pressed a few coins in her palm.

When she returned home, Pedro was squatting on the dirt path playing with pebbles. He looked up at her. "We're sailing." Paquita caught her breath. "Tomorrow I'm buying the tickets. Salvador sent money and says he's already got us a place to live in New York."

# 7

The SS Borinquen docked at Hubert Street on a Wednesday in April. The year was 1937. Paquita and Pedro shivered in the residual winter winds that sifted through their flimsy clothing.

Ensconced in the South Bronx, Paquita and Salvador worked hard. She cleaned, cooked, and took care of her husband and child. He secured a job as a bellhop at a Manhattan hotel. Without warning, from beyond unfathomable oceans and unscalable mountains, the Second World War resonated in their lives. Salvador volunteered in the Navy and was expediently sent overseas. During his two years of absence, to make ends meet, Paquita worked as a janitor in a coat factory on Sixth Avenue. Warily, she descended into the bowels of the city and entered the subway stuffed with human masses, shrinking from the hands of masturbators and pickpockets.

She remembered going into the factory restroom one morning, draped with her buckets, brooms and mops. One of the pressers was there, hunched over the sink. Her name had something to do with color. Maybe it was Lila. Paquita could not remember. She did remember how the woman sobbed into the sink, scrubbing her hand raw with a soapy brush. When she calmed down and drank the coffee Paquita got for her, she told her story.

She was on the subway that morning, minding her own business, crammed in as usual, chin held high to facilitate breathing, when she felt something smooth and hard poking at her hand. She attempted to inch away, but her arm was stuck in the hard mass of the crowd. The train swayed and the entire mass swayed at the same rhythm. Then something wet and sticky clung to the back of her hand. At her stop she elbowed her way out, propelled by a wave of passengers. She stood on the platform when the acrid odor of semen on her hand hit her. She cried all morning, until finally the factory supervisor told her to go home. She never returned.

In the factory, Paquita wondered what had happened to Lila, or maybe her name was Rosa, she thought, something to do with color, and she scrubbed a lavatory sink vigorously. A moan pulled her out of her reverie. When the moaning increased in volume, she rushed to the sewing room. Graciela, one of the seamstresses, writhed on the floor, her working smock collecting the nubs of cloth, colored fabric strips, and bunches of curled thread that carpeted the floor. She screamed desperately, her eyes frothy white and fixed on an inescapable horror. Graciela's moans became hoarse, enormous bellows that produced an excitement in Paquita that was almost joyful.

Paquita approached the circle of women surrounding the afflicted Graciela and avidly took in the scene. She rubbed her hands against the skirt of her blue uniform. Then another worker fell on the floor, her body twisting painfully, as though every bone had been fractured, and howling like a disemboweled dog. In a matter of minutes, three more women were felled as if by a virulent, vengeful spirit. What horrors had befallen the factory? Paquita wondered. The supervisor, a peroxide blond, attempted to explain to the factory manager what was going on while she nervously applied a thumb to the corners of her mouth. The supervisor usually paraded proudly among the sewing machines communicating the desires of her patrons because she was bilingual. With the commotion, she lost her usual haughtiness and spoke quickly, in staccato bursts, flapping her arms. Paquita stood next to her, but she did not understand the English jabber. The supervisor turned and spoke to her in Spanish: "Paquita, help me carry these women to Mr. Stein's office. They've calmed down now. And get some wet towels to wipe their faces, okay?"

Paquita complied and clambered up to Mr. Stein's office where the women lay on the wooden floor, gasping for breath, their faces streaked with tears and sweat. Paquita and the supervisor wiped the women's foreheads with wet towels while Mr. Stein busied himself supervising the other workers to enforce the daily production quota.

"I don't know what's wrong with these women, okay?" the blond supervisor said. "Getting ridiculous attacks like that. It's a circus in here. The mister is real mad, says he's tired of these tricks to get out of work. Says that if we're used to this kind of behavior in Puerto Rico, things are different here, okay? We gotta change all these bad habits and act like decent human beings. Says he won't tolerate no more hysterical women in his factory. You can imagine, I almost died of shame, okay?"

Paquita started to feel edgy. It dawned on her that if these were nervous attacks, she could be in trouble. She was frequently afflicted by the condition, though rarely in front of strangers. She remained uncharacteristically silent, mentally praying to the Virgin to help her not fall prey to the same sudden curse as the others.

The mister rushed into the office gesticulating and jabbering frantically. The supervisor interpreted what he said with a few words. "Dammit, more attacks." The blond pushed Paquita aside and ran to the sewing room.

Pandemonium reigned in the huge room. The stricken women beat against each other in anguished contortions. Screams caromed off the walls and beams while the sewing machines sat idly in rows as if peering down disdainfully at the writhing bodies on the floor.

*"¡Ay, Dios mío!"* Paquita moaned and rubbed her hands together. "What's happening here? This must be a curse, a spell cast on us by a jealous enemy. Maybe it was Juana who was furious when the mister kicked her out of here like a dog. Virgin of Perpetual Help, I have never seen anything like this."

"Shut up, Paquita, okay? Just give me a hand here." The impatient blond shoved her forward.

Stein's boss made a miraculous appearance. No one knows where the factory owner came from. He had never been seen at the plant before.

"What's going on, Stein?"

"Oh, Mr. Rosenberg, you shouldn't have bothered to come. It's nothing." Stein wet his lips nervously.

"What're you talking about? I see a bunch of sick women screaming all over the floor, and you say it's nothing?"

"But don't you understand? They're Puerto Rican," Stein said scornfully by way of explanation. "That's the way they are. These people get hysterical over nothing. Trying to get out of work, if you ask me. It's cultural, what can I say? These people are all the same. Probably wanna collect disability or something."

Rosenberg pushed Stein aside and rushed to make some phone calls. The calls brought in the police, ambulance, and firemen, all sniffing like hounds, investigating, inquiring. Over Mr. Stein's protests, they shut down the factory.

Every morning, the laid-off workers congregated at the employee entrance expecting some news. The blond supervisor appeared a week later and announced that experts from the fire department discovered something from the heating system leaking into the sewing room, and that was why the women had gotten so sick. It was something that affected the nervous system. Some kind of gas. "It was just an accident," she said. "Those things happen. Okay? Everything is cleared up now, so come back to work on Monday, okay?"

Relieved that she still had a job, Paquita walked back to her tenement apartment from the subway station on Willis Avenue. She peered at the signs around her which were as impenetrable as hieroglyphics. She stood in awe of the many symbols, knit into different combinations, offering messages to the fortunate ones who could decipher their mystery. She admired how her cousin Panchita could read *La Prensa* every evening. Sometimes while visiting, Paquita would pick up a Bible that was kept on a small end table in the living room. When she spread its pages open, no matter how hard she tried, she could not succeed in discovering the deep secrets of the silent words. In front of a Lucky Strike advertisement, she bent her head to the side, approached the printed words—her eyes stinging with effort—and tried hard to unravel the secret tangles. She failed to see whatever there was to see. She just could not see.

Eventually, Paquita learned to read when she was driven to the effort by need, but she never learned to speak English. She ambled down the streets listening to the strange sounds, guttural, coarse, sometimes brutal in their sharp timber. A day came when she stopped perceiving the stiff foreign accent, and she only heard the warm cadence of Spanish. When the familiar tongue wafted among the strange noises, the tips of her ears almost tensed as she recognized its decipherable, sonorous melody.

A laconic Salvador returned unexpectedly from the Navy. He held an honorable discharge and somber visions of distant seas and lands. He never spoke about the war. His shyness had been transformed into a brittle distaste. He spoke only when necessary, when he had something important to say. Every evening after work, he attended classes to acquire a dental-technician diploma under the GI Bill. When he finished his studies, he locked himself up in a workroom he prepared in the apartment and tinkered with his tools until bedtime. He married Paquita, because that was the way things were done in New York. Paquita adjusted complacently to the role of housewife and mother. Before her menopause, they attempted to have a child. But the child refused to be born. Pedro, cured of his asthma, attended school. That was the way things were done in New York. Both he and Salvador learned the new language that eluded Paquita forever.

Pedro was raised as if he were a sickly girl. Paquita did not allow him to play, go out, have friends, much less girlfriends. In her incessant need to dominate, to control her world, she always remained in ambush, waiting like a watchful cat, the tip of its tail quivering, for the slightest infraction of her inflexible rules. If Pedro had not soaked the dry beans when she returned from playing cards in the afternoon, if the neighborhood gossips told her they had seen him necking with the Italian girl who lived in the next block, if he refused to dress according to the sartorial code devised by her, a hail of insults and harsh slaps fell on him.

When Pedro's sixteenth birthday came around, the war still blazed. Preferring the ravages of war to the dominance of his mother, he forged his birth certificate and volunteered for the Army. He was promptly dispatched to Germany. This gave rise to numerous apoplectic seizures appropriately timed by Paquita.

Despite his mother's collapses, tantrums, fainting fits, and diverse insults, Pedro married the neighborhood Italian girl on one of his home leaves. It was Salvador who paid for the son's rebellion. To Paquita, he was the husband who could not engender children, the strange man who read daily newspapers in two languages, who insisted on studying with GI benefits, and became a dental technician. The husband who never touched liquor or gambled or took her to the Puerto Rico Theater to see the latest Libertad Lamarque movie. The man whose only vice was to smoke two packs of Camels a day. That man became Paquita's bull's-eye. She accused him of real or imaginary infidelities. She took his money to bring Tomás, her eldest son, his wife María, and their four children from the island. She took more of his money to bring her only living daughter Consuelo, her husband Regino, and six more children from the hills of Manatí. She bought plane tickets for Ramón and his orphaned child Blanca. She got them settled down one way or another. Ramón and Tomás got jobs at the carton factory, and Regino was placed as the super in a neighboring building. Paquita bought warm clothing at the thrift shop for her flock of children and grandchildren. Slowly she fashioned her empire, locking in her subjects, oppressing them with her favors and gifts. Paquita knit her web like a spider, and to rule absolutely, she hunted constantly for a daily ration of discord among her subjects.

Paquita hated her sons' wives. They were lazy gossips and wretched ingrates, she frequently said. Even *la difunta*, the "deceased one"—her name for Isabel, Blanca's mother—did not escape her injurious offense. She maintained that Ramón should have married Delia instead. Delia was such a nice girl, but that Isabel was so crazy about Ramón, she had cast a spell on him and turned his head and just like that—she would snap her fingers—he left Delia and married her instead. But since God sees all and hears all, *la difunta* suffered like hell from her disease and then left poor Ramón stuck with an orphan who's like a scared mouse because, every time we have company, she hides behind the sofa like a cockroach when the light goes on, she would say.

Pedro's Italian woman was a whore who cuckolded him while he was in the Army. She had no doubt about it. They even saw her in a bar kissing a tall, dark-haired man. And look at that girl she had, she doesn't look like her mother or poor Pedro. But he was blind, and no one could say a bad word about her. She even forced him to move far away from the family, the bitch.

You could forget about María, she would say. That peg-legged anemic was the biggest slob she'd ever seen in her life. The kids were always in filthy rags, the poor things. And poor Tomás came around all the time sniffing around the kitchen like a hungry dog.

*¡Ay!* she didn't know what to do with those boys. She made all kinds of sacrifices for them. She even tolerated their wives, but her heart broke when she thought of all the suffering those wretched women caused them. And Ramón, Paquita would carry on, he was always chasing skirts. He'd never settle down. On 141th there was a widow, her name was Fela, who was really good and was crazy about him. But Ramón said she was too old for him; he liked young chicks. "What chicks are you talking about?" Paquita would say. "You need a woman who'll take care of you, who'll have your meals ready on time, who'll keep your clothing and apartment clean, who won't cuckold you. Look, Fela's a widow and she has money in the bank. She works hard, has a nice apartment, and she only has a grown son who's on his own. And she really loves the orphan, God knows why. The other day she bought her a really nice woolen skirt, and she's always giving her money for candy." Let's see if he'll change his mind about this, Paquita would add. Years weigh on people, and the older he gets the more difficult it'll be to find a decent woman. I don't know, one of these days that boy is going to catch a disease running around like that with all those whores. My heart sticks in my throat when I think about it. The other day he was seen with

a married woman. Lolita told me everyone is talking about it. What a mess if the husband catches them! *Ay*, Virgin of the Seven Miracles, keep him safe and sound for me!

The barrio nags listened to her laments and nodded their heads in solidarity. What mother did not understand the disgraceful liaisons of their sons? With so many good women on earth, they always wound up with the whores!

As to her only living daughter, Consuelo, Paquita could only find her physical appearance to criticize. "Poor thing, she's so plain, doesn't look at all like me," she would say. Yet Paquita zealously launched into a task of rapprochement with Consuelo, anxiously imparting her own skills of exemplary housewife and the ins and outs of living in New York.

"The poor thing, I could hardly recognize her when we picked her up at the airport. She had a thin cotton dress that came down to her ankles, and she could hardly walk with a pair of white high-heeled shoes that were too narrow for her. How did she think she could fit her fat feet into them when she was used to roaming barefoot in the brambles? And she's such a *jíbara*, such a hick, she's afraid to talk to people. But don't worry, I'll teach her to behave so she doesn't embarrass me by acting like a clod," Paquita would announce with determination.

# 8

Gambling is an act of faith, an expression of hope that allows the poor to face their deprivation without despairing. Faith in numbers, the lottery, card games, horse races and hope in the possibility of better days, relieve the burden of a present that mirrors the past, a present relentlessly foreshadowing an irreversible future. To accept the inevitability of such a future is to embrace defeat. Faith is hope. Hope is illusion. The illusion of hitting the numbers or winning the lottery is far more enticing than the possibility of heavenly reward. Promises of deferred gratification, in a dimension that may not exist, attract few believers. Innocence of spirit is scarce in the ghetto.

Paquita was certainly not among the few who possessed it. In an outburst of adolescent piety and to relieve her conscience, she went to confession once to the Manatí town church after walking barefoot for kilometers from her village, El Cuco. The Spanish priest listened to her sins and angrily told her that for her transgressions she would burn in the eternal fires of hell. Stripped of any hope for eternal paradise, Paquita eventually converted to a faith that offered the possibility of immediate escape from her grim surroundings. Despite the repeated warnings of Salvador, who detested gambling with a passion, Paquita lived for the excitement of secret raps, clandestine shop backrooms, encoded dreams that promised gratification. She gambled enthusiastically, and at times, hit a number or won at cards. These successes fired her with greater hope.

In the beginning, gambling was merely another distraction in the routine of her world, like the Tuesday matinee or the visits to her cousin Panchita in El Barrio. But soon, she was hooked. Winning no longer represented a little farm in Puerto Rico for her old age, but an elevated emotional state that made her lightheaded, like a pull of marijuana. She invented a variety of illnesses with the corresponding visits to physicians to explain her frequent absences and her need for additional funds. She consulted a neighbor who had a dog-eared book that interpreted dreams numerically. It was easy when Paquita's dreams involved numbers. Then she could bet on them directly. It was a more complicated matter when they had to do with events and objects, such as a wedding or a cup. These had to be converted by her interpreter —owner of the book—into numbers. Her interpreter, who was busy with a factory job and several children, taught Paquita how to read and write so she could consult the book herself and make the daily lists for the numbers' runner. Every week, Paquita bought clandestine Irish lottery tickets. Every Friday afternoon, she met friends in neighboring apartments to play Spanish cards. And every day, she played the numbers.

When Ramón came to New York with Blanca and left the child in Paquita's care, it was the blessing Paquita had anticipated when she sent him the airplane tickets. Training the little girl was time-consuming, but Paquita knew she would reap the benefits soon enough. At the age of four, Paquita instructed her granddaughter to climb on a stool and wash dishes at the kitchen sink. The little girl, whose motor coordination had not matured completely, broke cups and glasses when they slipped from her tiny hands. Paquita solved the problem by thrashing Blanca with any object at hand. Her beatings were so creative, Blanca developed an extraordinary level of fine motor coordination for a child of her age. Besides doing housework and errands, Blanca accompanied her grandmother on her daily visits to the numbers' runner, dispelling any suspicions Salvador might harbor.

One cold afternoon, Paquita entered the dilapidated tenement building where a numbers' runner lived. She held Blanca tightly by the hand and rapped at the door of apartment 1A. "Strange, there's no one in," Paquita said pensively. As she turned to leave, two corpulent men with long coats appeared and grabbed her arm. Blanca burst out crying while Paquita yelled, "Shut up, you little demon!"

The gigantic men flashed glittery silver badges and barked some orders. Paquita did not understand a word they said. One of the men pinned her to the wall, while the other snatched her handbag and spilled its contents on the hallway floor. Her change purse, comb, mirror and handkerchief were strewn on the filthy floor. The man then tore the lining out, examining the handbag meticulously. When he found nothing, he shoved the handbag into her chest.

"What's the matter? I haven't done anything. This is an injustice. I just came to visit a friend," Paquita said lamely.

"Get outta here!" one of the men ordered, pointing an authoritative finger toward the street.

Well versed in body language, Paquita gathered her belongings from the floor, stuffed them quickly into her torn handbag and rushed out, pulling Blanca behind her. When they rounded the corner, she leaned against a lamp post, her knees rubbery.

"Who were those men, Mami? Why did they take your handbag?"

"Shut up, devil," Paquita snapped. The little girl winced when her grandmother squeezed her arm. Paquita's eyes shone wildly behind her eyeglasses.

"Don't you dare tell anyone about this, hear? Nobody. If Salvador finds out, he'll kill me."

Blanca nodded quickly, her eyes round as saucers.

In the apartment, Paquita double-locked the door. Too impatient to wait for Blanca to do it herself, she dragged the girl to the bedroom and peeled off her coat.

"Now take your panties off," she ordered.

Blanca obeyed. Her grandmother unclasped a safety pin that secured a small piece of paper to her panties.

"It's a good thing they didn't search you," Paquita said as she clenched the list of numbers in her fist. "I figured something was fishy. Last week they arrested Tino. And now they're after Moncho. Have to be more careful. Look, I'm still shaking like a leaf. And my knees are jelly. I've had the fright of my life."

Blanca wanted to ask a million questions, but she knew better. She knew that to ask questions was to risk confirmation or denial of the obvious. Her grandmother never explained things to her. She only slapped and scolded. "Shut up. Children should be seen and not heard," she admonished constantly. Blanca attempted to solve the puzzles that would spring in her mind. So she invented plausible explanations, relying on her limited experience to form logical connections in a confusing adult world.

The episode with the detectives did not curtail Paquita's activities. It merely tested her ingenuity, though Saturdays were particularly difficult because Salvador was in the apartment all day long. Unable to find excuses to go out, she paced through the apartment rendering more than the usual dose of insults and beatings. One Saturday, she decided to take drastic measures. She hid in the bathroom and scribbled her list of numbers. While Salvador was busy in his workshop, she called Blanca into the kitchen, handed her a few dollars, and sent her to the corner pizza shop.

Blanca followed her grandmother's instructions carefully. She slid behind the counter of the pizza shop and pushed a blue door with a "Do Not Enter" sign on it. Tony the Italian sat in the backroom with a short fat cigar bouncing in his mouth. She dug into her coat pocket and handed Tony the money and the list. The smoky room made her eyes water.

"Who're you, kid?"

"Paquita's granddaughter."

"Oh, yeah, yeah. Good kid."

Blanca ran back to the apartment with the oppressive feeling that men with silvery badges were practically stepping on her heels. The thought of going to jail was terrifying. Her cousin Samuel used to say that jail was a place where men became beasts. If that happened to men, Blanca shuddered at the thought of the horrors little girls would have to endure.

After her successful initiation, Paquita had Blanca play the numbers whenever Salvador was around. When the little girl realized that the men in dark coats were not returning, she ambled to the pizza shop with great serenity, immensely proud to perform a task acceptable to her demanding grandmother. Tony the Italian even gave her a free soda once in a while.

At times, she returned from the pizza shop when Ramón was on one of his visits to give his mother the weekly allowance to cover Blanca's expenses and to inquire about Paquita's precarious health. On these occasions, Blanca would stare at her shoes and ask for his blessing. Holding her breath, she waited for his perfunctory "God bless you" and an indication that he was finished with her. Blanca would then go solemnly to her room where she spent her time observing the enormous white flowers on the blue background of the linoleum floor.

Ever since she peed on his lap, Ramón avoided any contact with her. On the evening of her wretched ignominy, Blanca had finished washing the dinner dishes when Ramón sauntered into the kitchen. It was a Saturday, and he was in a good mood. The previous night he had scored an amorous conquest he had thought hopeless, and Saturday nights always held the promise of love. Blanca, dress hiked up in front, looked at him timidly from a corner of the kitchen, absorbing his smell of recently applied brilliantine, her mouth gaping, head tilted. Owing to his inordinately good mood, in an uncharacteristic display of compassion, he picked her up and sat her on one of his strong thighs.

Blanca cuddled against the broad chest of the big man who was her great love. She was fearful of calling any attention to herself, so she dared not move a muscle while her father talked with Paquita about a dream he had which involved number 106. Her arm fell asleep, but still she did not move. Then a throbbing fullness pressed against her bladder. She squeezed her thighs and shut her eyes tightly, dizzy from the effort, sucking in the aroma of Ramón's brilliantine. Before she could contain it, a warm flow escaped from her. Ramón jumped and shoved the girl to the floor. He stared at the dark stain on his navy blue trousers.

"Look, Mamá," he screeched, "what this devil of a girl did. She peed on my clean pants, and I just got them out of the cleaners. I'll fix you," he yelled at Blanca. He removed his belt and glowered at the girl huddling in a corner.

"Come here, you sow."

Fearful of angering Ramón further, she inched stoically toward him to accept the punishment she thought was quite justified, considering the magnitude of her offense. He belted her hard. Paquita urged him to hit harder, because if he did not teach the girl a good lesson now, she would grow up like a twisted tree and then it would be too late to straighten her out. She took full advantage of the incident to cast invectives about how lazy, slothful, good-for-nothing and insufferable the devil's orphan, as she called the girl, was.

"You don't know what I go through with this demon. I did you a big favor when I took her off your hands," she cried over and over.

Ramón needed no further excuses to ignore his daughter. Once, when she was unusually brave, she asked him to come see her on Christmas Day. He promised to do so, and she waited and waited all day looking for him through the window. He never showed up.

# 9

Paquita flitted through the South Bronx barrio inquiring about other people's health and regaling everyone with her latest misfortunes. None of her friends or acquaintances believed her capable of a dark thought and much less of an improper act.

"Doña Paquita is such a nice person," they whispered among themselves. "She even took in that orphan who doesn't talk, and her husband is always working and never takes her anywhere. And she's always ill, the poor thing."

Paquita rejected the indulgences of others with a sneer. Since her menopause, she avoided sex, which she considered a depravity. The only repository of tenderness and care was her own body, constantly flattered by the pleasures of hypochondria. She visited doctors as frequently as a pious old woman goes to Mass. The more arcane the illness diagnosed, the more serious it appeared, the more satisfied she felt. If someone had the misfortune of commenting favorably on her apparent physical well-being, she tended to respond, clucking with annoyance. "Oh, you're mistaken, my friend. Appearances can fool you. On the outside I seem well, but only God knows the misfortunes I carry inside," and she sighed deeply.

She was unable to wash dishes or do the laundry because she developed a skin allergy to detergents. When avoiding detergents did not relieve the itching and swelling of her hands, astute doctors identified her illness as a sensitivity to the waters of New York.

Since her asthma lacked the characteristic wheezing that denoted bronchial constriction, the doctors determined that it was precipitated by emotional distress. This diagnosis elicited great pleasure from the patient, who was convinced of the dark powers of emotional upsets to reduce her days on earth.

She was beset by mysterious pains in her chest, attacks of morbid nervousness if someone or something upset her, sudden vertigo when least expected, and all types of intestinal ailments. She constantly entertained friends and relatives with her latest afflictions. Yet the multiple ailments never stopped her from card playing, buying Irish lottery tickets, and playing the numbers. She went weekly to the Puerto Rico Theater on 138th Street, took the subway to the Park Avenue market, visited friends in Spanish Harlem, and spent hours in the local *bodega* conversing with the patrons who gathered there. Her multiple afflictions compelled her to travel to Puerto Rico frequently; the benign climate of the island made her feel better. After all, she was not allergic to the waters there.

On one of her many protracted trips to the island, Paquita left Blanca in the care of a chubby lady who had a small mongrel dog and a husband. The lady was very nice to the girl. On Blanca's first day of school, she plaited her black hair tightly, powdered her face with talcum, and took her by the hand to P.S. 34 on Brook Avenue.

Still holding the little girl by the hand, she spoke to the principal, a large man with a brightly buckled belt. The lady signed a number of papers, and Blanca found herself sitting in front of a blond woman with a perpetual smile. The woman demonstrated how Blanca should hold the pencil and mark some drawings in a thick booklet of pulpy paper. Blanca had never held a pencil before, and she scratched her head nervously. She did not understand a thing, but in order to please the strange woman and not show her ignorance, she assumed her most knowledgeable face and with awkward lines marked all the drawings in the booklet. This seemed to have delighted the strange woman no end, because she constantly nodded her head and smiled so widely her mouth seemed to devour her nose, eyes, and forehead. Blanca stared at her apprehensively.

When Blanca entered her first classroom, the happy illusions she had entertained about school disappeared. She flinched at its aura of decay. The teacher smiled brightly and led her to a small chair where Blanca was surrounded by rag dolls with lusterless eyes. The teacher spoke to her in the strange language Blanca had heard many times, her voice so loud and gesticulating so violently Blanca thought she was a madwoman. When she sat on the assigned chair, Blanca felt a painful squeeze in her arm. She reared up like a cobra. A boy giggled behind her, flapping his dirty hands in the air. She cried all day.

During that year in a class for the mentally retarded, Blanca drew pumpkins in October, colored pine trees in December, and cut out white bunnies in April.

She also picked up some English.

When Blanca was able to communicate in English, school authorities no longer considered her retarded and placed her in a classroom for children without the deficiency of not knowing the English language. Her first grade teacher was a black-haired woman with fiery eyes. She had long crimson nails, which seemed to Blanca like the claws of a bird of prey. Her disdain for the children was only surpassed by the terror the pupils felt for her. When Blanca mispronounced a difficult word during reading lessons, extra motivation to get it right was imparted by a strong pull on her braid or collar. When the teacher sought some variety, she dug her nails into Blanca's arm or rapped her knuckles with an ever-present ruler. Before turning around to write on the chalkboard, she warned the children that she had two eyes behind her head. She saw everything that happened while her head was turned, she said. Blanca had no idea what effect this revelation had on her classmates, but it terrified her to think that those hairy eyes, always open like caverns, stared at her pitilessly. She dared not stir in her seat.

By the time Blanca made it to the fourth grade, she was not only at the top of her class, but what was even more exciting, she had fallen in love with Ralph.

No one knew whether Ralph was an anglicized sobriquet for Rafael or Reinaldo. It was a certainty, though, that Ralph was the unvanquished holder of the title of Don Juan for the fourth grade. At thirteen, Ralph was an experienced older man despite his retention in a couple of grades during his checkered elementary school career. His handsome features and continuous hunt for females made him irresistible to girls who derided the childish boys their own age. They ignored the fact that Ralph could not read well, and that his genius was limited to disseminating his charm among grammar-school girls and some older ones at the junior high school on 142nd. None resented having to share him. It was a tacit pact. If they wanted to go steady with Ralph—and they all wanted to—they must accept the briefest of relationships. After all, such a specimen could not be found every day, and fortunate were those who enjoyed his attentions even if for a week at the most. Ralph was an equal-opportunity lover. He dispensed his liberal affections on Puerto Rican, Irish, Black, and Italian girls, and even on Bonnie, the Quaker.

Blanca, who looked at him with the eyes of a sick cow, went steady with Ralph for a week. Unfortunately, because it was the week of Washington's birthday, it was only four days long. Later, when Barbara's turn came up during a week of five whole days, Blanca felt a little stab of jealousy, but she still conferred on Ralph the bovine looks usually reserved for photographs of Elvis Presley.

School girls eyed Ralph constantly as he strutted in his tight pants, a plastic comb protruding from his back pocket. They would not deign to glance at the immature boys who hated and envied him. Rumors were rife to the effect that Ralph practiced French kissing, despite the fact that none of his girlfriends admitted to having indulged in that singular pleasure. Yet, the charge was repeated so many times it became an accepted truth.

Blanca's four-day turn with the hero of her fantasies slipped away before she knew it. She consoled herself with Luis, a boy her age who read well and had a cute birthmark on his upper lip. Walking her home one day, Luis was agitated, darting glances from side-to-side.

"What did you get in the math test?" Blanca asked.

"B."

"Mrs. Kaufman was in a bad mood today. Did you see how she rolled her eyes to the ceiling when Aurora dropped her social studies book on the floor? And she scolded me because I came in from recess sweaty and red in the face," she chattered on.

Luis looked into each building they passed.

"She said that no wonder I got asthma attacks. That I shouldn't be skipping rope because then they might have to take me to the emergency room, and that it was inconsiderate of me not to think of the problem this would cause others. Did you see how she wagged her finger at me and called me irresponsible?" Blanca inquired.

"Yeah."

"Hey, what's wrong with you? Cat got your tongue?"

Suddenly, Luis grabbed her arm and said, "Let's kiss."

Blanca flinched and stared at his birthmark. "Oh, I don't know," she stammered.

"Come on," he coaxed. "It's real good."

Unable to speak coherently, he squeezed her elbow. When he tried to say something, he failed to find the necessary words of persuasion. But her presence was essential to fulfill his daring plan, so he pressed on. He would convince her no matter what it took.

"What's the matter, you never kissed a guy?"

Blanca had only experienced kisses vicariously, observing teenage couples hidden in hallways or behind the guardhouse at the park. But she nodded and let him drag her into a building. After all, she had been Ralph's girl, and no one had to know they had only held hands once.

Luis explored the dark hallway quickly. He pulled her behind the stairwell strewn with empty beer bottles and dense with the stench of urine. Blanca's hands were sweaty, cold and sticky. She had no idea how to proceed, where to put her arms, how to make her nose disappear. In the movies, she noticed that the heroine dreamily closed her eyes just before the hero kissed her. Blanca clenched her eyes like fists while she pressed her books against her chest. The mingled odor of urine and beer hit her in the stomach, just as Luis gave her a quick peck on the lips. The abrupt peck seared her lips. She opened her eyes to the sight of Luis, mouth twisted, pulling nervously at his collar. He seemed in pain. She ran away from him and the awful smell of urine.

A kiss should offer a pleasure as great as licking a chocolate ice-cream ball plopped on a sugar cone. A kiss should feel as good as patting a puppy. She had always imagined it that way, tasty and soft. But that cold, tasteless buss? Really! It seemed quite stupid to her. But no, maybe not, she began to reflect. In the movies the heroine closes her eyes, the hero rubs his lips against hers, and they remain pasted together for a very long time. The heroine always seems on the verge of fainting, and the hero prepared to kiss her forever. That was it! Stupid Luis should have rubbed his lips against hers for a very long time. For ages and ages. Oh, God, but with that stink of urine, she might not have been able to stand it. Maybe behind the guardhouse at the park. But she could not suggest anything like that to him. He was the one who had to think about those things while she pretended she was an innocent damsel. Blanca's mental analysis served no useful purpose. By unexpressed agreement, Luis and Blanca never spoke of the episode again, nor did they consider themselves a couple after the crushing disappointment in the stairwell. Thinking about Luis' brief peck and comparing it to the passionate kisses in *Love Is a Many Splendored Thing*, she was sure William Holden felt like a furry puppy when he tasted Jennifer Jones' comet of chocolate ice cream—Blanca went home. She sucked in the smells that floated from the bakery downstairs. The aroma of kidney beans bubbling on the stove filtered through the apartment, and she felt hungry. There was nothing in the refrigerator. She poked in her coat pocket and found a coin. Enough to buy a corn muffin at the bakery. But Paquita had been cooking. That meant she would be home soon. Blanca decided to wait. Soon she heard the door slam.

"Your blessing."

"May God bless you," Paquita mumbled as she put a bag of groceries on the dinette table. She removed her coat.

"Blanca, take the garbage out on the way to the laundromat. And hurry, you know Tomás is waiting."

Blanca rolled her eyes to the ceiling. She took a shopping bag stuffed with garbage to the basement where the super burned it in an enormous coal boiler. Tentatively, she went down the wooden stairs, feeling the edge of each step with the tips of her shoes. At the bottom, she took a few steps, hand held up in the air, until she felt a long chain. She pulled on it and a bare light bulb went on. The basement was musty with the smell of coal, ashes, mice dung, and rotting food. Rats scuttled away from the sudden light, and she released the garbage bag as if it were red hot, pulled on the light chain, and ran up the stairs. In the hall, she twirled in the light, happy to have survived another incursion into the rat-infested basement.

She strained under Salvador's old sailor canvas sack full of dirty laundry and lugged it two blocks to the laundromat. Once the clothes were in the machine, she sprinkled them with powdered detergent, inserted coins in the slots, and shoved them in.

In the canvas sack she had stashed two empty soda bottles found in a garbage can on the street. She ran to the corner of 138th and crossed the street to a dilapidated little store where a wizened old man exchanged bottles for used magazines and comic books. Sitting in the hot rumbling laundromat, she read the juiciest stories in *True Confessions* and raced through *Little Lulu*. Her grandmother objected to her wasting any time reading at home when she had so many errands to run and chores to do.

As soon as Blanca returned to the apartment, Paquita handed her a heavy basket of food and rushed her out again. Blanca spilled into the night, a cold wind slicing into the skin of her face and bare hands as she walked ten blocks to a tall, wrought-iron fence. She climbed to the spiked spear points, careful not to drop the basket. The wind grazed her bare legs. The basket redolent of rice, beans, and stewed beef made her mouth water. She held the basket to her chest with one hand, and when she had slung a leg over the fence, taking care not to stab herself with a spear, she transferred the basket to the other hand. She eased herself down until the food was safe in Tomás' hands.

Half a lung had been removed from her uncle Tomás in the sanatorium for TB patients. The Catholic hospital, administered by nuns, served spartan food that lacked the seasonings, sauces, and rice Tomás enjoyed. Hospital meat, tasteless and of ambiguous color, was not even salted. Orderlies handed patients tiny packets of salt and pepper to use according to their taste. Tomás complained about the food on one of Paquita's visits, and from then on she sent Blanca every day after dark to feed her son because "the food eaten by those Americans tastes like seaweed, and that's why it's not nutritional," she would say. Tomás had observed that in the evenings, right after nightfall, the nuns retreated to their prayers. With this information at hand, Paquita scheduled food deliveries after dark to avoid detection.

Blanca stared at St. Francis of Assisi standing stonily in the garden, certain that he frowned at her in disapproval, while Tomás ate in the darkness and Blanca hovered over the fence waiting for the empty basket.

She always returned late, tired and famished. One night she climbed the creaking stairs of her building and unwittingly disturbed a drunk who lay sleeping in the shadows of the first landing. Furious for being abruptly awakened, he went after her, stumbling up the stairs like a wounded bull.

His fingers were like windmill vanes attacking the air. His old black hat and gnarled fingers were taken in by Blanca's frightened eyes. The rest of his body was buried under a dark, filthy coat. Blanca ran up, holding the food basket close to her body. She tripped and almost fell into the man's claws. The drunk's breath, heavy with alcohol and vomit, drove her on. Her chest ached when she reached her apartment. She banged on the door and looked back just in time to see the drunk stumble down the stairs. Trembling, she told her grandmother about the drunken pursuer. Paquita smacked her on the head.

"Shut up already. I'm sick and tired of your stupid stories. There's some food on the stove. Eat it and go to bed. I got enough problems on my mind."

That night, Blanca feared that, as soon as sleep swept her away, grimy fingers would wrap themselves around her neck and she would never escape. She forced herself to think about other things. So much had happened that day. She thought hard about skipping rope during recess. She tried to concentrate on Mrs. Kaufman, Ralph, even Luis and her first kiss under the stairwell. But her thoughts raced on without control. She thought of the drunk chasing her up the stairs, which made her think, inexplicably, about dark spirits. And that was what she hated thinking about most of all. When her grandmother forced her to a seance, Blanca feared she would disappear in a world of frightening beings. It was always the same pit in her stomach, the same fear.

A medium, eyes dark and glossy as coals, spins her hands in concentric circles over a bowl of water which sparkles in the glow of tapered candles. Then she closes her eyes, palms flat on the table, and sits still as a statue. Votaries, mostly women, gather somberly around the candle-lit table and mumble unintelligible prayers. Blanca's pupils dilate when she takes in the shadowy faces with their clenched eyes as they plead vehemently for the realization of something that Blanca knows for certain will be horrible. When the medium speaks with a voice thick as engine oil, it always comes as a terrible surprise.

Just as the earth rumbles a warning beneath the surface of the sea before a tremor is felt, the medium splits her lips far apart and moans. Blanca sees her uvula swing like a bell clapper. Her eyes are like dark suns. She speaks in a deep baritone, her words like fingernails scraping glass. The medium caws, a white dint appearing at either side of her nose. Holy water slops out of the bowl, guttering candles contort as if in agony. A shadow swoops down. The spirit speaks.

Blanca slams her eyes shut to escape the assault. The voice crushes against the wall of her heart. She clamps her eyes more tightly, damming the flood she knows will swallow her. Pure terror, blind terror, nameless terror. Another voice screeches next to her. The spirit approaches. Or maybe another spirit has surfaced, railing against his sentence in Purgatory. It is the hour of her ruin, the final hour when the voices of tortured spirits rage against unrealized destinies, aborted lives, violent deaths. Blanca is certain she will die this moment, her flesh torn to bits by demented spirits.

She does not breathe. Suddenly she sucks in a mouthful of air. An icy current grazes the hem of her skirt. Silence stills the voices. The medium gasps and collapses like a rag doll.

A light comes on. Paquita and the others plunk coins and dollar bills into a large crystal bowl and file out. Blanca's knees feel glutinous when she steps out into the night with her grandmother. She is always relieved to have escaped the tortured spirits once more. But she never sleeps after a seance. She sees spirits in every shadow. Invisible fingers jiggle the window pane with every gust of wind.

On one such night, she felt her bladder swell uncomfortably, but she was too frightened to cross the dark hall to the toilet. At dawn she fell asleep and dreamed of a porcelain bed pot on which she sat and sighed contentedly.

The next morning, a pungent odor awakened Paquita's suspicions, and she uncovered the amber stain Blanca had carefully hidden under her blanket. When the girl returned from school, Paquita waited red-faced, pale eyes flashing behind her lenses.

The instrument selected for the occasion was a thick leather belt with a gold-colored buckle in the shape of a large S. She made Blanca strip and tied her arms behind her back with a woolen scarf. She wrapped the belt around her fists and the buckle dangled in the air. "Get over here," Paquita said. And the girl stepped toward the shadowy line of pain. Then with intense, almost joyous vigor, Paquita beat her with the heavy buckle, turning the girl around so as to render an even beating.

"Take this, you swine, you filthy bitch. I should stick a stopper into your thing. Take this. Smell, smell the pee, you pig, and see how you like it."

She grabbed Blanca by the hair and rubbed her face into the soiled sheet. Having rested a bit, she beat her again, not sparing shoulders, head, back, until the shiny S was emblazoned in welts and blood all over her body. A thick silence punctuated the hard blows and Paquita's gasps when she brought the belt down. Blanca knew that crying would prolong the beating, so she stilled the ache behind her eyes and waited. When Paquita tired, she grabbed the girl by the hair again, shook her several times and shoved her into a corner. She raised a fist, triumphantly clasping a handful of hair like a winner's trophy. She then kicked the girl and walked away with a final threat.

"Next time you pee in bed, you'll see how I fix you up. I'm getting a cork and I'm stuffing it into your thing. You'll see, you filthy pig."

# 10

Salvador stretched the evening newspaper in front of him. Blanca glanced warily his way, but his face was slammed shut. She longed to hold his hand, talk to him. But she was frightened. Not of him, but of the consequences of her own voice intruding on the heavy atmosphere that hung in the living room.

The loud clang of pots in the kitchen was a sure sign of anger. The inevitability of another fight struck her, and she felt the familiar grip of fear. Tonight, like every night during the last two weeks since Salvador had been sleeping elsewhere, a rancorous storm swept through the small rooms.

"Blanca Rosa, come here this minute," her grandmother's voice was high and thick with anger. When Paquita used her two names, Blanca knew she was in trouble. In the kitchen, Paquita pointed at a pile of pots and dishes in the sink. To no avail, Blanca shrunk when she passed by her grandmother. She received a swift cuff on the head.

"You lazy, good-for-nothing. When did you think you'd do the dishes, *mañana*? No, you probably thought I'd do them for you," and she smacked Blanca's head again for good measure. Paquita made sure Blanca got started on her chore, took a deep breath, and went into the living room.

Blanca could mimic every hurtful word. She knew the dialogue by heart.

"So, your belly's full, and now that I've cooked and cleaned and looked after you, you're off to spend the night with the whore."

"Paquita, please shut up. I'm sick and tired of your insults. You know I can't sleep here. I'm a nervous man."

"Nervous, hah! You think I'm some kind of idiot? I know what you're up to with the whore. And don't talk to me about your so-called jumps."

Just as she got wound up for a long session—she had the ability to quarrel for hours—he put on his hat and coat and stomped out.

The vigorous fighting over someone Paquita always called "the whore" started about a year before, and with the passing of time the accusations intensified by angry increments. Under the stress of Paquita's diatribes, Salvador developed a particular strain of nervous attacks whose symptoms appeared only when they slept together. If Salvador made the mistake of lying on the marriage bed in the company of his wife, he was afflicted by a seizure that coursed through his entire body and caused uncontrollable tremors. Appropriately, he named his ailment "the jumps."

As soon as his head dropped on the pillow, the seizures acquired independent intensity and, like invisible elves, invaded his body. There were times when he twitched so violently, he fell out of bed. Paquita was also kept awake with his constant shaking and jolting. Several nights, he tried sleeping on the sofa since the discriminating jolts only took hold of him when he slept with his wife. The implied insult only aggravated Paquita's insomnia. She stood half the night glaring down at him, her curly hair sticking out wildly. She yelled and shook her fist in his stony face until one night his face cracked open. The disgust he had fought so hard to conceal spilled out and Paquita staggered back, bewildered.

The next evening when he returned from his new job at a jewelry factory, he had dinner and locked himself up in the dental workshop he had built in the apartment. Not having the resources to acquire a license to practice his trade, he did so furtively, locking the workshop during the day to avoid detection by a city inspector. At ten, he announced he had rented a room in a nearby boarding house. Blanca braced herself for the onslaught that was sure to ensue, but surprisingly, not a word passed through Paquita's lips. Salvador pecked her on the forehead, gave Blanca his blessing, and gently closed the door behind him.

The second the door was shut, Paquita sprung into action. She put on her coat and tracked him like a bloodhound. That first night of vigil was followed by others. Paquita needed to know whether Salvador slept in the rented room and whether he slept alone. She hid behind parked cars, like a thief stalking a victim. For hours she watched what went on in the boarding house until the cold night and her numb limbs forced her back home.

Paquita sniffed around hungrily during the day, too. She badgered the occupants of the rooming house, interrogating them relentlessly about Salvador and his nocturnal habits. Convinced of his infidelity, she was tireless in her attempts to catch him in the act. She had never believed that story about his seizures, or that she made him so nervous that he could not sleep with her. There was another woman. She had no doubt. And she knew her identity. It was only a matter of catching them together. They were sly. They certainly were, but she would outfox them.

Paquita engaged in a constant quest for information as to the whereabouts of "the whore." She waited for Blanca to come home from school one day, and they took the subway to El Barrio. On the station platform, swarms of people gathered in tightly ribbed nets.

"Sit on the bench, Blanca, and don't move until I come back," Paquita warned. "You hear me? Don't you dare move. I have to go to a place where they don't let children in. If they catch children there, a policeman comes and takes them away to prison. So you stay here without moving. I'll be back soon."

Blanca had no idea what a "soon" could be. She sat for a long time in the subway station and saw hundreds of faces. No, she was convinced she saw at least a million as she desperately searched for her grandmother. When the limit was reached of what she considered to be a soon and Paquita had not returned, she started sniveling, convinced that her grandmother would never find her amid the shoal of people at the station. She gripped the edge of the bench to keep from being carried away by the crowd.

Maybe her grandmother had flown off to Puerto Rico again. She had done it many times, and Blanca had to stay with people who were called foster parents. But they were not parents at all, only indifferent strangers. Paquita didn't have a suitcase, though. Unless she hid it somewhere so Blanca wouldn't see it. Or maybe she had just abandoned Blanca forever, fulfilling a frequent threat. Just yesterday, when Blanca fell in the school yard and bruised her knees, Paquita beat her with a wire hanger saying, "It wasn't because you were praying that you fell, you bitch. I'm so sick of you. Just wait and see. One of these days I'm just going to get rid of you forever."

Throngs of people wove in and out of the station, tore in and out of trains, bobbed up and down the stairs from platform to platform, yet no one looked at her, no one saw her. She felt strangely invisible among all those people who did not recognize her existence. Stunned by the blind masses scurrying like armies of ants, she no longer heard the screech of trains, the hurried steps, the clang of the turnstile. A lump stuck in her throat, and she burst into tears. She clutched the edge of the bench for comfort. Paquita was furious when she returned and caught her crying. She gave her a swift blow on the head so she would have a good reason to cry.

Paquita dealt with Blanca directly. Her ramrod rule allowed complete control with no need for circumlocution or hesitation. But with Salvador, it was another story. Paquita had to behave more conservatively with her husband and control her impulse to slap his face free of the disgust he held behind his hard look. When she sat across from him at the dinette table, it infuriated her to see him eat so slowly, deliberately chewing his food, always so careful about everything. So she attacked him with accusations and insults, her only weapons, attempting to break down the barrier that concealed his secret transgression. But she knew Salvador had the devil's temper, and she was always conscious of an invisible barrier which, if crossed, could scorch her with violence.

"Imagine," she told a friend once, "I was yelling at him one day, and instead of hitting me, he punched the wall and broke his hand in several places. If he had hit me, he would have smashed my face. That's why sometimes I get scared when I yell at him. I'm afraid he'll lose his temper and beat me bad."

But Salvador waited out the storm, tolerated her vituperation impassively, and did not fight back. Nor did he defend himself. That alone made Paquita more suspicious. She knew he was passive with guilt. And she knew why.

The truth that always lurked a step ahead of Paquita swung about one day and waited for her to catch up. It exploded one Saturday morning like the bloated belly of a dead dog in the heat when Salvador went out to buy the newspaper. He returned to the apartment, face ashen as a lava stone. Blanca sat on the floor, legs tucked under her skirt, playing quietly with a paper doll.

"Where's Paquita?" His voice was sharp as a blade.

"She went out, Papá."

"When?"

"I don't know."

"Was it a long time ago?"

"Yes, I think so."

"She took a key, didn't she? A key from my workshop, right?"

Blanca placed the paper doll on the linoleum floor.

"Tell me the truth, child!"

Blanca stared hard at the laced fingers on her lap.

When they moved to this larger apartment, Salvador divided a room in two with high wooden boards and a door in the middle. Half became Blanca's bedroom and in the other half he installed a dentist's chair, tools, and drills. After dinner, he spent hours making smoothly textured dentures and dental bridges. When he had no dental mechanic work, he created lovely pieces of gold jewelry punctuated with cultivated pearls or the semiprecious stones he bought at the jewelry factory where he worked. Not having a license to operate these enterprises, he kept the tiny workshop locked while he was out. That way, he said, if a government agent came to investigate, and God knows they're everywhere sniffing into honest people's business, no one could discover his sideline and drag him to court on the trumped up charges the government always brought against honest men whose only crime was trying to make a living.

His garrison had a weakness, though. Salvador had not considered it necessary to build the wall to the ceiling, so there was a narrow space between the ceiling and the top edge of the wall. Paquita studied the scalable wall, the width of the space above the wall, and with a ladder borrowed from the building superintendent, shoved Blanca into Salvador's workshop. From the other side, Blanca unlocked the door so Paquita could go in and rifle through Salvador's privacy. Feverishly, she found what she sought, an unfamiliar house key.

"Here's the key to the whore's apartment." Her angry scowl erased any hint of triumph she may have felt for finally succeeding in her quest.

She got her handbag, and before rushing out the door, said to Blanca, "If Salvador comes asking about this key, don't say I took it. You hear me? Don't you dare say I took it because he'll kill me."

Blanca blinked back tears as Salvador towered over her.

"Tell me the truth, Blanca. I won't hurt your grandmother. I just want to know if she has the key. It's an important key, you know," he said gently.

The girl could not lie. Maybe for him she would have lied, but not for her grandmother. Forced to choose loyalties, Blanca chose the one who kept a first-aid kit with a red cross on it and pulled it out of a drawer whenever she scraped or cut herself. The man who took her to the movies once and comforted her when she hid under the seat because an enormous gorilla escaped from a laboratory cage and kidnapped a pretty young woman who slept so innocently, a shapely arm curved over her blond curls. The man who helped her with homework when he was around.

"Yes, Papá," she said.

Salvador dashed through the door and flew down the stairs.

Blanca looked through the window and waited. The neighborhood was animated with people running Saturday afternoon errands. Cars idled at the red traffic light. Then she heard a riot of voices.

Paquita rushed in gasping. She held a fist to her chest. Salvador rushed in after her, his face as white as limestone, fists clenched and bloodless. Blanca hid behind the armchair.

"Give me the key," he roared.

"So you want the key, huh? Why are you so interested in this key? Because it belongs to the whore's apartment, doesn't it? Don't deny it anymore, I finally caught you. Bet you never thought I'd find out where you moved her to in El Barrio. But I did. And I went to the whore's place just now, pushed the key into the lock and it opened, just like that," Paquita snapped her fingers. "I'm sorry she wasn't in, because I was ready to claw her eyes out. But one of her brats was there, and I gave him a good whack on the head."

Paquita's face was scarlet. Her body sagged, deflated like an airless balloon.

Blanca trembled behind the armchair.

"Give me the key or I'll kill you." Salvador's words whistled low and cold.

"Go ahead, kill me. Why don't you get it over with? There's nothing else you can do to me now. First you go to bed with Consuelo, my own daughter, the very same I carried for nine months in my belly, and then you kill me so you can bed her in peace."

Blanca had some difficulty understanding why Papá and Aunt Consuelo went to bed together, but a sick misgiving lodged in some deep recess of her mind as she fathomed her grandmother's fury.

Salvador pulled at Paquita's handbag. She dug an elbow into his ribs, kicked his shin, and ran out. He stood for a while in the middle of the living room, gasping for breath. Then he settled in his armchair and waited.

Voices and a clatter of feet rushed up to the apartment like a flood. Paquita appeared more composed when she arrived accompanied by Ramón and a big, blond policeman with the biggest feet Blanca had ever seen. Some curious neighbors straggled in also, titillated by the captivating scent of scandal. They all spoke at once, some in English, others in Spanish. Paquita accused Salvador of attempted murder in

Spanish, while Salvador defended his position in English and a neighbor translated and put in his two cents in both languages. No one was reluctant to express, at the top of hearty lungs, whose side they were taking in the matter at hand. Ramón, who had never distinguished himself for his valor, stood ill at ease under the lintel, ready to slip out at an appropriate moment. The clamor peaked in confusion when a thin man, shrieking something about the defense of maternal honor, hurtled into the room brandishing a six-inch switchblade. With a lissome twist, the big-footed policeman snapped the man's hand and unarmed the otherwise dauntless son Tomás. The avenging son now stood crestfallen and handcuffed, his illusions of gallant maternal defender suddenly snipped by the big-shoed Irishman. As far as Tomás was concerned, the Irishman had not been born of a mother.

The clang and clatter of voices spilled down the stairs and into a wire-screened wagon that drove them all, participants and spectators, to the police station. Hiding behind the armchair, Blanca heard her grandmother's voice rise above the din.

"It's all that devil of a girl's fault with her big mouth. She'll pay for this when I get back."

# 11

Because she had heard that God was merciful, Blanca knelt behind the armchair, palms pressed together, and implored for delivery, to be struck by a bolt of lightning. She longed to fracture into tiny pieces, and that her fragments be spilled into the wind. Then she would be nothing, because she could never be gathered together again. And that which is nothing feels nothing. Huddled like a fetus behind the armchair, she was desperate to die. Death was the only escape from her plight.

It was hard to curl into herself and become as tiny as possible. She still ached from the last beating. A broken saucer had caused her latest fall into disfavor. On that occasion Paquita chose a broom and beat her again and again until her anger was spent. The insults were as painful as the blows, and she could still hear the scalding words beating to the rhythm of the broom.

"Take this, you worthless piece of shit. You good-for-nothing bitch. You can't even take cats out to pee. Good-for-nothing trash. Take this and this and this so you'll learn to be careful. How many times have I told you, rotten whore, not to break things. Get out of my sight now. I can't stand you anymore. And don't cry, or I'll really give you a good flogging so you'll have plenty of reason to cry."

Bent over in pain, Blanca scuttled to her bed. She wept as quietly as she could, lips tight as seams. No one would hear a peep from her. The welts crisscrossing her body throbbed. She licked her wounds like a mongrel and fell asleep.

Terrified of another beating, she now prayed behind the armchair. But since loving God is loving without being loved, there was no response to her desperate plea. Death did not save her from this longest of days. All she could do was wait for Paquita's return, husbandless, and with an ideal target for her monstrous wrath.

That evening a tight-lipped neighbor rushed Blanca to the emergency room, an eardrum ruptured, ribs bruised, a concussion, and purple hematomas tattooed on her body.

Paquita, in the meantime, escaped to Puerto Rico.

Once released from the hospital, the authorities deposited her in a foster home, with a family approved and licensed by the city to take charge of children in times of crises. For this act of charity, they received due compensation with federal, state, and city funds. Her black and blue sadness cut a jagged tear in the core of her existence through which she would forever peer at the world.

Before fleeing to Puerto Rico, Paquita barged into the welfare office with a grandson-translator in tow. She denounced her daughter Consuelo, whom she claimed was receiving financial benefits from Salvador, her lover, Paquita's very own husband, would you believe it? Paquita's voice rose several octaves. She argued for the justice of suspending Consuelo's welfare benefits. Consuelo and her six children should suffer the penury she deserved, since her husband Regino, plagued by his wife's infidelity, had divorced her. Shortly after the divorce, he was found stabbed to death in his apartment. Wasn't that a coincidence, she hinted slyly.

Wait your turn, lady. You have no proof. There's nothing we can do. Can't you see we're busy? Paquita, recognizing her defeat, clung to her grandson-translator's arm and hurried to the subway station. She had much to do before she left.

The itch for revenge dulled any other sensation. Somehow she had to get even. Convinced of the betrayal, Paquita had accosted Consuelo without mercy. She treasured a fistful of hair she wrenched from her daughter's head in a tussle launched when they ran into each other on the street. Consuelo defended herself from her mother's attack, and Paquita retreated bearing the rancor of bloody scratches her own daughter carved on her face.

The boy, one of Tomás', stood sullenly beside his grandmother. He stepped back in embarrassment when she started mumbling to herself. In front of Paquita, almost at the edge of the platform and facing the track, was a short, long-haired woman. Paquita's heart slammed. It was the whore, she was sure of it. She's wearing a new coat, but it's her all right. Paquita approached the woman stealthily, like a cat on the prowl. Now she would pay for it all, and what judge would condemn her when he knew the dimension of her suffering, the proportions of the betrayal? She was so close to the woman she could sniff her cologne and catch a glint of the bobby pins that gathered strands of long black hair at the sides of her head.

Instinctively, perceiving the approach of a hostile presence, the woman swiveled suddenly, and Paquita gasped when she saw the face of a stranger. She had come so close to murdering an innocent woman. Her knees gave way. Clasping the arm of the unsuspecting victim for support, she held a fist to her chest and sank to the ground. The next day she flew to Puerto Rico.

Removed from the barrage of insults and beatings, of lies and betrayals, Blanca gathered the picture-puzzle fragments of her being in a bright cheery apartment where she listened to The Platters on a record player, watched Felix the Kat on television every afternoon, and played house with the daughters of her foster family. Her bruises faded, and soon she was laughing and babbling, certain at last that someone was listening. She stopped hiding from strangers and happily skipped with Elba to the market where she would help her select aromatic spices and firm vegetables for the delicious sauces she poured over her roasts. They chattered in the kitchen, and while Elba got the pots and pans out, Blanca rinsed the coriander and green peppers, shook out the excess water, and drained them in baskets. Though it made her cry, Blanca enjoyed peeling and chopping onions and pounding a mixture of oregano, garlic, and peppercorns in the beautifully carved oak mortar to make a fragrant *sofrito*. Sometimes Elba allowed her to stir the sauce with a big wooden spoon as she introduced Blanca to the art of cooking.

It was summertime, and with no school or errands to occupy her time, she learned to roller skate in the park and read many books in the library. Elba had her hair cut at a beauty parlor, a haven full of colored pots and creams and scents where the most fascinating metamorphoses took place.

Soon, much too soon, it was all over. The chill warning of winter was in the air. Dead leaves spun dizzily on sidewalks and tiny patches of grass. Blanca's cardboard suitcase was ready when the social worker knocked on the door. Her hand disappeared in the social worker's smooth palm, and the two pairs of eyes looked steadily ahead at the solitary hall.

Blanca shrank when she recognized the old neighborhood. Firemen milled in front of the Willis Avenue firehouse as they whistled at pretty girls. Saint Luke's loomed haughtily between two tenements. Behind the church, nuns presided over a parochial school where only the Irish and Italians could afford to send their children. The social worker parked on St. Ann's Avenue, around the corner from Woolworth's on 138th. She led Blanca into a scruffy building and knocked at a ground-floor apartment. There she delivered the girl to Goyita.

The door shut behind Blanca, and Goyita looked down at her.

"You look just like your father, child. Here we are. This room's just for you. Do you like it?"

The room was small. It contained a real bed with a pink chenille bedspread and a ruffled bolster. A doll with a flounced skirt and a poke bonnet sat in the center of the bed. On the opposite wall there was a chest of drawers with a tiny altar on top. On a white, delicately crocheted mat there was a statue of the Virgin draped in blue and white holding a hand to her chest, framed pictures of the Sacred Heart of Jesus and Saint Michael the Archangel, fat candles of different colors, and a glass of holy water.

"That's to protect us all from the evil spirits," Goyita explained.

Blanca sat on the edge of the bed and picked up the doll. She touched its blond curls, pink and white clothing, and then looked up timidly.

"That's for you. I got it at Alexander's yesterday. What a mess! People were crawling all over the place for the Labor Day sale. I picked up a few things here and there. Not bad." Goyita observed her brightly enameled fingernails.

Blanca hugged the doll, inhaled the aroma of new rubber, and gently patted the nylon strands of hair. And it wasn't even her birthday, she thought.

"Take your jacket off, kid. Are you hungry? Yeah, I thought so. Let's get you some milk and something sweet. You like jelly doughnuts? What kid doesn't, huh?"

In the kitchen, Goyita switched on the radio. "Wish I could yodel like that," she said admiringly, and hummed to the country-western tune on the radio.

"You really look just like Ramón. It's incredible. Speaking of your father, I better start dinner. He'll be here any minute."

When Goyita moved in with Ramón, she pleaded with him to bring Blanca to live with them. Unable to have children, Goyita was eager to pacify her maternal stirrings. Ramón, attempting to still his occasional pangs of conscience, as well as his concubine, acceded unenthusiastically.

Permissive in her new role, Goyita allowed Blanca to trick- or-treat on Halloween dressed as a gypsy. After school, she let Blanca stay home to play grown-up. The girl dabbed drops of Goyita's *Christmas in July* behind her ears and smeared her face with the multicolored sticks and creams Goyita generously applied to herself every morning.

On Saturdays, while Ramón had a few beers with his friends at the neighborhood tavern, Goyita and Blanca roamed department stores. Goyita trained the girl well in the art she had most adeptly perfected. She planted her small sentinel at a strategic location in the store, with instructions to cough when she saw the security guard. While Blanca stood watch, pretending to examine the merchandise, Goyita stuffed her capacious handbag with whatever baubles she could fit into it. When they got home and shut the door against the pursuers Blanca was certain would accost them, she wobbled weakly to her room and sat on the bed while Goyita followed and pulled out stockings and petticoats, crayons and coloring books and lots of costume jewelry. Amazing how much she could stuff into her handbag!

Goyita enrolled Blanca in after-school catechism lessons at St. Luke's, insisting that she must make her First Holy Communion. The girl had never endured any formal training in the mysteries of Catholicism. Her belief in an ambiguous higher being resulted from a process of osmosis whereby she involuntarily absorbed reports about the existence of an infinitely endowed god and his sycophantic saints, angels, and virgins. Fear of the devil had been effectively transmitted to her as well. She knew of the dark being who tempted humans constantly and was the cause of all the wrongs of the world. Her theology was supplemented by the Manichean stories she overheard regarding the constant conflict between good and evil spirits, the frequent curses of her Uncle Tomás, who defecated on God and the Holy Host all the time, and the dusky secrets of spiritualism. Dragged to many seances by her grandmother, Blanca had been instilled with the fear of evil.

Ecclesiastical liturgy made Blanca dizzy and nauseous. Kneeling at her pew in Saint Luke's, Blanca felt a hollow sickness that snaked from her stomach to her flesh and crawled into her head. With a doleful countenance, Sister Martha led the girls through their catechism lessons. She made sure her charges fulfilled all ritual requirements, kneeling during the mea culpa and pounding their narrow chests with an exaggerated semblance of penitence. Oblivious to the sinful burden Sister Martha said they had been born with, the girls giggled every time the nun clicked her tongue in disapproval when they confused the sequence of the Act of Contrition.

After school, Blanca was always hungry, and she held her head in her cupped hands while she knelt. A smile of satisfaction washed over the nun's face. Sister Martha pushed a forefinger under the white wimple to scratch her head. "Put your head up," the nun snapped at the famished Blanca, whose face was green with sacrifice.

The girls lined up for confession. Although the confessor was only a voice and shadows, Blanca never confused him with God. Blanca was last in line, and under the supervisory eye of the nun, she looked up at the statues and carvings in the church. Blood spurted everywhere. From whip lashes, thorns, crosses, lance wounds. Blanca closed her eyes and lowered her head. She longed to be outside lolling in the spring sun. She could not recall committing sins that were so horrible Jesus had to die for them, and nervously she invented a few sins that, she hoped, would not cause too much distress.

The confessional had the odor of worn pennies.

"Bless me, Father, for I have sinned." She hurried through the sign of the cross. "This is my first confession." (I haven't had the time nor the inclination nor the freedom to sin too much, but here goes.) "I disobeyed my father once." (He asked me for a beer while he was watching a wrestling match on TV, and Goyita, who was already in the kitchen, said she would get it for him.)

"I said a bad word once." (My schoolmates were whispering about a girl who had been raped, and like an idiot I asked, "what's rape?", a question which caused much hilarity. Joe, the leader in this sort of discussion, took me under his wing to explain what he called the facts of life. But I didn't believe him for a second. Who does he think I am, an idiot? Anyway, after what Joe said, I'm convinced that rape is a nasty word.)

"I've told two lies." (The ones I just told you.) "Oh, my God, I am heartily sorry for having offended thee, and I detest all my sins..." Then she strayed from Sister Martha's strict instructions and asked the priest, with great disquiet, whether her sins were mortal or venial. Much to her relief, the priest assured her they were only venial, and she atoned for her sins with two Our Fathers and two Holy Marys, kneeling before the blind eyes of Jesus and his acolytes.

The day of her First Holy Communion seemed to have unfolded from the pages of the most beautiful fairy tale. In a white dress and veil, holding a tiny Mass book and a white plastic rosary that resembled nacre, Blanca looked like an incipient bride ready to take her perpetual vows.

The holy host adhered to her palate, though, and with great difficulty she attempted to pray quietly as she detached the dead Jesus with the tip of her tongue. It never seemed logical to her that Jesus would choose to enter the souls of his worshippers through the digestive tract. He should have preferred holy water dripped in the eyes of the faithful, or aromatic oils smoothed over the forehead like ashes. But if the priests, regally dressed in purple and gold, said that this was the way it had to be done, who was she to question the rite?

Goyita beamed proudly. She had filched the cutest lace handbag from Alexander's for the occasion and forced Ramón to purchase the required attire for such a solemnity. Blanca paraded loftily through the neighborhood, like a queen strolling in her garden. Nothing frightened her that day, even when she passed by the dreaded basement window. This was where a skinny old man with a crow's face lurked. He offered candy to little girls on their way home from school, asking them to come in and play with him.

Blanca was happy that day, but she was devastatingly punished for every second of joy. As any happiness she experienced carried with it an exorbitant price, she suffered the consequences of her peaceful joy during her stay with Goyita. She had to pay for her emancipation from her grandmother's tyranny, for leaning happily toward the sun, for healing her psychic amputations. Paquita's absence offered her liberation from a hatred that had begun to spring from her innermost being and that remained frozen in her like a dead embryo. She had been freed of the guilt born from that hate, a guilt that seeped into all her experiences. Since freedom has an exorbitant price, Blanca paid for the days without beatings, the sunny afternoons when she fashioned roller skates out of empty beer cans bent in half and scraped happily on the sidewalk, the nights when she curled up in bed and read comic books. Blanca paid deeply. She paid with interest. The interest of her debt accumulated unrestrained because, in an act of unforgivable hubris, she had dared to be happy.

She started to pay her debt on the afternoon she returned from school and Goyita was not home. She waited at the stoop until her father arrived from work, and together they went into the apartment. Goyita had taken her clothing, her jewelry, her cosmetics, her perfumes. She took the radio. Blanca ran to her bedroom and stared at the bare chest of drawers. The absence of Goyita's altar attested to the reality of her disappearance. Ramón searched the drawers and wardrobe for evidence of her sudden flight. He mumbled curses under his breath. He cursed Goyita, then all women, and rushed out of the apartment without a word. Alone and frightened, Blanca examined her feet as they dangled from the armchair. She yearned for the soothing warmth of a cocoon. A dog barked in the distance.

Ramón gave off the harsh stench of rum when he returned at dawn. His eyes were swollen and his chin sprinkled with black dots. Blanca asked for Goyita. When her father did not respond, she asked again and again. "Shut up!" he shouted finally, and she did not ask again. In his bedroom, Ramón cried in that peculiar fashion men have, trying to contain the racking sobs that were hoarse and hollow. He shook and bellowed like a wounded elephant. It seemed to Blanca that his tears would never soothe his sorrow. Blanca also cried.

Death was one of the patterns of her life. Since the silent death of her mother, Blanca would face death many times. People around her seemed to be always dying. Or disappearing, which was the same. Once, on the way to a Sunday outing at Orchard Beach, Blanca, Salvador, and Paquita strolled to the subway station. At the corner of Brook Avenue and 139th Street, a crowd circled a figure on the sidewalk. It looked like a big rag doll thrown on the pavement. Blanca snuck through the crowd and saw a boneless man, arms and legs in strange angles, brains splattered on the sidewalk. The eye Blanca could see was a purple puddle. The neighbors murmured among themselves, stunned by the aftermath of his unfortunate story. After sipping all kinds of sinful concoctions in a lifelong attack of desperate thirst, the man's spirit was left empty. He jumped from the roof of a six-story building in search of the ultimate sensation. When he made the irrevocable jump, spectators saw him reach for a fire escape in apparent repentance. But he could only hold on for a few seconds. His desperate screams were cut short by the hard pavement that collected his reluctant sacrifice with indifferent scorn.

Blanca remembered the man in his puddle of blood, and now she wanted to die, too. Death would strike easily. One only had to stop breathing. But the more she tried, the more her rebellious lungs inflated and expelled mouthfuls of air that returned anxiously to her nostrils.

Without Goyita, her father no longer cared for her. So he deposited her again, like a sack of old clothing, at the dank basement apartment of a co-worker. Rafael lived there with his wife and six children. He required additional money for his vices, which consisted of a few beers on Friday nights and playing the numbers. Ramón quieted his conscience for this new desertion by paying him for Blanca's care. For him, Blanca long ago had become a transferable object.

While she lived with Rafael, his wife, and six children, Blanca never saw her father. She ran through the barrio streets with her broken shoes and torn clothing, visiting friends and schoolmates during the dinner hour, hoping she would be asked to stay. To protect herself from the cold that always snuck through her threadbare coat, she wore layers of soiled clothing. Forced to share her sparse clothing with Rafael's two daughters, she layered her entire wardrobe over her body like onion skins. She had three grayish panties, two undershirts that had once been white, a blue cotton dress that had acquired a yellowish hue, a woolen skirt with orange and green stripes, and a navy-blue blouse that she clasped in front with two plastic buttons and a safety pin. She also wore several pairs of socks of nondescript color which soaked through when it rained or snowed because her only shoes were like sieves. Blanca's shoes were so worn out that the soles had come apart, and she held the flaps together with strings. She scratched her head violently, showering her shoulders with lice.

On the night Blanca willed to die, Rafael returned to the apartment unexpectedly. His wife had gone out with the girls, and the boys were playing handball at the park. The man was scrawny and his eyes were half-closed. Blanca was frightened when she looked up from her school book and saw him stagger in. Rafael crossed the kitchen, seemed not to notice her, and went into the bedroom.

Then he called.

"Girl, come 'ere," his voice greased the air.

"What for?"

"I'm gonna show you something real nice."

Blanca suspected that nothing nice could emerge from his request, but her years of unquestioned obedience to adults had indoctrinated her well. Her heart thumped like a door batting in the wind. She went into the dark room. Rafael was sitting on the bed.

"Come 'ere."

Blanca lingered at the foot of the bed.

"Hurry up, I don't got all night."

The girl approached hesitantly, balky, her head bent down. Rafael took her hands.

"Whatsa matter, you afraid a me? Come on, all I wanna do is play with you."

Rafael released her, and from the crooked wound of his zipper pulled out the thick beak of a condor. The little girl covered her face, and under the shield of her hands, shut her eyes hermetically to erase the horror she had just seen. He grabbed her stiff hands and forced them on the condor's beak, so fat and swollen it seemed ready to swallow her small hands. The stench of rum and perspiration made her heave.

"No, no, I don't want to," she sobbed. "No, no, no," she shook her head violently, eyes shut, cancelling horrors.

"Grab me, you asshole, grab me tight, shit, and don't let go or I'll kill you." A slap burned the side of her head.

Blanca wept, condemned to visions of blood dripping from her terrible wounds. The man's fingernails dug into her shoulders as he howled and shook like a dying beast. A gush of smelly liquid stained her. Terrified, she searched for her fallen hands on the floor, certain that they could be found floating in a pool of blood.

Rafael opened his eyes and with a dark smile said, "You're my girlfriend now. Me and you gonna play a lot from now on. Just you and me."

Then his face clouded. Icily, he warned, "Don't go telling nobody 'bout our little game, you hear, 'cause you're dead meat. Look, see this knife? You know who this knife's for?"

Blanca didn't respond, she just stared at the gleaming blade.

"This baby's for you, little girl, to stick it in your heart if you go blabbin'. So it's our little secret, right?"

The man fell on the bed, exhausted.

"Get atta here."

Blanca ran to the park. She washed her hands again and again at the water fountain, scrubbing them with dead leaves. Then she clambered on a swing and propelled herself into the sky, feeling the cold air on her cheeks. She no longer cried, but concentrated on the coming and going of the swing. She pushed herself higher and higher until her heart drowned in her stomach.

Miriam, Rafael's oldest daughter, woke everyone up the next morning.

"Rebeca, Blanca, get up it's late. Hey, Blanca, your eyes are real swollen. What's the matter?"

"Nothing."

Blanca put on her coat over the clothing she had slept in, took her books from the top of the radiator, and ran to school.

She hurried to the cafeteria before she missed breakfast. Standing in line, she wearily observed the boys sparring and the girls who watched the boys, whispering and giggling. She put cold cereal and reconstructed milk on her tray and approached the long tables.

"Hey, Blanca, come 'ere," Susana yelled and flapped her arms.

Blanca sat next to her.

"Carmen brought a real nice rope today. We'll jump rope after lunch. Listen, don't get too close to Socorro. Jenny told me she has lice. And I tell you, I don't wanna catch lice again after what I went through when my mother rubbed kerosene on my scalp." Susana wagged her head. "And now, you know what she does? She washes my head with dog-flea shampoo. The stuff stings and it stinks, too!"

Blanca ate slowly, trying to relieve her stomach ache.

"Hey, how come you're not saying something? What's the matter?"

"Nothing. I don't feel well, that's all."

Blanca hunched over her cereal bowl, not daring to look at her friend. She was afraid her secret would slip out and thrash on the table like a dying fish.

"Hey, if you go to the nurse, maybe she'll send you home. That's cool, you can miss school."

"No, no, it's not that bad. I feel better already after I ate," Blanca said quickly.

"Up to you," Susana shrugged. "The bell, hurry, or we'll be late."

Blanca threw the uneaten cereal in a huge metal garbage barrel and went up to class. Mrs. Wasserman asked her why she refused to remove her coat. Blanca said she was cold and opened her reading book, but the letters and words were incomprehensible. Her workbook remained blank, and she was unable to smile even when Heriberto, the class clown, made a cartwheel in front of the chalkboard and was banished to a corner where he stood facing the wall.

Mrs. Wasserman waited for two weeks while Blanca refused to take off her coat and answered all questions with an "I don't know" and a shrug.

"What's the matter, Blanca. You're not doing your homework, the work you do in class isn't as good as it used to be. All your grades are going down. You can't go on like this. Why aren't you working hard the way you used to, doing your homework, participating in class? Why don't you borrow books from the class library any longer?"

Blanca shrugged and balanced her weight on one foot and then another while she stood by the teacher's desk.

"Well, if you want to talk to me about anything, let me know. But I expect you to work as hard as you did before."

Her attempt at a note of austerity did not hide the compassion Mrs. Wasserman felt for her favorite student.

# 12

Public School 9 was a red-brick structure built at the turn of the century. It loomed on 138th Street across from the Puerto Rico Theater like a huge armory vigilantly surveilling students, teachers, and staff who scuttled in and out its wide staircase. P.S. 9 did not inspire teachers to draw out the best in their pupils. Teachers never expected the children—who were mostly Puerto Rican and Black, with a smattering of Irish and Italians too poor to have fled the ghetto—to occupy the ivy-scented halls of distant universities or mark history with distinguished feats. Teachers felt gratified beyond their expectations when girls turned twelve without "getting themselves pregnant," and boys managed to elude reform school. Their biggest success consisted in steering the little lambs into a trade that would keep them off the public dole, such as auto mechanics or sewing.

Teachers and principal lingered at the shore, their backs turned to the island of isolation in which the children lived. From the periphery, they looked away and refused to learn the language of the dispossessed. Teachers were often overheard in the lounge by the girls who cleaned up after them. They expressed shock that little girls would have their ear lobes pierced, a savage tribal custom that, they thought, had to be some form of child abuse. They criticized when children were absent from school to care for younger siblings if a mother had to run errands, or if they had to translate for a sick relative in the hospital. They accused children of cheating when they copied from each other's homework. When the children explained that they were only helping out a friend, they were doubly punished for lying as well as cheating. And their diet was atrocious, teachers said, eating disgusting food like black-blood sausages and boiled green bananas.

The children of P.S. 9 were, at best, no more than question marks. If the children were hungry, suffered abuse, needed assistance to realize their potential, their silent appeals for help fell on stone hearts. Most teachers were at P.S. 9 not because they wanted to be, but because inexperience or limited pedagogical abilities did not allow them access to a more desirable school district.

There were exceptions. Mrs. Kalfus, a second-grade teacher, once kissed Blanca's swollen cheek when she had a toothache. Years later Blanca, who forgot much of her disrupted childhood, remembered that kiss. In the fifth grade, Mrs. Wasserman kept a collection of children's books in the classroom. These were precious books about princesses who slept under flowery canopies and were always loved by handsome princes. There was a book about a girl who owned a black horse and galloped gloriously on the sandy beaches of a place called New England, and about two-story white houses inhabited by happy people and dogs and cats and canaries and lots of dolls. That school year Blanca read the books in Mrs. Wasserman's collection over and over again until they were etched in her memory. She transformed the stories into dreams of possible worlds. Because Blanca was a manipulator of symbols, she took the only symbols at her disposal and dreamed them possible. She hid them in a quiet nook of her mind, and from there they gave her light and comfort.

Blanca read in two languages. She had taught herself to read in Spanish after a cousin arrived from Puerto Rico and brought with her a book. The young woman recognized Blanca's hunger for words and offered the book to her like a sacrament. Blanca avidly spread its pages, but could not read it because it was written in Spanish. Hungrily, she pored over the first book she ever owned. She searched through its pages and scrutinized the drawings. Then she went back to the first page, the first sentence, the first word, the title. Familiar letters, letters she knew, words that she knew also, but did not know she knew. Oh, the pain, the pain of those intractable symbols. She wanted to possess them, drink them, devour them. Her hunger for those words did not wane. She held the book tightly, the words wiggled and swam and titillated. Then she split the words like ripe pomegranates and spilled the letters like seeds. She gently gathered the seeds into their shells one by one, again and again, over and over, until each word burst in her mind like a blossom. The world was never the same after that.

Blanca read with desperate thirst in her two languages. If there were no books at her disposal, she read labels on olive jars and tomato sauce cans. She read street signs and cigarette packets. She stood for hours in front of the newspaper stand and gulped words until intoxicated. The attendant always knew she was there. He would shoo her away like a fly. And like a fly, she zoomed back for her honey. One day he asked her name. She said Blanca. And he said that's a pretty name; it means white, doesn't it? She said yes, how do you know? And he said oh, I know many things, which surprised Blanca because he was blind.

When does conscious life begin? Is it born from the astonishment we feel when we discover that deception lies everywhere? Or is it the smell of another's distinctive sweat, or when destiny marches on, echoing cruelties? Is it born from lost pride or the humiliation of a slap? Or is it when we realize that gods mock and sneer? Could it begin with the explosion of a perfect silence?

Blanca's conscious life began when she lay on her cot and her rum-colored eyes shone with imaginary scenes. It was when Blanca discovered fantasies and daydreams. She was an Amazon galloping on a white horse, or a princess sleeping amid veils of tulle. In her fantasies, Blanca was a ballerina, a movie star, a cabaret singer, a championship horseback rider, a modern sculptor, a teacher who stunned students with her beauty and wisdom. Once she discovered the magic of fantasy, there were many occasions during the day and night when Blanca fled to a private, secure world where she found silence. A world without grandmothers or fathers or fake parents or beatings or desertions or betrayals. Even when night terrors preyed and she woke up trembling, she floated away to green meadows and strolled by clear streams until a sweet sleep claimed her.

The children were filing out to the lunch room, and Blanca lagged at the end of the line.

Mrs. Wasserman narrowed her eyes. "Why are you limping, Blanca?"

"My shoes broke, Mrs. Wasserman, and the tacks are sticking into my feet."

"Are you still living with your father and stepmother?"

"No, Mrs. Wasserman."

"Who do you live with now?"

"Some people my father knows."

"I thought so. Your stepmother always sent you to school with clean and freshly ironed clothes."

When Blanca did not respond, the teacher sent her off to lunch. The next day, when the dismissal bell rang, she asked Blanca to stay for a few minutes. Mrs. Wasserman brought out a big box from the closet and placed it on her desk. She opened it and took out a pair of black patent leather shoes with wide buckles, socks of the whitest hue, a heavy dark blue coat, and two beautiful dresses, one woolen and the other corduroy. From the bottom of the box, Mrs. Wasserman brought out a white brassiere of simple cotton with a label that read 28AA. She smiled. "It's time you wore one of these. You're growing quickly."

The basement seemed unusually quiet and still when Blanca came up to the door carrying her treasured box from school. Genara was always in the apartment waiting for her children to come home. Blanca was accustomed to Genara's silence when she unlocked the door for her every afternoon and Blanca put her books away and went out again. Rafael's wife hardly spoke to her. Blanca was an added burden, another mouth to feed, another bother. She already had six children, why take on the responsibility of another? But Rafael insisted on taking in the orphan who always made a mess at the table with her books and papers, she fumed to friends and relatives.

"Look, woman, her pa' gives me good money, and we don't spend a dime on her. We hardly feed her, for Chrissake. In school she gets breakfast and lunch, and if we give her a bite of something left over from dinner, that's it. If I ask her pa' for extra money for clothing, he dishes it out. And it's money that goes straight into my pocket, because he don't even ask how she's doing. And you know he don't come to see her. So in this little business, I'm the winner. Shit, don't complain no more, I'm sick of your naggin'," he emphasized with his *caudillo* voice.

Genara's dislike was obvious, and Blanca spoke to her only when absolutely necessary. She tried to stay out of her way as much as possible. She was terrified of Rafael. She spent time out of school roaming the streets like a stray cat, in friends' apartments, and looking for something to do in the neighborhood park with its swings and slides and bunches of teenagers who hid behind the guardhouse to pet, drink, and shoot dice and heroin. She returned to the basement as late as possible to finish her homework and sleep. Sometimes, Miriam and Rebeca played with her, but Genara disapproved of time spent with the orphan, as she called Blanca. The four boys had their own interests in the streets. To them, Blanca was another piece of furniture in the crowded apartment.

Genara had seen the light and received the spirit in her soul. She was a member of the Pentecostal Church of the Seventh Day and went out every evening to attend services. She returned about ten, exalted by the brothers and sisters who had spoken in tongues. Frequently, she took her reluctant children to services, hoping that they too would be blessed with a pledge of salvation. Since she was not interested in running into Blanca in the afterlife, the girl was not invited. Blanca was left behind, without a key to get into the apartment, to roam the dingy streets, pacifying hunger pangs and the bitter cold with constant movement. She never returned when she knew the man was in the apartment alone.

But that afternoon, when Blanca came from school with her treasure trove, it was Rafael, and not Genara, who opened the door.

The girl stared at the brick skirt of a building through the narrow half-window. Dumped on the bed like an empty sack, she concentrated hard on the uneven rectangular lines drawn on the soot-blackened wall. She could see a red curve, the beginning or the end, she was not sure, of a letter scrawled in the night by a disgruntled neighbor wishing to preserve his immortality. The letter bobbed as she did. At times it became a blur. She followed the red curve intently with stark wide-open eyes, head twisted to the side. In the depths of her self-inflicted daze, she knew this lonely pain would always be with her.

She walked very slowly to school, as though holding a large ball between her legs. Mrs. Wasserman's eyes almost burst in anger. She called the school authorities who called the medical authorities who called the police authorities. The swift rescue climaxed in social-services offices and court. The neglectful father apologized.

"I'm a widower. I gotta work and had no one to take care of her. I didn't know what was going on. I swear on the sacred Bible, I didn't know."

Blanca was taken to live with Conchita, her new guardian, inspected and licensed by the city to care for children in crises. She took antibiotics provided by the city for a stubborn infection and wore clothes provided by the city. Blanca, whose life was continually regimented by municipal fiat, perceived that an omnipotent, omnipresent, and omniscient being must surely reside in the mayor's office, sitting in front of a great city map and pushing pins with colored heads. One of those little heads, red maybe because it was her favorite color, represented Blanca. She felt calmer knowing she was taken care of by this faceless amorphous being.

It was a long time before she removed her heavy blue coat.

# 13

The past fills my nights and all my days. I try to escape the terror of nightmares and open my eyes only to find clusters of faces and images in the hospital room groping at me from the lonely distance of childhood.

I am drawn to the window like a plant to a source of light. Through the iron bars I see the old elm, but surprisingly it is not surrounded by the stark outline of familiar city buildings. Instead, medieval red-tiled roofs layer a hill. The silence of mirrors flickers in the room and startles me. I rub my eyes with the heels of my hands. All I can see are bucolic pastures dotted with cows chewing placidly under the billowy clouds. A cemetery looms beyond a row of weeping willows. My heart beats so hard I can hear it thud in my temples. I dash to the bathroom and splash water on my face. When I return to the room, I fall into bed and shelter my head under a pillow.

The kingdom Paquita had carefully wrought for her own satisfaction disintegrated when Consuelo and Salvador committed the ultimate betrayal and shattered a time-honored taboo. Her dominance destroyed, Paquita fled to the island in self-imposed exile, liberating her subjects in the South Bronx, who heaved a collective sigh of relief. She fled from the betrayal that haunted her every hour, believing that on the island her pain would find relief because, as the song says, *la distancia causa olvido*, distance brings forgetfullness. She was bereft of the strength needed to hold on to her subjects, to govern her kingdom. So she surrendered her realm and lived only for her hatred and anger. She continued to fan the flame of her rancor, letting it burn slowly, because she knew it was the flame that would keep her alive in the new role she assumed: the lonely martyr.

She had lived alone on the island for two years, nurturing her bitterness until loneliness gripped her. She needed to fill her silence. She needed, as she needed a continuous source of oxygen, someone who would love her unconditionally. And she remembered the orphan.

Paquita appeared from nowhere in the yard of P.S. 9 where Blanca skipped rope after lunch. The old woman approached the girls who waited their turn to jump and sang:

"Strawberry, chocolate,
cream on top,
tell me the name of your sweetheart,
a, b, c..."

"Blanca," Paquita called, and the girl froze when she heard the voice of her nightmares.

"What's the matter with you?" Paquita said angrily. "The social worker said it was okay for you to come with me as long as your father signs." Paquita held out a sheaf of papers. "Here's his signature for the principal. You have to translate for me, so let's go to the office and get this over with."

Before Blanca realized what was happening, they landed in Puerto Rico. Distant cousins greeted Blanca and Paquita at the Isla Verde airport. Blanca tugged uncomfortably at her collar while they asked her questions or talked to Paquita. When the car sped from Avenida Norte toward the narrow streets of Villa Palmeras, Blanca stared at the strange world that flashed by in vivid colors and signs of Mueblería Alemañy and Carlos Ruiz, Abogado Notario. People were unburdened by coats and the compelling need to rush because of the cold.

She inhaled the sweet scent of palm trees and adjusted her vision to the brilliance of a sun that seemed to lie on top of her head.

Paquita and Blanca penetrated the alleys leading into a society of little houses bunched at the rim of San José Lagoon. The *coquís*, tiny frogs known only to Puerto Rico, sang in brambles and bushes of red and yellow hibiscus that sprouted from tiny patches of land. When she went to bed that first night in Puerto Rico, Blanca listened to the babbling stridency of the neighbors' radios and blinked in the darkness while the *coquís* sang. Blanca wept under the mosquito net, envisioning her sentence in a new prison, bound to Paquita, her jailer, forever.

On the island, Paquita's world shrunk to the dimensions of a fist, and she had nothing left but ghosts in her pocket. Paquita no longer played cards with friends, went to the cinema, or played the numbers. Perhaps it was the inevitable loss of every trace of youth. Or perhaps she was subdued by the husband who lived in her memory, locked in the embrace of her only daughter. Whatever the reasons, the result was that Paquita suddenly grew very old. In time she no longer beat Blanca, and her insults lost their sting. Faced with a kingdom in ruins, Paquita contemplated a great void. She realized that Blanca was her last vassal. She did not have the strength to dominate her granddaughter physically, but years of beatings had achieved the irreversible mental bondage that would not allow Blanca to break away. Paquita's will remained strong, and she would continue chipping away at bits of Blanca's mind and soul. She would convince the girl that she was merely an extension of her grandmother. No more. No less. The girl became the center of the old woman's center. So it was that Paquita controlled every second of her granddaughter's life and made the girl her reason to be and to exist. It was the girl who would sacrifice her youth to Paquita, who would love her, obey her, and never ever leave her.

When Blanca started school and talked about her friends, Paquita shook a finger at her. "You don't have any friends," she would say. "Those are your schoolmates." Then she would jab her own chest with a forefinger. "I am your only friend, and don't you forget it."

She looked after Blanca to guarantee an imperishable presence in her life. "Damn parasites," she murmured when she noticed Blanca's bloated abdomen poking under her skirt. Well-versed in home remedies, for she had been a spiritualist once, she forced a tablespoon full of castor oil into Blanca's reluctant mouth.

"See if you spill the worms with this. I've told you a million times, don't walk barefoot on the soil. Worms go right through the soles of your feet. It's hard to be rid of them once they're in. And don't throw up or I'll give you another spoonful," she added when Blanca heaved.

She warned Blanca about eating pineapple or coconut during her period because she would contract TB. To insure healthy blood with adequate hemoglobin, she made her take Lady Pinkham elixir daily.

"Look at all the people in your family with TB," she emphasized when she dragged her every year for chest X-rays to the community clinic.

Oppressive attention to Blanca's health was only one dimension of Paquita's harsh rule. She also commanded absolute love with its absolute concomitants: blind obedience, indisputable loyalty, and mute respect. Since the world of children is without alternatives, Blanca acceded uncomplainingly to this twist of destiny. She had the obligation of kissing her grandmother and asking for her blessing before going out and upon returning and every night before going to bed, a repugnant duty performed without conviction. She held her breath when approaching the humid and mottled cheek so as not to catch a whiff of the damp skin which made her stomach shrink. Blanca was afraid of smelling like her grandmother, whose clothing was always damp with an acrid sweat, and she found ways of grazing her lips against the old woman's skin for the shortest possible time. She devised innumerable stratagems such as talking to her quickly about an event of the day when she came near the moist cheek, diverting Paquita's attention enough so that she would not notice the hastily tossed kiss.

On Saturdays, Paquita got Blanca out of bed at dawn. There were many errands to run, and God helps those who rise early, she said. Blanca scratched the mosquito bites on her legs and arms and rubbed herself with eucalyptus alcohol to relieve her itchiness before they clambered up the alleys to the wide iron gates of the cemetery at Eduardo Conde Avenue. They walked all day, entering and exiting grocery stores and pharmacies. Paquita introduced her granddaughter to shop owners and store clerks, initiating her to the world of errands in the new barrio.

When Paquita determined that the house required a good cleaning, she made Blanca kneel and scrub the cement floor with a heavy brush soaked in a mixture of water, detergent, and ammonia. Paquita supervised from a wicker rocking chair where she sat, legs splayed, to catch some fresh air. Paquita only used underwear when she went out. In the house she sat with her legs wide open and her dress hiked above her knees showing the gray hairs of her aging pubis. Blanca made a valiant effort not to look into the darkness of her dress while Paquita ordered her to clean here and there.

"Look, that corner needs more scrubbing. It's still dirty," Paquita barked.

The strong odor of detergent and ammonia turned her stomach, but Blanca would not raise her head while she silently scrubbed. Sometimes she would be compelled by tedium to speak, but without looking up.

"Could you give me half a dollar to buy a novel I saw at Farmacia Archilla?"

"What're you saying? A novel?" Paquita fluttered her arms as though she were shooing a swarm of flies.

"You spend your life with books. One of these days you're going blind or crazy from so much reading. Anyhow, I'm not letting you throw money away on stupid novels. You think money grows on trees?"

Paquita had never gone to school. She bitterly railed against her mother for keeping her home to help raise her eight younger siblings. So Paquita was unable to recognize the intellectual existence of her granddaughter. She was like the experimental cats Blanca had read about. Not allowed to see vertical lines until after the critical period of brain development, they never acquired the capacity to perceive verticality. So it was with Paquita. Never having been exposed to the world of ideas, she could not perceive its existence. She considered Blanca a corporeal and emotional being whose body and soul she was driving to the definite goal of loving Paquita above all else. She made no allowance for detours.

Every afternoon when the sun inflicted its severest punishment on any who dared to remain awake, Paquita took a siesta after turning on an electric fan at the foot of the bed, allowing the air to cool her uncovered graying triangle. In the meantime, Blanca washed and ironed their clothes, kept the house clean, scrubbed floors and walls, polished the furniture, and did all their shopping. To break the boredom of her chores, Blanca reflected on the destiny of a blind person or of someone afflicted by madness. She certainly did not intend to stop reading, as her grandmother suggested. If what Paquita said was true and she was fated to become blind or crazy as a result of her reading, she decided that given a choice in the matter, she would choose madness. She made this decision easily. A blind person cannot read without Braille, while a madwoman, locked up in her cell like a monk, can read as much as she wants. Convinced that her destiny would be estrangement, she made faces like an insane person, a gurgling little laugh rising in her throat.

In the evenings, Blanca, hot and tired from running errands and doing chores, would sit on the front steps of the house for a breath of cool air. There was no distant horizon where Blanca could lose herself and escape her confinement. All she saw were the dark alleys and tiny patios of the neighboring houses scraping against each other.

One evening, a dark moon hung in an air bloated with humidity and Blanca saw a light go on in the house across the alley. A young man's face peered through the open shutters. Blanca had seen him come home from work earlier with a brown paper bag under his arm. She started to turn away when the young man, guessing her intention, signaled with his palm, asking her to stay. Blanca was curious, and she waited while the young man's face disappeared when he turned his back to her. He seemed to be climbing on something, and Blanca could see his torso and his trouser belt. She guessed he was propped on a bed because he wobbled inordinately. When he caught his balance, he turned around, smiling like an elf. Looking straight at Blanca, he clutched his penis, which he had extracted without her notice, and he masturbated peremptorily. Blanca stalked into the house and went to bed.

An overwhelming sense of loss washed over her. She wanted to go away, disappear somehow, but she could not escape the emptiness that drowned her. She could feel the emptiness like bruises that throb and hurt for days after a beating. She covered herself up with the sheet. The night was hot and sticky, but she could not face the darkness outside.

She would wait out the night, wait for the comfort of sunshine.

Just as sunshine was a comfort, so was school. Antonio B. Caimary Junior High School stood wide and flat on the hill of Villa Palmeras. The facade was decorated with red bricks bearing the inscription in Spanish, *There is no worse darkness than ignorance*—Shakespeare. From the second floor one could see Eduardo Conde Avenue flanked by shops and congested with people and cars.

When Blanca registered in school, her sentence with her grandmother was shortened. She enjoyed classes and was especially pleased with her new language of learning. Until that time, her Spanish had been limited to the Spanish she heard around her, the Spanish spoken by persons with little or no formal education. Now she had teachers who spoke the language. She had never met a Puerto Rican teacher before, or a Puerto Rican physician, or a Puerto Rican attorney. When she walked down Eduardo Conde Avenue, she read signs on doctors' offices, lawyers' offices, pharmacists, all in Spanish and all Puerto Rican! For the first time, Blanca understood that she did not have to be Jewish or Irish or Chinese to be a doctor or a lawyer or a teacher or a pharmacist. She understood that in a leap she could arrive at a world of books, of ideas, that she too could have a sign with her name in big letters and diplomas inscribed in Latin hanging from her wall. If other Puerto Ricans had done it, then she could do it, too. What do you know? she thought. She was truly amazed.

During her first year in Puerto Rico, she struggled to progress in her maternal language. She acquired the Spanish rules of accentuation, broadened her vocabulary, and erased Spanglish from her lexicon. She discovered the cadence of its song, the melody of its rhythms, its semantic repository, the logic of its syntax. Blanca read *El Sombrero de Tres Picos, El Final de Norma, La Carreta* and she recited poems of redeemed lovers in her Spanish class. Language would never again be solely a tool for communication. Language became a refreshing balm— aromatic and strong—producing a pleasure so intense that she started talking to herself for the sheer pleasure of listening to it. She composed songs and wrote poems and stories. Divested of her usual diffidence, she chattered happily with her schoolmates and promptly became the school's maven of the English language.

"Hey, *americana*, help me with this English lesson." Pablo ran after Blanca, brushing his hair from his forehead.

"My name's Blanca. I don't like to be called *americana*."

"Okay, okay," Pablo acceded quickly. He was more interested in the knowledge Blanca could impart than in her name. Right now he would call her Queen Isabella if that was what she wanted.

"What's the matter with the English lesson?"

"Can't understand a thing. Mr. Ramos didn't explain how to do this. Look."

They sat under a guava tree. Blanca explained some of the mysteries of the English subjunctive, and slowly the fog of concern lifted from Pablo's brow. He took a ripe guava that had been lying on the grass, split it in two with his thumbnails, and inspected its womb carefully to make sure it had no worms. He then offered half to Blanca. The guava was sweet and delicious. The recess bell rang and they ran to class.

"You're OK!" Pablo yelled in gratitude.

Her mother's presence was stronger in Puerto Rico. Blanca met people who had known Isabel, and they told her stories of her mother's life in the shantytown. Blanca walked through the same places her mother had walked, saw the places where her mother had lived. Blanca loved her island where the sun almost always shone and flowers peeked through stones. She ran about capturing the aromas of the barrio, the crows of roosters, the garrulous prattle of matrons. Blanca embraced her island and no longer missed the guttural language, nor the roguish friends, nor the muddy snow. She finally felt that she had come home.

# 14

I rummage through the drawers looking for a notebook when I hear voices approach my room. The door flings open, and an orderly wheels in a pale, heavily sedated woman. A nurse follows briskly. I sit quietly on my bed and stare at the grim lines of the patient's mouth. With the help of the orderly, the nurse unstraps the unconscious woman from the gurney, hoists her up on a sheet, and swings her into the freshly-made bed. They speak to each other as though I were not present.

"Any more ECT patients today?" the orderly asks.

"One this afternoon. At two," the nurse responds.

"Okey doke."

The orderly wheels the gurney out. The nurse tucks the sheets, pulls the covers over the patient, and checks her pulse and blood pressure. She jots notes on the chart tacked to the foot of the bed and secures the side rails.

When the nurse leaves, I stand beside the woman's bed and listen to her gentle breathing. The woman is young and slight. She seems so vulnerable in the baggy hospital gown. The grim set of her mouth speaks to me of sorrow and pain. I edge closer and clasp her small hand. I read the name on the plastic bracelet. A lovely name. "I'll be with you, Celia Oliveras," I whisper, overcome with unexpected tenderness.

When Celia wakes up hours later, she looks at me with empty eyes. The nurse returns and urges Celia to walk to the bathroom. Celia clings to the nurse's arm and shuffles down the hall unaware of her surroundings. Later in the evening, before bedtime, she seems to recognize me. Before I can say anything, Celia's eyes glaze and she falls asleep again.

I think about the tragedy of imprisoned women. Whenever I feel a trap closing in on me, as I do now watching Celia breath evenly in her own private captivity, I am reminded of that caged woman I saw so many years ago.

By a series of coincidences, Paquita discovered the address of a distant cousin she had not seen in many years. Her cousin lived in a barrio of Puerto Nuevo, not far from Santurce. Paquita had precise directions on how to get there. She and Blanca took the bus called *la machina*. It was called the merry-go-round because it went in and out, round and round, all the barrios from Old San Juan to the plaza of Río Piedras. In Río Piedras they boarded a public car en route to Puerto Nuevo. They were the first ones in the car and sat in the coveted seats in front. They waited half an hour until the driver crammed the back seats with passengers.

The house where Paquita's cousin lived was filled with children running through its dark rooms. The cousin kept thick drapes drawn from dusk to dawn in all the windows, from ceiling to floor, so the sun would not fade the furniture.

Paquita and Blanca sat on a sofa covered with a transparent plastic that stuck to Blanca's sweaty thighs. While the two older women talked about living and dead relatives, they heard intermittent groans and moans interspersed with low giggles from what sounded like the voice of a hoarse woman.

"It's the retarded one," the cousin asserted, pointing her chin toward the back yard. "Do you want to see her, Paquita?"

The tiny back yard was enclosed by a chain-link fence dense with ivy. A large cage with weeds growing all around it stood next to a yellow hibiscus bush. The cage was rustically built in the ground with boards and reticulated wire. The women peered into the cage. In a corner where shadows offered some solace from the pounding sun, they could barely make out a human figure crouching next to a mound of feces. Paquita took a handkerchief out of her handbag, and pretending to cough, placed it over her nose.

The caged woman came out of the shadows and waddled toward them. She tilted her head to the side as she looked out. She had layers of grime on her face. She started jumping and laughing, her flat breasts hanging limply. She poked dirty fingers through the wire mesh and held on to it. She stared at Blanca and whimpered like a small animal.

Paquita's cousin explained. "That's my youngest daughter. An accident. Some accident, huh? I was too old to have more kids and look what happened. You don't know how much trouble she's given me. Here I was trying to bring up four older kids born a year apart, but she was more trouble than all of them put together. I had to do everything for her. Then she got bigger and wilder, and I couldn't even find a school that would take her. So my husband built this cage to keep her 'cause of all the grief she was giving us. She hit the other kids, and the neighbors complained about her yelling all the time. A lot easier this way, I tell you. I hose the cage down once in a while, but when she gets her period it really stinks something awful, so I have to clean the cage every day."

"Does she talk?" Paquita asked.

"She talked before we put her in here, but she lost it. All she does now is moan."

Blanca was entranced by the trapped woman and her severed possibilities. This woman would never hear her voice composing sentences. She would never wear patent leather shoes and furrow new paths with her steps. The caged woman would never know the pleasure of a cool shower on a hot afternoon, a warm meal, humming in the night while she sewed a dress, the feel of a friendly hug, a kiss. She would never have children, smell the fresh fruit at the open air market, write a letter, sing a bolero, attach words to her thoughts, or create ideas with urgent brush strokes. She would never look at herself in a mirror and brush her hair.

Blanca looked into the dull eyes blinking in the light and anger raked through her heart. She returned to the dark house where the cousin brewed coffee.

Celia shows me a photograph of herself, young and pretty, looking out at the world with dreamy and audacious eyes that remind me of the Olympia painted by Manet. In the hospital they emptied her eyes of dreams, and with electrical charges dimmed her audacity. Where was she when the picture was taken, staring at a spot above the camera, so far away? I wonder if her eyes will ever gleam like that again.

She looks up from the photograph. "I'm losing control of myself. Something else has taken over, but I don't know what. I don't know who I am anymore. I just don't know what's me."

Haltingly she tells me her story. Celia's husband signed her into the psychiatric ward of the hospital, complaining about her depression, rebellion, and emotional instability. Staff psychiatrists confirmed the diagnosis.

Celia married at sixteen to a man twenty-five years her senior. She became pregnant immediately after her marriage and gave birth to a boy who was born on Christmas Day. A year later Marisol was born, a reminder for Celia of her native island drenched in sea and sun. Her husband Juan owned an electrical appliance repair shop and liked to boast that he had no need for a formal education to make a good living. He was a big man, skin burnished by the sun of his ancestors. Going back to his years in the Army, he liked to sport a military haircut.

His wife owed him absolute obedience, respect, and the fulfillment of her conjugal duties. These included the satisfaction of his elementary needs, such as laundered and well-pressed clothing, a house so clean you could eat off its floors, meals on schedule and in abundance, and the relief of his sexual tension. She also had to keep the children quiet when he watched his wrestling matches on television and when, after quaffing a few beers, he settled down in the sofa to snore like a blessed soul.

Afraid of being overheard, Celia whispers urgently in my ear. "I can remember my name and where I am, but I don't remember yesterday. The day was erased from my mind. It's as though it never existed. But somewhere deep inside I know there was a yesterday. Isn't that strange?" We are in the common room pretending to play cards. She pauses and looks behind her. When she is sure no one is near, she leans closer.

"I don't remember how long I've been in this place or my son's name. They've ripped out strips of my memory. Whole chunks are gone. Dr. Carroll says it's temporary, that memory will gradually return. I'm so scared, though. I don't think I believe him. I don't want any more shock treatment. I just can't stand it any more."

Celia fumbles with her cards.

"How many times are they doing it?" I ask.

"Six or more. Dr. Carroll says it's only effective if it's done all those times. But I don't want to. I can't bear it. I'd prefer anything else to this. Right now lots of names crowd in my head like a crazy mosaic. You know, like names in a Russian novel? And I can't stop it. It's terrifying that I can remember the names of people I hardly know and I can't remember my own son's." Celia slaps a hand of cards on the table and looks away. She stands up abruptly.

"I'm really tired. Think I'll lie down."

I nod and walk her to our room. I help her change into a nightgown and get into bed. I sit on the edge of the bed, hold her hand, and caress her hair as gently as I can. But I find nothing to say. How can anyone annihilate the fear we all feel of brain damage, of the subtle penetration into our most intimate and deepest thoughts? How can we fight the most terrifying of tyrannies?

"Maybe you shouldn't subject yourself to shock treatment any longer. Can't you tell them to stop?" I ask finally.

The weary cast in Celia's eyes mists with fear, a fear that speckles her irises gray. She fears the psychiatrists, her husband, the formidable depressions that weaken her. I feel Celia's unnameable fear and make it my own. I squeeze her arm in solidarity.

"Of course not," I say emphatically, answering my own question. "They'll just think you need more of it."

I wait until Celia falls asleep, thinking how remarkable it is that we have lived such parallel lives. I also escaped an intolerable home life and wound up marrying a tyrant. As I said before, life is a repetition of patterns. I escaped my grandmother's subjugation only to fall into the snare of an equally oppressive tyrant. But then, for me, love has always exacted the harshest of penalties.

# 15

Paquita developed angina pectoris, a hearing problem, high blood pressure, and diabetes. Despite a worsening of her glaucoma, she noticed the young men who ogled Blanca. She warned the girl constantly about the depravity of love. To insure that Blanca never surrendered to the clutches of lust, Paquita concealed herself behind bushes and tree trunks to spy on her when she returned home from school. She had warned Blanca to relinquish the company of others because "he who does something alone, pays for it alone."

Hiding behind a parked car one afternoon, Paquita watched as Blanca walked from school with a friend. Pablo carried her books, a chivalrous custom of the times, and they chatted contentedly, deeply absorbed in their own conversation. Paquita shadowed them, hiding behind a bush before leaping in their path brandishing a black umbrella like a Saracen's sword.

"What're you doing with my granddaughter, you mongrel? Take this, so you'll learn not to seduce innocent girls," Paquita cried, showering blows on Pablo's head with her umbrella. Pablo shielded himself inadequately because of all the books he carried. He took advantage of a pause while Paquita caught her breath to shove Blanca's books back at her and barrel down the street. Paquita, who was by now panting heavily, clasped the girl by the wrist and dragged her home where she gave her a swift cuff. "He who does it alone, pays for it alone," Paquita declared, followed by "Birds of a feather flock together," proverbs that Blanca could not apply to the situation at hand no matter how hard she tried.

There was not much to do after the swift fall of twilight. Blanca and Paquita confronted the hours of darkness that loomed ahead before bedtime, each in her own way. Paquita got entangled in her contemplations. She let the night sweep her back, way back into the past where she festered like a wound. The bitterness of her losses fueled the grudge she held close to her heart. She wanted vengeance so badly, she cried tears of rage and impotence. Salvador and Consuelo succeeded in robbing her of her self-esteem and reduced her to a lonely old woman without a husband, without a family. In the still hours of the evening, she hungered for revenge and wished the most dire of fates on the two lovers.

For Blanca, these were hours of unbounded silence. A time when she wished with all her might to forget what she remembered and to tear ahead to that place in her dreams where possibilities existed. But she was racked by an anger and a hatred she could not escape.

The frozen embryo of hate that Blanca sheltered since childhood was at first like dots on an umlaut, tiny and insignificant. But when nourished, hatred swells. Aroused by pubescent hormones, Blanca seethed with an anger that clotted every pore, an anger that clouded the contents of her consciousness. Blanca never answered back when her grandmother yelled, and she obeyed Paquita's mandates without protest. But she fingered her hidden rosary of anger and hatred. The two were interchangeable, indistinguishable.

In her grandmother's presence, Blanca never dared show her feelings. She became adept at quashing the irritation that threatened to poke through the folds of her hate. With apparently sweet tolerance, Blanca submerged her disgust at Paquita's artless attempts at affection. She buried the memory of beatings and insults behind a smile. The memory was very much alive in her mind. Like the spark of a firefly, it glimmered in her lonely nights. But anger is caged thunder, impossible to rein in for long. Alone in her bedroom, while Paquita slept, it broke loose with a quiet intensity that awakened no witnesses.

As soon as it was dark, Paquita sunk into a hammock and brought her transistor radio to her good ear. She listened to WKAQ and hummed popular tunes as she pulled on a rope staked to the wall to rock herself back and forth in her hammock. Blanca pored over books and notes at the dinette table under a pool of yellow light. At ten, Paquita got her chamber pot. It was the signal that Blanca too must go to bed.

"Bless me," Blanca said.

"May God bless you." Paquita leaned forward to collect Blanca's hasty kiss.

Blanca's bed was crowded in a tiny room with a chest of drawers and a mirrored wardrobe. She lay fully clothed, an arm flung over her eyes. Her thoughts were gathered in layers, and she shuffled through them like a deck of cards. She heard the old woman's snores ending in a prolonged whistle. Blanca stood up, intending to get ready for bed. She pulled her nightgown from the wardrobe and stared at her reflection in the mirror. A festering rage boiled and curdled until she could no longer bear its molten steel. She clenched her fists, grit her teeth. She choked on an angry scream and it roared in her head. At that moment she held up her impotence, the helplessness she abhorred, and sunk her teeth into her arms. She pummeled her face and dug her nails into her cheeks. Hewing down, down, down, chin, chest, abdomen. Death, death, she yearned for death and destruction. Blanca would finally kill the old woman when she succeeded in killing herself.

Some evenings Paquita tucked away her thoughts of revenge and, with Blanca in tow, called on her niece Elena who lived on Fajardo Street. The street snaked down from the cemetery to the shantytown of La Playita and ended abruptly in the San José Lagoon. The most valuable houses, built of masonry instead of wood, stood proudly on the slant just off Eduardo Conde Avenue.

Elena lived on Fajardo Street with her husband Lito and Margarita, their teenage niece. Margarita's father was one of Lito's brothers, a drug addict who had been arrested many times for theft. Margarita's mother, a bewildered teenager, left her infant daughter in Elena's care one day never to return. Elena and Lito raised the girl as their own. But recently Fernando, Margarita's father, had been released from prison on probation and he had moved with the family.

Before Margarita's arrival, Elena and Lito had tried to have children of their own. After several miscarriages, Elena was forced to have her tubes cut. The emptiness of their home was partially alleviated by a mongrel they baptized Bobby, a vanilla cookie addict given to ferocious barking from the balcony. He managed to frighten the cowardly cars that fled away when they heard his valiant barks. When the dog's habit of lustfully humping visitors' legs became a source of embarrassment, Lito gave a bottle of rum *cañita* to the barrio's castrator to scoop out the dog's testicles and dampen his concupiscence. Elena still remembered the horrifying howls of the tortured dog and how she vomited when she mopped up the blood. Lito, who assisted with the kitchen table surgery, washed his hands with pine soap afterwards and shared the castrator's bottle of *cañita* that night.

When Paquita and Blanca passed through the gate, Margarita was in the front yard practicing twirls and leaps in her white-tasseled boots. She was a popular majorette, and her dream was to march in the Discovery Day parade in San

Juan. She did a cartwheel and revealed the ruffled panties under her short white skirt. With precision and a certain degree of angularity, she back-twirled and did double baton tosses. At the end of her performance, she walked over to Paquita and Blanca and bowed gracefully.

"Did you like it?" Margarita asked, out of breath.

"I don't know why you bother with that business." Paquita dismissed her and walked into the house.

Blanca and Margarita giggled.

"Well, that's real encouraging." Margarita tossed her baton and Blanca caught it with two hands.

"You know how she is." Blanca handed the baton back to Margarita. "Nobody can do anything right in her book."

Margarita shrugged.

Elena's voice startled them. "Margarita, Blanca, what're you two doing out there in the dark? Get in the house before the mosquitoes eat you alive!"

Bus Number One lumbered to the stop. Although there were vacant seats, Blanca preferred to stand so as not to wrinkle the starched pleated uniform she had pressed that morning. She noticed other Central High School students, the boys in gray trousers with razor-sharp creases and white shirts and the girls in blue, pleated skirts. When she got off the bus, she faced the high school's sparkling marble staircase, wide as an ocean, cresting proudly toward an ample three-story building on Ponce de León Avenue, the hub of Santurce. Under the light of the gleaming tropical sun, the school was like a Greek monument with its graceful doric columns. Cement benches under the almond and tamarind trees of the front yard were always packed with students waiting for the bell to ring.

Señorita Ortiz was madly in love with Lope de Vega.

"Oh," she sighed deeply, interrupting the biographical narration of her idol's life, "had I lived in Lope de Vega's time, I would have fallen into his snare," she said, fluttering her thick black lashes.

Her students doubted Señorita Ortiz's assumptions, since she lacked the female charms that would have attracted an amorous adventurer like her adored Lope. She was tiny and had a disproportionately big head. Wrinkles trellised her face and trailed down her arms. Her hands were long and dry, tipped with scarlet fingernails.

Señorita Ortiz struck panic in the hearts of her pupils by pitching at them surprise questions of philosophical depth about the motivations of literary characters or their authors. One morning she discoursed on the daunting Doña Bárbara and asked suddenly, "Is jealousy a sign of love?"

The students sat very still, staring at their hands, without moving a muscle, for any movement could be misinterpreted as willingness to respond. Blanca considered her notebook. Although she had an opinion, she shuddered at the prospect of proffering the incorrect response and suffering Señorita Ortiz's derision. Like the day Manolo used the Puerto Rican slang word *ñoco*, for amputee, when referring to Cervantes, and she threw him out of the room under a barrage of insults. Blanca felt the weight of the teacher's glare. Blanca's heart lurched when she heard the voice, scoffingly predicting a wrong answer.

"Well, Blanca, you're always sitting there without saying a word. What is your opinion?"

This is it, Blanca thought. This is the day of my ruination, my total destruction. In unison, the other students sighed with relief. Shuffling feet and clearing throats echoed through the classroom.

Blanca stood up slowly, and squeezing her fingers one by one to reassure herself that they were still there, she launched into a discussion on the true significance of jealousy in a relationship and her opinion that jealousy only existed in people who had a low concept of themselves. While Blanca spoke, convinced of the good sense of her arguments, she watched in amazement as Señorita Ortiz's face dissolved into stunned surprise and then split into a smile. "Well, Blanca, that was a good argument." When the bell rang at the end of the period, Blanca knew she had won her over.

Margarita was waiting for her in the hall.

"I saw Lorenzo when I left the office. You should see him, he's such a cutie today," Margarita said.

"What were you doing in the office? Don't tell me you're still pining for Señor Morales, or Lorenzo, as you call him." Blanca rolled her eyes to the ceiling.

"They told me the secretary was absent today, so I took a chance and walked right into his office. I invented an excuse about my mother wanting an appointment to see him."

"Margarita, how could you lie to the principal? But, tell me quickly, what happened?"

"Since you insist." Margarita curled her fingers, blew on them with two short breaths and polished her nails on her blouse. "He told me that his secretary made all his appointments, so I should come tomorrow to see her. Oh, Blanca, he looked at me with those big brown eyes. My soul is wounded. I'm crazy, absolutely crazy about him."

"You know it's a lost cause, don't you? You have a powerful rival."

"Who, Señora Cuevas?"

"The same."

"Bah, I'm not worried about her. She's married; it's an impossible love."

"Well, missy, he's married, too, you know. Or haven't you noticed the pictures of his wife and children on his desk?"

"I don't care, I adore him, and I will always adore him."

She pulled out a neatly folded piece of paper from her notebook. "Look, I wrote a poem, a la Bécquer. But I don't dare give it to him."

The conspiracy brought their heads together.

"I know what you can do," Blanca said. "Mail it anonymously and he'll never know who sent it."

"What if he thinks that stupid Señora Cuevas wrote it?"

"When he asks her, she'll deny it, won't she? That's all there is to it."

"Good thinking. I'll mail it after school today. Hope he likes it. Here, read it and tell me what you think. But do it soon, I want to send it off right away. You know my father, that jerk, not Lito, he spies on me all the time. I have to be careful with stuff like this," Margarita said.

The girls chattered noisily as they walked into typing class. "Wonder who our substitute teacher will be today," Blanca said. They were struck silent when they realized that Señorita Ortega was back in school after a month in a mental institution. The principal had found her after class standing on a pupil's desk unscrewing light bulbs and carefully placing them in a large wicker basket while twittering happily about planting her tulip bulbs as they did in Holland.

She kept a heart-shaped box of Swiss chocolates in her desk. Between periods, she surreptitiously popped a bonbon into her mouth and ate it quickly before the next class arrived. She was wiping her teeth with the tip of her tongue when the students walked in. The girls giggled nervously when they saw the teacher and scurried to their desks. They sat, backs straight, at their typewriters. The typewriters were so old, students joked that Columbus had brought them to Puerto Rico on his first voyage.

Señorita Ortega did not allow them to look at the keyboard at any time. Margarita placed her fingers in the wrong position on the keyboard and typed a line of gibberish.

Blanca's fingers wedged between a couple of keys in her old Remington, and she had great difficulty extracting them. It was not going to be a good typing day. A subdued giggle had begun to swell in the classroom when Señorita Ortega, eyes flashing like knives, stared down at them. Afraid of provoking another breakdown, Blanca continued typing without looking at the teacher, although she almost snapped a pinky when it lodged between the ñ and the accent. Blanca's only consolation was that afterwards they had World History, her favorite, which was sometimes taught by an inexperienced and highly-strung student teacher. But, despite the student teacher's stammers and frightened eyes, Blanca was irresistibly charmed by the exploits of the brave Macedonians.

That afternoon, Blanca got off the bus and lingered at a storefront window that displayed party dresses dripping with golden spangles. Young boys carrying sheaves of straw raced down the street. She said hello to Don Nicanor who stood under a mango tree, wiping his forehead after arduously climbing Fajardo Street. When she arrived home, she was planning to ask for permission to go to Elena's to help make *pasteles*, the grated plantains stuffed with pork that Paquita loved. What she really wanted to do was return Margarita's poem so it would go out in the afternoon mail. Blanca hoped her grandmother was in a good mood and had no errands in mind for her. Blanca especially dreaded having to go anywhere with her grandmother. It could be extremely embarrassing.

Like the time they went to the Electric Company to protest a bill which exceeded by much Paquita's estimates. She complained to a clerk, beginning her protest in a calculatedly soft voice. Blanca lingered nearby and glanced around, pretending she was not with Paquita. The clerk checked the records.

"Sorry, señora," she said politely. "But your bill is correct. I can't find any error."

Before the clerk had finished pronouncing the final syllable, Paquita had already interpreted the message relayed by the woman's gestures and tone of voice. She gathered all the histrionic skills she could muster (it was not in vain that she had watched all those Libertad Lamarque movies at the Puerto Rico Theater in the Bronx) and with an agility which would awaken the envy of a gymnast, hurled herself on the floor, writhing and screeching violently. Blanca had witnessed these "attacks" many times, and she inched to a corner while office clerks and customers surrounded the stricken woman.

Paquita left the general manager's office and had difficulty finding Blanca who was almost invisible, pressed as she was against a wall. Clasping the bill in her fist, she smiled slyly and said, "I solved the problem. Let's go."

Dispensed from running errands with Paquita that day, Blanca rushed out before her grandmother changed her mind. Elena stirred a sauce she was making in a huge pot while Margarita arranged green bananas, plantains, yucca, onions, and chunks of marinated pork on the table. They wore kerchiefs on their heads so strands of hair would not get into the food.

"There's another kerchief in the drawer, Blanca," Elena said.

Blanca put on the kerchief and washed her hands. They sat at the kitchen table and started paring the vegetables.

"Isn't Paquita coming to help with these *pasteles*?" Elena asked.

"No, she's got asthma today."

They worked in silence for a while, chopping and grating.

"I just ran into another pervert." Blanca announced.

"Really? What did he do?" Margarita asked.

"The usual, he was standing in an alley covering his unzipped pants with a folded newspaper, and when I walked by, he flashed it."

"Did you look away?" Elena asked.

Blanca nodded. "Okay, then," Elena said. "A decent girl can't look at those things. Men are nothing but trouble, and the less you know about their secrets, the better off you are. You two have to be very careful with men; they're all the same." Elena pared a large plantain fiercely. "All they want is one thing, to take advantage of innocent girls. Be very, very careful, you hear me?"

Blanca and Margarita nodded vigorously as Elena regaled them with the catastrophes befallen on women who deviated from "God's will." Like the woman who had the misfortune of conceiving while she menstruated and her baby was born with a dog's head. "It died, thank God," she said with conviction.

"Now, let's put these things in the refrigerator and finish up later. I'll go change so we can run some errands before the shops close," she said in one breath. When Elena was gone, Blanca slipped the poem into Margarita's pocket just before Margarita's father stumbled into the kitchen, eyes glazed, and reached for a beer in the refrigerator.

Elena, Margarita, and Blanca walked slowly under the heat. Elena unfurled a blue umbrella to protect them from the steaming sun. Men flirted with them, blowing kisses and uttering terms of endearment. When they arrived at the post office, Elena was furious because a cad had said to her, "Hello *chinita*." To her, there was no worse insult. "How dare he call me that!" she said angrily. "Do I look Chinese to you?" she inquired. Blanca and Margarita shook their heads emphatically, though if truth be told, Elena had a definite Asian cast to her features.

While Elena bought some stamps at the post office, still mumbling curses at the man who dared call her Chinese, Margarita slipped the poem for the principal into the mail slot. She joined Blanca, who was reading the FBI's Most Wanted list. Later, Elena bought a bottle of orange-blossom water at Farmacia Imperial because her nerves were so shaky. They were worse, she claimed, after the Chinese-calling incident. Then, to their dismay, they ran into the terror of all the women and children of Villa Palmeras and Barrio Obrero combined. Blanca covered her nose and quickly looked away.

A one-eyed man dressed in filthy rags staggered to the corner and held on to the lamp post. He was called Ether-Sniffer. A steady source of income was provided by the sharp razor blade in his scrawny hand. When he laughed at the horrified women who stared at him, he revealed blackened toothless gums. The stench of ether, perspiration, and caked and fresh blood exuded from the man's scarred flesh.

For the entertainment of pedestrians ready to pay up, he took a sniff of ether from a soaked rag and slashed his arms, face or chest. The length, depth and location of his wounds depended on how much a customer was willing to pay. A quarter bought a shallow gash in an arm or a leg. A dollar procured a bloodier spectacle. He gouged an eye out with the tip of his blade once for a reward that must have been extraordinary.

"My stomach's turned inside out," Elena said, and they rushed away from the staggering man who offered bits of his flesh for sale.

# 16

Most patients participate in obligatory group therapy sessions conducted by Dr. Hackson. A psychiatric resident assists Dr. Hackson in this endeavor. Dr. Stevens is a thin young man who had been on the verge of dying from diverse illnesses during his first years in medical school. He talks to me a lot because he says we have an affinity. I have never understood what that could be, but I listen to him when he is in a talkative mood and speaks to me in confidence of his own afflictions. He has suffered every illness described in medical texts. Sometimes he has diagnosed himself as having several diseases simultaneously. While in regular medical practice, anytime he would examine a patient, he would dash afterwards to scrub his hands and arms with a hard bristle brush which almost peeled his skin off. His fears having rendered him unable to examine patients physically made psychiatry his only option in the medical profession. Today, sitting next to Dr. Hackson, he looks rather blanched, but he smiles at all of us while he scratches the palm of his hand.

I sit with some of the other patients in straight-backed chairs arranged in a circle.

Dr. Hackson begins the session. “Does anyone have comments about last week’s session? Or those of you who have not participated before, would you like to comment on anything?”

I suppose this is an open-ended question. Not very effective, though. No one responds.

“Well, how are you feeling today?”

Another bomb.

Dr. Stevens, with his starving hamster face, tries to break the ice and impress his supervisor.

"I heard a great joke the other day," he says. "Do you want to hear it?"

"Good idea," Dr. Hackson says. "Laughter is very therapeutic. Recent studies indicate that laughter helps patients with varied illnesses to improve. Proceed, Dr. Stevens."

The young resident slides to the edge of his chair.

"A man runs into a friend on the street. 'Hey, I want to congratulate you. This is one of the happiest days of your life,' he says enthusiastically. 'What're you saying?' his friend asked. 'I don't get married until tomorrow.' The man responded, 'That's why I said today is one of the happiest days of your life.'"

The doctors beam. Miguel grimaces while Castule stares at his hands and fidgets uncomfortably in his chair. I look out the window, my mind hopping from image to image.

"Does anyone want to tell another joke?"

This is group therapy? I wonder.

Debra, the hospital aristocrat who likes to believe that she is Zelda Fitzgerald, clears her throat.

"I know a very good joke," she asserts in her Southern-belle accent. "I heard it in a Virginia hospital. I think it's quite appropriate, if I do say so myself. Now listen, you all." With a slight movement of her hand, she brushes her hair back.

"Once a man was driving in the city when he had a flat tire. Well, wouldn't you know, when he starts changing the tire—all those big screws that hold the tire? Well, you know, they all rolled down the street and fell into a sewer. The man ranted and raved until he heard someone whistle. Well, he looked up towards a stone wall that surrounded the state mental hospital. There, sitting on the wall, was an itsy-bitsy man, in his striped pajamas, waving to him, to come closer. The man was a bit scared, mind you, but he went over. The patient said to him, 'What you gotta do, you see, is take a screw from each of them three other tires and you use them on the spare tire. That should get you to the nearest garage.' Well, the man just couldn't believe it. 'What a great idea!' he yelled. 'With a mind like yours, how come you're in a loony bin?' he asked. To which the patient responded, quite haughtily I must say, 'I'm here because I'm crazy, not because I'm stupid.' Isn't that a hoot?" Debra says as she cups her mouth with a dainty hand and shakes with laughter.

I had heard the same joke in two languages and did not find it amusing. Celia clears her throat. "Well," Celia begins speaking slowly. "I find this very upsetting."

"What do you find upsetting, Celia?" Dr. Hackson asks.

"Instead of telling jokes, I think we should talk about our feelings, our pain. That's why we're here, isn't it? Because we're all in pain?" Celia looks around at the other patients. "I've never seen anyone cry around here. It's as though crying were a sign of weakness, or that people feel so hopeless—it's not even worth crying. I don't know."

"Man, these people are too drugged to cry. Except me, I don't get a thing to help me out around here." Miguel interjects.

"Well, I cry," Celia continues. "And one day, I was sitting in this room watching TV. I heard the news about an unemployed family man who was so desperate he called the television station and told the news director that at two o'clock that afternoon, to protest the economic state of the country, he was setting himself on fire. The news director asked him where he was doing this and sent a reporter and cameraman to the place. The man got there with a container of gasoline, poured it over himself, and lit a match. The match went out and he lit another and another until he finally succeeded. He became a human um,...what is it called?" Celia turns to me anxiously.

"A torch?" I say.

"Yes, that's it, a human torch. In the meantime, the camera rolled on and the reporter talked into his microphone. They actually showed the man on fire on television. They never tried to stop him. They didn't even call the police. But they made sure they covered the incident on the six o'clock news, though. That's all that mattered to these people. When I saw this, well, I cried my heart out. And what did all of you do? You turned away, looking somewhere else as if you couldn't stand the sight of me. You all turned away," she repeats. "I felt so alone."

"Why is this important to you?" Dr. Hackson asks.

"Well, crying is good for you," Celia says emphatically. "I just read the other day about some scientists who discovered that tears contain some kind of hormone, and when someone cries, it reduces emotional tension. It's calming to cry."

"I cry when I peel onions, and I don't feel no calm," Miguel says.

Celia looks at him impatiently. "Scientists say it's not the same!"

"What do they know? If they're so smart, how come we're in here?" Miguel looks directly at Dr. Hackson.

"That's an interesting question, Miguel." Dr. Hackson replies evenly.

Celia continues. "I insist that this is important. I don't think we should be ashamed of crying or uncomfortable when we see others cry. I think that in this place we all try, at least when we're together in the common room, to present some kind of mask of well-being that doesn't exist. We only reveal our true feelings when we're lying in bed and the lights are out."

"That's very interesting," Dr. Hackson contributes while Dr. Stevens nods. "Does anyone want to comment on what Celia just said?"

Silvia raises her hand timidly. "Well, um, I feel that if I ever started crying, nothing, no one in the world, could stop me. That's why I don't cry. There are so many tears in me, that if I let only one drop escape, then the others are going to rush out and drown me." Silvia bites her lower lip, clenches her jaw, and says nothing else. Several patients nod slightly.

"This is a very important topic, but it's time to stop." Dr. Hackson looks at his watch. "We'll continue next week. Good day."

I stand up before anyone else and rush to the bathroom, understanding finally why psychiatrists were once called alienists. My bladder is so full, I find it painful to walk. I had difficulty remaining still until the end of the session, but I could not leave while Silvia's hoarse voice tolled. I sit on the cold toilet seat, and with a sigh, I release a gush of warm liquid. I shiver and wipe myself from back to front. I glance at the blood staining the toilet paper. I pull out more paper, roll it in a wad and wedge it between my legs. I beat a path to my room and comb through my travel kit for a sanitary tampon. As I rush back to the toilet, a hot flow burbles down my legs. When I lock myself in the toilet stall, blood courses down my legs and a puddle forms at my feet. The blood has the scent of secret uterus, torn ovaries, pulsating cervix. I squeeze the muscles between my legs as I quickly unwrap the tampon, but no sphincter can staunch the flow.

When Blanca started menstruating at the age of twelve, Paquita embarked on periodic inspections to insure, according to her, that the blood was red enough and no health problem presented itself. Paquita also subjected Blanca to routine vaginal inspections to insure that she was not running around with any man or to check any impulse the girl might have to do so. The inspections always occurred on late afternoons, just before dusk. She ordered Blanca to her bed, where the teenager raised her skirt, removed her underpants, and spread her legs like scissors. The old woman adjusted her eyeglasses and with a knitted brow pulled Blanca's thighs farther apart until the vagina revealed its inner folds. During these examinations, Blanca covered her face with a pillow. The examiner squeezed her thighs hard while she looked at whatever she had come to see. When she released Blanca's thighs, they were blotched with white indentations and red bruises. Blanca never knew what sign there could be in such a cursory examination to reveal that she was engaging in acts of depravity, as Paquita called sex.

I think of these things as I lie on my stomach with a pillow wedged under the pelvis. I am keenly aware of my body's imposition, its regal mandate over my life. The sight of so much blood induces me to consider how much I loathe myself. I hate myself, yes, I do, though there are days when I forget the hatred. I hate myself for the restitution I make for sins I never committed. For my stolen childhood, my mangled youth. For the humiliation of having to be who I am not. For fearing people. For wanting happiness. For the tears aching behind my retinas. For the nocturnal terrors that torture my sleep. For my iron defenses. For the outrage, the torment. For my stubborn will. For the insults that hammer in my mind. For the swallowed anger. For the violated trust. For the invisible scars that scorch my memories. For the precipice that constantly taunts me from its edge. For the submission sustained in the shackles of tyranny. For the omnipotence of adults, the subjugation of children. For the madness which tempts me constantly. For not daring to dream. For my mind which never ceases to rush on like a runaway film on a granular screen. For memories that refuse to die. And forgive.

# 17

She met Felipe Rodríguez at Central High School. That was his name. Just like the famous singer. True to his namesake, Felipe also sang. His voice, soft and thrilling, haunted her nights when she fell asleep with images of his strong dark fingers strumming the guitar.

Though Garcilaso de la Vega stoked her mind with stars, it was Felipe who was there in the flesh wanting something that plunged her from the depths of fear to the pinnacle of enticement. She sought literature and stars and ran away from Felipe's thrall while wanting to be close to him. She ached for him to touch her, want her, hold her. But she was deathly afraid of her want and the power of his touch. Until one day at lunchtime, when he held her behind the almond trees in the back yard and pressed his lips against hers. Her heart pounded joylessly, expecting the pain and the punishment. Afterwards, when Felipe looked at her without contempt, she sighed at her reprieve.

On a weekend, before performing at an event, he headed toward the lagoon in search of her. Knowing he could never come near her while Paquita was around, he hoped at least to catch a glimpse of her. He stood at a corner lamp post and was lucky to see Blanca in the patio, bent over a corrugated metal tub as she scrubbed clothes on a wooden wash board, revealing her smooth arms and tawny legs. Later that night, he died in an automobile accident.

When Felipe died, a sense of desolation, a vortex of pain and loss, overcame Blanca. There seemed to be a place in her core where words did not exist, for she could not name her pain. All at once, she felt the awful hurt of all her losses. Felipe's death brought it all back. Inexplicably, she felt a need for her mother that was so great she craved to reincorporate, to reemerge with that being who had been her being. She felt like an infant, unable to attach words to her terrible losses.

She went to bed and closed her eyes. She could feel the steady drip of tears behind her brow. She listened to the cries of a child, mute yelps, swallowed moans, from the loneliness of a gutter. The hurt child, cur in a corner, voiceless, weightless, formless, like air, punished to a total silence that shrieks from her belly, trying to break out like a wave, shattering all dams in a prolonged scream that perforates thunder, that invades agony, that drowns the wind. The girl who in her dog's corner tries to devour herself, feeding from her own flesh, swallowing chunks of lips, tongue, cheeks. Trying to consume herself. And cease to exist.

Since religion embraced all that she did not comprehend, Blanca turned to the Church for consolation. Despite her grandmother, who hated nuns with a passion and priests even more, Blanca went to confession every Saturday after doing her chores. On Sundays she attended San Juan Bosco's nine o'clock Mass, having fasted since the night before so she could receive Communion. She usually arrived early and lingered at the sidewalk talking to the boys from the Youth for Catholic Action. Although Paquita tolerated these religious incursions, she would not allow Blanca to become a Daughter of Mary because then she had to allow her to go to meetings and spend money on a blue and white uniform and the related paraphernalia that went with membership in such an august entity.

Blanca's religious zeal offered her the opportunity to escape the confines of the house and Paquita's company on Saturdays and Sundays. She knew her grandmother would never accompany her, since Paquita had sworn never to step inside a church. When Blanca returned from Mass, Paquita waited for her, swaying in her rocking chair in the front porch.

"What did the tricky priests say today, eh?"

"Oh, please don't say things like that. The sermon was really good this morning."

"Priests!" she spat. "They're all a pack of hypocrites. I bet they passed the little baskets around, didn't they? Because if they don't get their money, they're not happy. That's why they say that whoever doesn't give them money is condemned to everlasting fire."

"But they have to pay rent and eat and dress like everyone else."

"So, they should go to work like everyone else. That's a lot of shit! What they do with the money is buy cigarettes and pay for prostitutes."

"You shouldn't say things like that, Mami," Blanca ventured to say.

"I'll tell you something," Paquita said. "Priests and nuns are no saints. You've heard what they say in the news all the time. How nuns get pregnant. And who's getting them pregnant if it isn't the priests? What they've got in those convents are houses of Lucifer. They smoke and drink and gamble and do everything, everything, I say. They don't fool me with their talk about God. I thought you were more intelligent, but I think they brainwashed you. Those jerks who even charge for the baptism of a poor soul. And if the father has no money, the kid remains a heathen. That's the way they are, and they're all the same, all of them. With thosc long robes, pretending they're so saintly!"

Only during Holy Week would Paquita refrain from attacking the Church, secluding herself modestly for the benefit of her neighbors. She believed appearances had to be maintained at whatever cost. Accordingly, she kissed stale bread before throwing it out and cooked codfish on Fridays during

Lent. During Holy Week, the whole neighborhood could hear what she called "funeral music" playing on her radio. This invariably included Beethoven's Ninth Symphony with its Ode to Joy and the Bach Fugues. Every Good Friday she allowed Blanca to see the *Ten Commandments* at the local movie house. Blanca saw the film so many times in her youth, she knew the dialogue by heart.

Despite Paquita's fervent desire to maintain appearances at all costs, she would not step inside a church. It was one thing to deal with God directly, as she did by respecting His name, although once in a while an expletive leveled at the Holy Host would hurtle out in anger. Because of some deep and unreachable fear, Paquita tolerated Blanca's church-going, although she would have preferred to prohibit it.

For Blanca, the dominical hectoring was like listening to rain. Blanca removed her Sunday clothes and prepared lunch while Paquita prattled on. On Sunday afternoons they called at Elena's. The adults chatted and watched the Spanish-dubbed version of Bonanza on television while Blanca and Margarita sat on the steps outside and exchanged secrets that invariably included boys. But it was not only from Elena or Lito, or even Paquita, they kept their secrets. They were more careful than usual because Fernando objected strenuously to Margarita's friendships outings. He forbade her attendance at parties in the neighborhood and going out with friends. Whenever she was home, Fernando sank into an armchair, inhaling deeply from his cigarette, and watched her like a hawk. Margarita was always respectful, but she asked for Elena's or Lito's permission when she wanted to go somewhere and ignored her father's prohibitions.

"Can't wait for him to get a job or something," Margarita whispered to Blanca. "He's making my life miserable."

"But he didn't raise you or anything. He's not really your father." Blanca said.

"I know, but he thinks he is."

When Bonanza was over at nine, Blanca and Paquita returned home. Paquita swung in her hammock, listened to her transistor radio, hummed old melodies, and relived her past. Because Paquita now lived only in the past. Then she fell asleep. At ten, Blanca helped her get to bed, ironed her school uniform for the next day, and wrote in her diary, a rather sterile task given the predictability of her days. She wrote in English, a secret language no one around her had mastered, and then hid the diary in her drawer under the petticoats so her grandmother, ever alert, would not find it.

Before falling asleep, Blanca heard the laughter of young hooligans throwing rocks at copulating dogs just to see them run, hitched together, down the alleys.

# 18

Potentially harmful objects were taken from me when I arrived at the hospital. Belt, pantyhose, shoe laces. My belongings were meticulously inspected for possession of mirrors, nail files, or any other object that could be transformed into a tool of destruction. The bathroom mirrors are metallic, and they distort the faces of those who are fearless enough to look into them.

I constantly think of ways to kill myself, to dull the clatter in my head. It is difficult here, but not impossible. I could swallow a pencil, insert a wet finger in an electric outlet, hoard my daily medication until I have enough to perform the deed successfully. I never stop analyzing strategies for self-destruction. Outside it is easier. I have the freedom to drink myself into oblivion, to jump from a tall building. The important thing is not to fail the next time. I feel so incompetent. It is so like me to botch something like this. I feel ugly, inept, stupid. I feel overwhelming impulses to slash my flesh with a razor, crisscrossing patterns on my body. I want to pull my cheeks out in fistfuls of pulp, to gnaw at my flesh, to die torn to shreds by wolves.

Dr. Hackson knows nothing of this. I have seen him several times, not counting group therapy, and if all goes well, I will be out soon. So I keep Dr. Hackson off the scent. Besides, why should I trust him? When I was in intensive care, strapped in bed and at my most vulnerable, he took advantage of my weakness and told me, quite peremptorily, that I had to sign myself into the hospital. I said no way can I do that. Having committed an enormous act of irresponsibility, I incongruously pointed out my maternal and professional duties. He responded bossily, "If you refuse to commit yourself, I'll declare you mentally incompetent and you're off to the state mental hospital. Indefinitely." "Where do I sign?" I said. What else could I do? Every time I think about it, I get so irate I have to force my anger down like a tablespoon of castor oil. But I can never let my anger show.

So I talk to him about my life, but only what I want him to know. Once I told him I wanted to be a perfect teacher. He pounced on that and gave me a spirited lecture on my unrealistic expectations. He claims my depression is caused by frustration at not being able to fulfill my self-imposed expectations, which are impossible to realize. I had never seen him brighten up like that. Then he gave me one of his self-improvement tapes, which I never play, and smugly sat back satisfied in the knowledge that he had done something for the rather substantial fee he charges my health-insurance company.

I lead him astray by maintaining my pose of an educated woman at all times. Although I talk about my past, it's really to clarify it to myself. But mostly, I discuss politics, history, philosophy. I compare my life to the brush strokes of Van Gogh—violent, exuberant, insisting on the metaphor, evading the clear and concrete. While he sits in his comfortable armchair, I propel myself in my child's swing and hide my true grievances, my wounds, my deepest wishes. He will never understand how much I want to die.

I look through my drawers and closet. There is nothing of interest. The drawers contain some underwear. The bra may be promising. Bring it up to the throat, one of women's most vulnerable regions. But not the most vulnerable. It certainly wasn't through the throat that Margarita's blood flowed. Margarita. Why do I remember her every time I think the unthinkable? Every time I structure the places where death can come to me?

On Palm Sunday, Blanca returned home from Mass. "Give me your blessing," she said.

Paquita wiped her eyes with a handkerchief and rocked in her chair.

"Why're you crying? What happened?" Blanca was startled.

"Oh, the tragedy, my child, the tragedy. Tragedies never cease in my life. They never cease. Until when, my God, until when?" Weeping she put her hands to her head and rolled her eyes to the ceiling to make sure that God was listening.

"Please, tell me what's the matter."

"Elena's neighbor was here. She rushed in and gave me the news."

The terrible news.

Margarita had been invited to a birthday party. Her father forbade her to go. Elena informed him in no uncertain terms that he had no right to tell Margarita where to go or not to go because it was she and Lito who had raised the child since she was a tiny baby.

Margarita left the house that evening in an amethyst gown, tightly gathered at the waist. Her father watched her through the slats of the louvered window as she walked down the street with two girl friends.

The household was dark after eleven, when everyone retired. Except Fernando. He waited, smoking in the dark living room, watching through the window slats.

Fernando doused his cigarette when he saw Margarita open the gate. She removed her shoes at the door and tiptoed into the kitchen for a glass of water. In the bathroom, she changed into her nightgown and brushed her teeth, unaware that her father had slipped into the kitchen. She closed the door to her bedroom and went to bed. She was lulled by the memories of that perfect evening in which she danced with the handsomest boys in the neighborhood. She recalled happily how they all rushed to her whenever a new piece began. On the brink of sleep, she heard, as in a dream, the bedroom door open. Steps approached stealthily. In the shadows, she dreamed a strident warning, and she swam to the shore of wakefulness, too late.

She tried to scream when her father's heavy shadow fell on her with the glint of a blade in his fist, searching for her under the sheets. But he clamped a hand over her mouth. She thrashed and kicked when her father tried to enter her with his dark weapon, his potent rum-soaked breath searing her lungs. Then she felt a sticky wetness in her back. She struggled, but still he penetrated and stabbed, his eyes blazing, hers wide as a skull's. With the loss of blood, she weakened quickly. When she no longer struggled, Fernando stabbed her sixteen times more as he climaxed in the lake of blood that was her bed. He finally quenched his thirst with the girl with wide-open eyes.

They say the eyeballs of the dead hold an image of the last things they see. Having sated his lust, Fernando stabbed his daughter's eyes to destroy the impression of his face imprinted in her eyes.

Elena and Lito woke up with the crowing of the roosters. They worked hard all day and slept so soundly they were not aware of the horrors of the night before. Sunlight aimed a finger at the bloody corpse. Elena and Lito clung to each other and howled, stumbling out of the house, tracking the floor with Margarita's blood.

For three days and three nights relatives and friends poured from hills and barrios to the little house on Fajardo

Street. The women chanted the Rosary while the men took long, hard gulps of rum and bobbed their heads whenever one of them spoke. They talked about the murderer's arrest, his lack of remorse. Blanca sat with Elena, who was numb with pain. Someone brought *El Vocero* with the bloody headline emblazoned on the front page. Lito tore it up angrily as tears streamed down his face.

After the funeral, Paquita and Blanca rode in the back seat of a neighbor's car. Paquita leaned forward to talk to the woman in the passenger seat. Blanca looked out the window. Her grief was so great, nothing could console her. She closed the window against the hot afternoon air and pressed her forehead against the glass.

# 19

The muffler of a passing car drags along the pavement outside and the clatter wedges in a fragment of my drowsy mind. The awful noise splits my senses open to voices, the clicking of heels and car horns. An opaque light and the sickening smell of rubbing alcohol assail me as well, and I wake up with a start. There are no strangers in the room, as I fear. Celia sleeps, covers pulled to her chin.

I had that dream again last night. Always a man with a gun or a knife. Sometimes I see him clearly. Other times, he's only a shadow. He never rushes. On the contrary, he stalks me slowly, deliberately, until he knows I am paralyzed with fear. I can never escape him in the dream. I wake up when he is about to strike.

Quite unexpectedly a chunk of memory stirs in my mind. It is like a photograph ripped in minuscule pieces which, when put together, is like an image reflected in rippling waters. If I tilt my head, the photograph becomes disorganized, mixed, confused. Then my mind's eye sees the shredded photograph glued together to form a new picture. Coarse seams hold the picture whole yet fragmented.

Felipe Rodríguez was dead. Margarita was dead. Death closed in on her. Blanca finally grasped the true meaning of silence, a word that reverberated in her head like a recurring nightmare. Every day seemed solemn to her. And she slipped into her solemn days in fear that even her own body, the body she had always known, was dying, too.

Deep stirrings of melancholy beset her. She could no longer hide the swell of her breasts pressing eagerly against her blouse, nor the annoyingly seductive curves that sloped from the waist down her thighs. Her attempts to walk with buttocks tucked in failed under the insistent sway of the hips. Baffled by her body's alchemy, she could not face her reflection in the mirror. Nothing was in place inside of her, and she felt that the silence of her body was a terrible betrayal. She had lost so much of herself that she no longer knew who she was. She went to sleep early to prolong the beauty of the night when her body finally did not matter.

Blanca was sixteen and worked at Franklin's, a women's clothing store in Barrio Obrero. Every afternoon after school and on Saturday mornings, she waited on customers, filled out sales slips, folded and arranged merchandise. The work was tedious, especially on inventory days, but after giving most of her earnings to Paquita, she had enough left over for driving lessons. Paquita was thrilled to plan all the excursions Blanca would take her on when she finished high school, worked as a secretary in a bank or an airline company, and bought a used car. Paquita had their whole lives planned out for them, but she had not counted on the effect the driving instructor would have on Blanca's despair.

When Blanca walked into the driving school that very first day and saw the instructor, she recognized the lust encrusted in his yellow eyes. She had seen that look in other men before, the way his indolent gaze slid over her body, calculating the measurements through her cotton blouse and flared skirt, imagining the color of her nipples, relishing the aroma that exuded from her pores. She should have escaped then, but she did not run away from him until later when it was too late.

She went back every Saturday, fearing what he could do to her, for she was well aware of the power of men. Yet she was betrayed by a sense of longing that washed over her whenever the man was near. The man was married, pure anathema, and old enough to be her father. He waited for her hungrily every week.

The seduction was carefully choreographed and executed. He began by rubbing his hand purposefully against hers while she gripped the driver's wheel. Then he placed his hand on her thigh. Finally, he kissed her. And she let him rub her hand, touch her thigh, kiss her on the mouth. Blanca was terrified of her own cravings, but she listened to his every word of seduction, holding her breath, afraid to move a muscle.

Until the Saturday afternoon when he drove her to a solitary place, and she knew with horrifying fear what his intentions were. She ran, but he was faster, stronger. He scalded her flesh with blows, split her lips, and she saw her own blood everywhere. He dragged her to the ground and fell on top of her. She felt a lance pierce her insides. Hurt, hurt, she felt a hurt so deep it cut into the private walls of her deepest intimacy and hurtled her into a darkness she had already known. How was it possible that this horrible pain was happening to her again? Would it ever stop? When she realized there was nothing else she could do but give in, she stared at the golden rim of the clouds. She concentrated on the lavender trail of the sun while the man galloped on top of her. The sky became a blur, but she stared at the clouds and the sun and the colors of the sky with stark, wide-open eyes.

When the man was done, he spoke. Not understanding what he said, Blanca carefully examined an empty beer bottle someone had discarded in the thicket. Her torn underwear was strewn near the bottle. In the fog of her thoughts, she heard the man's voice calling her baby, telling her how delicious she was. Her skin crawled with disgust. Hatred burned in her heart. She tried to sit up and a shard of pain ripped through her insides. Her face throbbed, and she could taste the blood on her lips. Fire blazed between her legs.

She felt faint, headless, and her consciousness tumbled into a gorge full of spiders. Screams dripped into puddles of viscous mud. A severed head, draped with cobwebs, chased her. She ran, flinging screams that gushed and slid stickily through the cobweb hair of the severed head. She groped in the darkness, searching among the spiders and their gummy nests. She stumbled on a mask so similar to her own head that she drove it into her neck and searched no more. Sitting on a tar rock, fire scorched her armpits, her groin, her ears. A shudder crawled over her, and she shed her dappled skin.

"Don't go putting little acts on, shit," the man yelled. "No phony fainting spells now, pretending you're sick or something. Look, my wife's waiting for me. Get up, *carajo*."

He pulled her to her feet. Blanca looked at the man and he averted his eyes nervously. In a deep recess of her eyes, he detected a boundless hole.

Blanca tried to escape, but the man pursued her, his lust a mad obsession. He wanted her all the time, needing her daily. And if he was unable to use her, he masturbated furiously with her pink nipples fastened to his brain. He needed to gnaw her armpits, taste her mossy pubis, root her soft belly like a wild boar. The stitches in his groin made his erection fat and desperate. He exploded in fragments of white jets, gushing somewhere in his heart or his brain, he was never sure. He needed to use her again and again, scouring her face with his milk-spilling manhood.

He made her his. She feared the beatings he threatened to inflict, but the most effective threat, the one that chilled her heart, was the threat of revealing their secret to her grandmother. He guaranteed her silent acquiescence during his constant onslaught. Her fear allowed him to use her, and while he used her, she nurtured her dark hate. But despite her icy hatred, she was convinced of the irreversibility of fate. Dejected, Blanca plunged into the everlasting shadow of silence, believing she had no other choice but to surrender to more punishment. It was not difficult. She had grown accustomed to punishment. In fact, she expected it as her inescapable fate. And he awakened a new source of hatred that made her forget, however briefly, the solitary cell with her aged jailer. A new hatred that flattened all of her hopes.

When they returned from an Isla Verde motel, they talked about the heat of August or the rains of May and planned their next outing, which had to be soon, very soon.

"I can't wait too long," he protested.

"I can't help it. My grandmother will get suspicious."

"Don't worry about the old woman. She's senile."

"No, she's not. She may be old, but she's alert and gets more suspicious every day. I can't think of any more lies to make up so I can go out. I tell her I have to go to the library for a special school assignment, or that I have to work late at the store, or I'm going to church. I don't know what else I can say."

"Just keep on inventing whatever tales you have to, because I have to see you more often. What we have to do is find a way to see each other on weekends, too."

"That's impossible!"

Yellow sparks in the man's leopard eyes lit up hungrily.

"I know what we'll do. On Saturday nights, late, when the old woman and all the neighbors are asleep, say, eleven or twelve, I'll throw a stone at your window. Then you'll know I'm there, open the back door, and we can go in your bedroom. That way I can get through Sundays with a little peace."

Blanca frowned. "Are you crazy? I won't do it. Never!"

The yellow eyes narrowed. "What do you mean, you won't do it? You'll do whatever I tell you." He veered the car to a street near the airport and parked. He squeezed her shoulders. "Unless you want me to tell your grandmother all about us."

"No, of course, not. But she can hear us, someone might see you. It's a lousy plan. I can't do it, I can't."

"Don't be a crybaby." He turned away with a scowl of disgust. "Listen, I'll be there tomorrow night. You better be ready for me."

That next evening, Professor McDowell ended his televised weather report. The Luis Vigoreaux and Lydia Echevarría Show was over at ten. Paquita switched off the new television set she received for Mother's Day from her sons and went to bed. From her own bedroom, Blanca listened to Paquita's breathing as it became deeper and deeper and she began to snore. At eleven she heard a clack on the slats of her jalousie window. Her heart faltered in a frenzy of fear. She tiptoed to the kitchen door and opened it. The man followed her to the bedroom. He undressed quickly and fell on the narrow bed pulling at her cotton nightgown. Blanca surrendered to another joyless night.

Time slipped by, and she could no longer ignore the nausea-ridden mornings and her constant vertigo. For two months she spread mercurochrome and tincture of iodine on her sanitary napkins to satisfy the monthly inspections of her grandmother, who said she wanted to make sure her menstrual blood was the right color. Only now did Blanca understand the true motive of those inspections. Miraculously, after Paquita contracted a gum disease and had all her teeth extracted, without any explanation, she had stopped her gynecological inspections.

The man did not waver. Unconcerned as he was by the future, he never considered the effects of his acts. He never looked back. He followed his instincts, all steered to satisfying his hedonistic needs, without weighing the consequences. He recognized no repercussions for his acts.

The man had a friend well-versed in women's affairs. He recommended a tisane brewed with avocado leaves, to be taken several times a day. The potion made Blanca throw up violently, but she still did not bleed.

Then the friend recommended a pharmacist who injected women with a hormone that was so powerful, it would bring about her period in no time. Every day after work, the man drove Blanca in his long green car to the dark alley behind the pharmacy. They entered through the back door. In a dusty corner of the storage room, Blanca hiked up her dress and pulled down her underpants. She stood like a mare with bare haunches in the air while the pharmacist injected a searing solution into her buttock. The pain made her stomach lurch. Her buttocks were black and blue after several injections, but her period seemed unreachable. She pounded her abdomen with her fists and threw herself down the stairs, but the embryo clung fast, refusing to release her.

The man's friend said, finally, "If the kid doesn't come out, you'll have to take drastic measures. It'll cost you, you know." And they made an appointment. Blanca felt very much alone when she took the bus to Parada 23 and spotted the street behind Immaculate Conception Church. She searched for a number, found it, and climbed the creaking stairs that led to a wooden mirador. A receptionist sat in the tiny waiting room. A musty odor was in the air. "Sit down, Señorita, the doctor's with another patient now. He'll be with you soon."

Blanca sat down and, deep in her dark thoughts, desperately prayed to Saint Judas Thadeus to help her with this impossible situation. If her grandmother found out, she would die of anger. She would surely suffer a heart attack if she knew that her granddaughter was carrying the child of a married man, a man with no future.

"Do it for her, Saint Judas," she prayed, "not for me. I don't deserve any favors. I pledge ten rosaries, two novenas and to go to Mass every Sunday for the rest of my life."

But she could not bring herself to make the most obvious promise. Convinced that fate would not let her escape her punishment, she never promised to break up with the man.

The doctor confirmed her pregnancy.

"I already know that. I came for an abortion," Blanca said firmly.

The doctor looked at her disdainfully.

"Who told you to come here?" he asked.

"A friend."

"Well, señorita," his voice filled with sarcasm when he uttered the word, "you either have this child or explode, because in Puerto Rico, in case you didn't know, abortions are illegal. So get out of here!"

Blanca was desperate. This was her last hope. What could she do now? She would have to kill herself. A suicide was preferable to a confrontation with her grandmother, which would surely end in one or two deaths anyway.

Her nights were sleepless. During the day, she forced herself to eat enough so as not to arouse the suspicions of her grandmother, though she had to vomit after every meal. Paquita's eyesight was not good, and Blanca passed the monthly inspections of her sanitary napkins.

As Blanca smeared her sanitary napkins with tincture of iodine and mercurochrome, trying to foil Paquita's inspections, the man explored the most mundane corners of his barrio. They were in a motel room when he gave her the news.

"There's an old woman in Caguas who does these jobs. A guy who works with me is her neighbor, and he said he's willing to talk to her about doing it. He'll let me know what happens in a few days."

Blanca skipped school, and she and the man set out early. They drove up the hills and slopes of Caguas and found the unpainted shack they were looking for. It was tightly shuttered and did not seem inhabited.

They were greeted by a gaunt old woman, blackened by years of sun and wind. A dog barked hoarsely in the back yard. Sunlight snuck through cracks between the wooden boards of the walls.

The old woman ordered the man to leave because "These are women's matters" and escorted Blanca to the only bedroom in the shack.

"Take your panties off and let me see you," she said as she opened the shutters.

"Hum," the municipal hospital janitor murmured while she examined Blanca.

She chattered about "these crazy girls who get into trouble left and right" when Blanca felt a cold tube enter her.

"Don't tense up now because it'll be worse," the janitor ordered.

And she violated her womb with a hot thick liquid. "Stay still for a while so it'll go deep inside. That's it."

The man, who in those days had lost the hunger of his yellow leopard eyes, picked Blanca up in the afternoon.

"You got to come back tomorrow early. Kid'll be out then," the hospital janitor indicated.

There was still sunshine when they returned to Santurce and the flowering flamboyant trees, drenched in a scandalous red, edged the road with their broad shade.

The next day, Blanca waited for the man at the scheduled time, in the usual place. The country shack looked stark in the bright morning sun. The man and Blanca sat on plastic and chrome chairs while the janitor shut the door and opened the shutters a bit so some air would come into the stale room. She chattered with the man about the "damn Populares."

"But Republicans are worse. I don't even vote no more," she said while she punctured the air with a long grimy finger. A few seconds after they had coffee, Blanca's womb contracted in terrible spasms. A ripping pain tore through her. She hugged her abdomen and bent over, crying.

"Well, the pain's started," the old woman announced unnecessarily while the man helped bring Blanca to bed.

"You can go now. Return in the afternoon. This'll take some time."

The man left without saying good-bye, occupied as he was by thoughts of the *lechonera* where he would indulge in a substantial lunch of roast pork, plantain fritters, and cold beer.

The old woman handed Blanca a pillow. Blanca was glad to escape the woman's biting odor of ammonia by pressing the pillow into her face.

"That's the way it is, my child. Pleasure today's sure to bring suffering tomorrow. How about some camomile tea to calm you down a bit. You're too upset. Don't scream now. There aren't any neighbors around, but someone can walk by and hear you. Bite into the pillow when you feel the pain coming." The woman hurried to put a kettle of water on the stove and gather some tea leaves in the backyard.

Blanca squeezed the pillow against her hard abdomen. Desperately she sat up, kneeled, lay down, trying to find a position that would relieve her pain. It was useless. She pressed the pillow to her stomach again and fell into a ravine of pain. Her tears were like flames licking her eyes. Blindly she moaned when the sharp pain bore into her. She fell into the fiery abyss of hurt. Blanca screamed into the pillow and a howl roared in her ears.

Time slogged by through the day. Cold sweat, like ice on fire, hurled Blanca again and again into her gorge of pain. The old woman applied cold wet towels to her forehead while she mumbled, "See if these girls learn not to get into trouble."

The contractions punched ruthlessly, a solid mass of blackness. There was no respite now. The pillow was drenched with tears and screams, moans and sweat.

"Come on," the janitor said. "We have to sit you on the toilet. Hurry or you'll mess up the bed."

On the lidless toilet, Blanca thrust a red crescent into the waters tinted with urine. The tiny body floated sorrowfully. Blanca stared at its bit of head curled into itself, its wisp of a back rounded in self-defense. Stunned, she slipped into a merciful blackness, as deep as her sorrow.

Hurricane winds blew wildly in the afternoon. Despite the storm warnings, the man's wife waited for Blanca at the bus stop.

"Got to talk to you," she said, curling a finger and tilting her head toward a quiet street.

Blanca stepped on the leaves that swirled in the wind. Her skirt billowed like a wind-filled sail as she followed the woman. She knew her secret life was unravelling and soon everyone would see who she really was. She held her skirt down, lowered her head against the wind and listened.

"I left him last night, and I'm filing for a divorce as soon as possible. He's a no-good lout who doesn't do an hour's worth of work. He's working now, I know, but it won't last long. When we owned the driving school, he did the least amount of work and gambled most of our earnings, so we went under. He's lazier than the upper jaw. I know you're seeing him, but I don't care. You're not the first and won't be the last." She paused to catch her breath. "How old are you?"

"Seventeen."

The woman nodded knowingly.

"I was seventeen, too," her voice traced a path in her memory. "Listen, I can testify on your behalf if you decide to take him to court for abusing a minor or something like that. It's statutory rape, you know. That's all I wanted to say. I never want to see his face again. So you're free to do what you want. But if you need my help, let me know, and you can send him to prison, the filthy lout."

Blanca listened to the bitter offer, but she was unable to mirror herself in the tired face that had walked where Blanca walked and had seen Blanca's future. She was suspicious of the offer. Too kind. What did she care about Blanca? She just wanted to harm the man, seek vengeance because he had another woman now. She was jealous, that was all. Blanca heard her out politely, but shut out the warnings. She drowned her suspicions, the accusations whispered in the deepest folds of her consciousness and the memory of her constant mistreatment at the man's hands.

"Don't forget," the woman repeated. "If you decide to prosecute, I'll be a witness of what he did to you. I know, he did the same to me."

Blanca spun and swallowed air as she rushed away from the woman. She felt that invisible forces were cornering her into an exitless trap. Her grandmother had received an anonymous letter claiming that Blanca was seen entering a motel with an older, married man. The old woman interrogated Blanca without mercy. Blanca admitted nothing. Paquita took the necessary precautions and told her neighbors, who would certainly spread the word around, that she had taken Blanca to the doctor for a thorough physical examination. "For a good listener, few words are necessary," Paquita asserted.

But all did not end there. A neighborhood woman came one morning when Paquita was hosing her spit of a garden, informing her that Blanca was going out with a married man and, to make matters worse, she said, he was dark-skinned. The old woman galvanized her hoarded angers and forgotten strength. For the satisfaction of the barrio gossip, she knocked Blanca down in the garden, rendering a hail of blows and insults the likes of which she had not inflicted in years, but which had been collecting like bile. The mocking eyes of the neighbor swallowed the beating greedily, and she rushed down the street to spread the gossip through the barrio, painting the scene witnessed with vivid and colorful embellishments.

Now Blanca ran down the street at the edge of hysteria. A vise clamped around her chest and chopped her breathing into small rapid dashes. Her grandmother was on the scent. How long could she sustain this web of deception?

The day a hurricane warning was announced and the scowling sky threatened, they rented a furnished room in a rooming house and eloped. Blanca packed some books and clothing in her suitcase, and looking at the empty wind, ran off with the man with yellow leopard eyes.

The wind robbed her of her own shadow. The hurricane swerved to Haiti.

# 20

I ask for a pen and some paper at the nurses' station. Back in the room, I turn on the tape player that the hospital provides for our therapeutic use and continue a letter started days ago to my friend Rosa. Often I am unable to speak freely during visiting hours. Too many people are present, too many nurses snooping around, trying to find out what we really think. So whenever Rosa comes to visit, I hand her a letter containing the important things I want to say, and during her visit, we talk about inanities.

Dear Rosa,

Will be free soon, if all goes well. Things march or, rather, walk in rhythmic and predictable steps around here. Days fuse with each other, and they seem more like waves than marks. Eternal recurrences. Calendars should be redesigned to reflect the passage of time in curves instead of numbers embedded in little squares. Considering how time progresses, instead of linear, it must certainly be circular.

I'm listening to *Esperanza Inútil* by Daniel Santos. Thanks for recording it for me. I remember the nights in San Juan when we curled up like cocoons, listened to boleros, and languidly inhaled our Galoises. I remember the nostalgic talks we had, the delicious tales we wove. I remember the tears we shared when we relived our disappointments and the past that made us like sisters.

Nothing changes here. Patients wander around, their eye sockets either too empty or too alive. Destructive wishes clang in our heads like migraines. We all have unsettled grievances, avenging ghosts that constantly torment us. Each person hauls around an individual tragedy. In this alienated, dissonant world we all have a story to tell. Variations on a theme. Gradually the stories fuse in a twisted path, a road going nowhere. Once you are on that road, there is nowhere to go, there is only memory.

Silvia arrived here on an emergency admission. She says she could hear howling in her head, loud and relentless, until she could no longer stand the torment. Her agony began after she went into a bar one night to buy a pack of cigarettes. When she staggered out two hours later, she had been repeatedly raped on a table by a gang of four while she screamed and screamed and the other customers clapped and whistled. When she talks, her voice is like a dry echo in a deep hole, and her eyes always blaze with an inner terror. No one has good posture in this place, but Silvia has the worst. She hangs her head when she walks, looking at her shoes. When she sits, she stares at her hands as though peering into the bottom of an empty cup. Her voice is still hoarse from all the screaming. I wonder if voice has memory, and Silvia's will always remember the violence it tried to denounce. A film of hurt mists her eyes when she talks about the nightmares she has while she's awake during the day, too. They must be terrifying labyrinths of pain.

Miguel rarely sleeps. His drug abuse awakened his brain permanently, and he roams the halls all night, his bare feet burning into the floor tiles. They took his shoes away after he tried to escape. The hallucinations induced by drugs soothed his anger. Miguel's father had him committed to a state mental institution before coming here, and what he saw there will forever fuel his anger.

Castule, the pyromaniac, is a small baldish man. He constantly says he's sorry, as though his very existence were a nuisance to the rest of humanity. If he walks down the hall where another person happens to be passing by, he says he's sorry. When he passes the other person, he effusively thanks him with his head sunk in his chest. He never dares to look into someone else's face. He's like a frightened bird, apologizing for the violation caused by his presence. Deep ridges cut into his face, and they deepen when his tortoise-shell wide-rimmed eyeglasses slide down the bridge of his nose. He always wears polyester clothing that was in style twenty years ago. Bell bottoms and safari shirts, that sort of thing. When he was a child, he lit old newspapers and set his house on fire. His mother almost died in the blaze. Castule hardly speaks, but once in a while he'll approach an unsuspecting victim and a gossipy whisper emerges from his raspy throat. He says he has sexual relations with his mother while his father takes photos. "Then," he says with great dramatic flourish, "I become a bat." When he finishes this grotesque story, he sneezes repeatedly and blows his nose with great force, saying he's sorry constantly while he adjusts his eyeglasses.

Celia is depressed like me. She's an amputated feminist whose husband, in the best machista tradition, institutionalized her. Shock treatment keeps her under control. She expected marriage to liberate her from an abusive, oppressing father. But marriage was just a continuation of her situation at home. She wanted to get a university degree, but her husband wouldn't hear of it. He slapped her around to keep her in her place. He warned her not to even think of leaving, because he'd have her declared an unfit mother and take her children away. One day he lit a bonfire in their backyard and burned all the poems she had written since childhood. He found them in an old shoe box she hid under the bed. She cried when she told me how he laughed into the flames, arms crossed over his big chest, and said, "Poetry, hah, that's a lot of crap." He put her away when she rebelled. She had refused to have sex with him, and instead of scrubbing floors, had started reading things like the *Leviathan*. Now, after many sessions of shock therapy, she feels they have burned her brain. Her depression, in the meantime, hasn't waned.

> No one knows the origin of Ursula's madness, which keeps the rumor-mongers harping busily. When she cries, she only sheds tears through her left eye. She's usually heavily sedated, but on rare occasions she escapes the chaos of her mind and she sits with her private nurse in the common room, her freshly brushed hair cascading on her slender shoulders, hands laced on her lap, chin held high, eyes cloudy with distance. But everyone is wary of her because no one knows why or when delirium suddenly shatters her peace. Because of this unpredictability, she is always alone with her custodian.
>
> And Nina, a little old lady, screeches constantly, her revenge on a life of quiet acceptance. She was calm on her birthday because of all the presents her relatives spread on her dresser. She'd forget she had received them though, and every time she looked toward the dresser, she would rejoice again, as if she had seen the presents for the first time.

The nurse brings the nightly sleeping pill. I fold the unfinished letter and put it away. I take the sedative with water from a styrofoam cup and brace myself for another bout of fitful sleep. Every night I drop off the edge of the earth, clawing at the darkness as I fall. I wander about in my dreams until I emerge from them early in the morning, exhausted by my active nocturnal life.

Sometimes, I dream of a force, a dark, invisible power that levitates me without control, crashing my head against the ceiling. When the dark force attacks, I struggle to wake up, to scream, but I can only see myself still as a statue, mouth wide open, terror clinging to my heart.

I fall asleep and start dreaming quickly. I sweep the hall of a women's club. Women who have maids, send their children to private schools, and whittle away their hours in health clubs, beauty salons, or as volunteers serving humanity, because that's what women of their class are supposed to do. While I sweep, a storm darkens the skies. The bridge players hastily take their coats and go home. I remain alone, making sure all is in order, the door and windows hermetically shut. A woman appears at the door. She is tall, elegant, in her mid-fifties, wearing a purple dress. With her gloved knuckles, she raps at the upper glass pane of the door. I recognize her and open the door. The woman asks whether I am alone. I nod. The woman walks to an intricately carved wardrobe, opens the door and takes out a blue plastic garbage bag. She twists it, wraps the two ends around her hands and turns around. She looks at me, an evil smile darkening her face. Her ice-blue eyes shimmer. I feel a chill in my bones while a shiver slithers down my spine. I scream and furiously beat the woman again and again. I wake up in terror.

Weary of nightmares, I try to decipher the dream while I consider the ceiling cracks now tinted with the shadows of dawn. At seven, I dress without enthusiasm and smooth my hair down with my fingers. I go to the common room after breakfast. It is essential that the psychiatric personnel see me there, engaged in acts of socialization or listening to the tapes Dr. Hackson gives me on *How to Overcome Unrealistic Expectations*. I surreptitiously replace Dr. Hackson's tapes with my beloved Daniel Santos.

I approach Celia, who is attempting to knit a large yellow square.

"What're you up to?" I ask her.

"Practicing for arts and crafts class. But I'm not doing too well."

Celia holds up a lopsided scrap of knitting fraught with irregular holes. She makes a face and we both laugh.

"I'm trying to make something I can give to my daughter for her birthday. She'll be ten next month." Celia folds her knitting on her lap. "I just hope she's taking her medication."

"What for?"

"She's got, um. Oh, what's it called?" Celia rolls up her eyes. "It's the illness that Alexander the Great and Julius Caesar had." She snaps her fingers urgently. "It starts with an e."

"Epilepsy?"

"Yes, yes, that's it, epilepsy," she points at me with her knitting needle.

Celia reads voraciously. She reads everything. Essays on dialectical materialism, treatises on the problems of the Puerto Rican immigrant in Enrique Laguerre's novels, the poetry of Clemente Soto Vélez. She is frequently seen dipping into the fat dictionary she keeps in her room like a valued piece of furniture. Yet her thoughts are crushed by words she cannot recall. Many times a sought-after word trembles on the tip of her tongue, tormenting her. Celia forms and reforms it in her mind, but is unable to capture the word. In an anguish-filled circumlocution, she often describes what she wants to say until someone offers the correct term or she finally pulls it from her memory, sometimes hours later. Words can flow from Celia like an open tap, but because she never knows when she will stumble in her speech, she hesitates to engage in conversation unless she has something pressing to say. I am one of the few persons with whom she can stumble without embarrassment. Although some people think she is not smart, I have long conversations with her and recognize the intelligence that hides behind her once-audacious eyes.

Now Celia's words flow easily.

"She has to take a drug that controls her attacks, but before that she had about two attacks a week. The poor thing would roll her eyes up to the sky until they were white, like a corpse. She'd foam at the mouth, shaking and jerking on the floor. It was ugly, especially when she lost control of her bladder."

"Do you know why she's epileptic?" I ask.

"Doctors say it's a problem in the neurons of the brain. But no one knows why neurons collapse, why they, um, um, how do you say it? Why the brain's signals get disconnected. It's something like an electrical storm."

"How about your son?"

"Oh, Noel is fine. Doing well in school, too. They both are."

I stand up.

"Going somewhere?" Celia asks.

"Taking a shower now. I missed yesterday's, and you know that it's not therapeutic."

Celia smiles. I pick up my soap and towel. On the way to the communal showers, my body odor wraps me in its heady musk. The odors of moist vagina and sweaty skin mix with the rancid sweetness that seeps from my pores. An odd scent drifts from my armpits, as though someone had entered my room one night, worn my blouse, and then returned it to the drawer soaked with perspiration. I do not recognize my own smell. I smell like a stranger. In the shower I scrub my body hard. I try to wipe out memories of the past. The more I think, the harder I scrub.

# 21

Stepping down from the platform at graduation, Blanca felt someone gripping her arm. Again, she heard the voice of her nightmares.

First Paquita cried.

"How could you, wretched ingrate, after I gave you my life? How could you stab me in the back? This is going to kill me, and you'll be responsible for my death. I don't know where to hide my face, I'm so ashamed. Because you, you left, but I'm the one who has to face the neighbors, the world. That this face full of wrinkles should have to suffer this shame, this dishonor in my old age. What will become of me now?"

Then she revealed her anger.

"May a bolt of lightning strike the monster dead. May God make him pay twenty million times for the wrong he has done me. I pray that a cancer consume him slowly. The damned son of a whore, I shit on his mother a thousand times. How he turned your head with his promises! He fooled you, you know, and you let him take advantage of you like an idiot. He brainwashed you and then filled your head with sweet talk. Maybe he'll have a bad end, the monster. What do you see in him? Tell me that. He's an ugly monster."

Finally, she exposed the bait.

"Here, I brought you a letter from the university." Calmer now, she wiped her tears with a pudgy hand. "Elena read it to me very carefully. They're giving you a scholarship if you start in August. Come with me and you can go study like you wanted to. Maybe you can buy a car to come and go to classes, and you can work in the afternoons to make the car payments.

If Salvador keeps sending me the same amount he does weekly, maybe I can help out."

When she noticed that Blanca stood silently in her cap and gown looking like a widow in mourning, she added, "What're you going to do with that monster who has no future? He's a low-life. He doesn't have a pot to pee in. That poor wife of his had to divorce him because he was so lazy. Now he has to pay child support for three kids. Look, he didn't even show up for your graduation. He doesn't care that you got honors. Leave him and come back with me. I'll tell the neighbors that he threatened you and forced you to run away with him."

She dug her nails into Blanca's arm. Blanca knew her grandmother well enough to realize Paquita did not want to live alone. She needed Blanca. Without her, the old woman was bereft of a servant, companion, errand runner, and a supplementary income. She needed a nurse, an object to vent her anger and frustration on, an ear that would always be there to listen to her voice and reinforce her existence. Why else had she shown up at Blanca's graduation brandishing her acceptance letter to the university? She was desperate, and Blanca knew it.

"You know how people are," Blanca said. "They're always going to say terrible things about me because of what happened. It's true that he has nothing to offer, but I have to marry him even if I divorce him later. I have no choice. My reputation will be ruined forever if I don't, and then I'll have to leave the country to start a new life where no one will know me."

"You're crazy, that's what you are," Paquita responded angrily. "But you, you're going to long for the worst moment you ever spent by my side. That man's gonna ruin you one way or another. He'll never change. God knows what he'll do to you."

Blanca responded quickly. "If you sign the papers, we can get married, and after I divorce him, I'll come and live with you."

Paquita looked up at her granddaughter with a glimmer of hope in her eyes. Maybe she could repossess Blanca after all.

"All right, but don't let the monster know about this because he's capable of anything if he finds out about our plan. He'll probably drag you away where I can never find you."

Paquita recognized something in the man that reminded her of needs she herself harbored. The thought disturbed her and she shook it off. She wept some more for Blanca's benefit and stomped away.

Amid the song of the acacia, Taína was born. After twelve hours of labor, the infant who had wailed in Blanca's womb entered reluctantly into the world of glaring lights and sounds in a definite snit. She refused to cry at birth and during the first two weeks of her life.

In the night, the man always searched for Blanca because there were no others. But his wounding insults tinted her eyes with a deep melancholy. His sexual grievances were many. She was too wide, too soft. Now that she had given birth, she no longer offered him the same pleasure. Then he penetrated the smaller orifice, and it became his only source of pleasure. Until one night, when Blanca sighted a mouse, claimed it scampered out of Taína's room, and brought the infant into the marriage bed. Wedged between her parents, Taína slept there every night, limiting the painful assaults suffered by her mother.

The man became afflicted by a particularly virulent strain of jealousy. He accused Blanca of having multiple lovers: her boss, her co-workers, the bus driver. Any man who came in contact with her was suspect. If she exercised to reduce her postpartum stomach, he asked crossly, "Who the hell are you getting in shape for?" If she wore make-up to work, he demanded to know why was she making herself look pretty. When she bought a new dress, he wanted an immediate explanation of why she had bought it and for whose pleasure. To dispel any positive notion she might have about her own physical appeal, he took advantage of a weight gain of several pounds to rail at her for becoming a fat unattractive sow.

He purposely remained unemployed with plenty of time on his hands. To obstruct Blanca's contact with men on her way to work, he drove her to and from the office every day and even had lunch with her. They lived with his mother María in a tiny house on Calle Loíza. While Blanca worked, and the man was at the racetrack, María took care of Taína. When not placing bets or listening to the races on the radio, the man spent his time calling Blanca at the office to make sure she was there. He never bothered to make up an excuse.

After childbirth, he could no longer fantasize about Blanca's innocence, despite her youth, and his sexual passion for her was replaced by another passion that soaked her patience dry. Blanca became his possession, his provider, his sole source of sexual pleasure, an object he could mistreat with impunity. He did not allow her a breath of privacy. She had to tell him everything she did or thought. She could not have friends because they would only pervert her. He had to be her only friend. When she wrote letters to old friends or relatives in New York, he read and censored them until she became so adept at self-censorship that her letters contained the limpest prose without any inner revelation or subjectivity. He criticized her reading habit because books would put unwholesome ideas in her head. If in the evenings, after a tiring day at the office, Blanca sat down to read, the man grabbed the book and threw it into the garbage, saying, "With what that stupid book cost you, I could have bet on a quiniella." Then he expounded for hours on his personal betting formula which would soon yield the most incredible riches when he won big at the horse track.

Christmas approached with carols promising false hopes of peace when Blanca, convinced finally that she had endured enough punishment, looked straight into the man's face and told him she was leaving. While she gathered her belongings, the man bellowed, eyes aflame. Dramatically, he locked himself in the bathroom and came out claiming he had taken a bottle of aspirin. He announced his imminent death and declared it would weigh heavily on Blanca's conscience. Aware of his histrionic abilities, Blanca cast him a cold glance and unflinchingly continued packing. He stood at the foot of the bed and forgot he was supposed to be dying.

"Got yourself a lover, huh? Bet he's waiting for you in a filthy motel. You whore. I dragged you from the street, married you, made a decent woman out of you. God knows what you did before you met me. You were no virgin, that's for sure. And here I am, suffering under the weight of all the horns you've put on my head, you filthy bitch. Still I'm willing to put up with you. And now look, you ungrateful whore, you want to dump me for another guy," he said.

His hurtful words cut notches in her own voice.

"Just leave me alone," she said, and slammed her suitcase shut.

She felt the hairs on the nape of her neck prickle when the man lifted his arm. The force of the punch slung her on the bed. Then he lunged at her. His face came close to hers, his breath bitter. "You're not leaving, whore. I'll kill you first."

His big hands tightened around her neck, and he pinned her legs under him. She struggled to escape the blunt, wide hands. When she tried to scream, his fingers dug into her flesh and squeezed her throat dry. She tried desperately to catch a mouthful of air. A wave of nausea washed over her. She was so tired, she closed her eyes while feebly beating his back with her fists.

"What are you doing, are you crazy?" María burst into the room still wearing the turban she used when she went out to do the shopping.

The man stared at his mother and then looked back at Blanca's pale face. He peeled his fingers from her throat and stomped out of the room. María followed him, scolding and waving her arms.

Taína woke up from her siesta and padded to her mother's side. With her tiny hand, she caressed Blanca's head.

Fear immobilized Blanca for two years before she attempted to leave again.

Taína became her sustenance. The little girl grew, parroting happily as she scrambled through the house, her legs wobbly, her laughter flooding the air with its happy peals. She sucked her thumb constantly, obliged to take it out by the necessity to yell or eat. She wiggled when she heard music on her father's radio, which was on all day long tuned to a popular music station. She asked for "aba" when she was thirsty, and dragged an old cotton diaper to the kitchen where she waited impatiently for her water.

She retold fairy tales to satisfy her sense of justice and retribution. In her version of Little Red Riding Hood, the girl always killed the wolf by shoving a knife in his neck. Wicked stepmothers and stepsisters always wound up in the bottom of the sea.

Taína filled Blanca's days and nights with the transparency of acacia honey. Blanca took in little sips of air all day, caressing her love, immersed in its warm waters, never finding bottom. She absorbed it like a fragrance, and she was lost in the constant flow that held them together.

She knew that someday Taína would leave to take tentative steps in the world's marshes. She would be torn from her, because her weight could only bring them both down. Blanca knew it would hurt deep in her womb where the deepest pain was felt. Taína would hurt, too, although her pain would be sweetened by expectations. But that day was far away. Now, Blanca examined Taína's stubby little fingers, her dark curls, her broad forehead, her caramel skin, so silky and smooth, her fragrance of new leaves. Her heart rejoiced when she heard the tiny voice laugh, baring her little teeth, packed together like grains of corn. They clung to each other like vines, and grew strong with their love. Nothing could deprive her of this love. Not even the man with the yellow eyes. Not even the old woman who patiently awaited her return to the cage.

Often Taína exploded in tantrums. She screamed and kicked on the floor, her face a storm of anger. Taína would mark the world with her protest, she seemed to say, protesting ahead of time all she was destined to see. Her protest presaged breaking the enslaving tradition of her mother. Could Taína possibly go back to that first link in the chain of her mother's oppression? Where was the beginning after all? Was it Blanca, or Paquita, or Paquita's mother? Or did it go beyond these abject women to a past so far back she could never hope to reach it? Taína would someday hear stories of hunger, of cruelty, of want. Paquita's mother, forced at the age of twelve to live with a widower who had four children, one as old as the bride. A child forced to raise children and bear children. Then Paquita, the unfortunate first-born who was also female. As soon as she could walk, she, too, became a child forced to raise another woman's children. The bitterness of a lost youth remained with Paquita as she dealt with her own daughters and with Blanca. Could Taína break the pattern? Could Blanca?

Those four years of marriage slipped through time like a dreamless night. Blanca's days passed slowly, all identical, so that their mere tired repetition insured the emptiness of her future. She forgot each day as soon as it was over. She would not weave memories. She got up, worked in the office, returned home, had dinner, bathed her child, read her a story, and put her to bed. Then she would go to bed. She dreamed that she woke up, went to work, returned, had dinner, bathed her child, read her a story, put her to bed, and then went to bed herself. With time, she listened to the alarm clock ring and had no idea whether her reality was a dream or the dream her reality.

Until the acacia spoke one afternoon with its pythoness tongue.

"Wake up! Even Segismundo awoke," it said airily. "Though dreams are only dreams, all of life is not a dream. Wake up! Taína no longer grows in your dreams. Don't you realize that your dreams are lost in reality and their reality cannot be a dream. Wake up! Sorcery tires me, and I cannot speak in enigmas any longer."

The alarm clock awakened her irreversibly on Taína's third birthday. The child spent the day kicking and screaming on the floor. Blanca called the old woman who had waited and tended her cage. They agreed on a day and a time. Blanca remained awake.

The man was waiting for her, as he did every evening at quitting time. Blanca approached the car door, opened it, and scooped up Taína. She fled down the street cradling the child in her arms and hailed a taxi. The man was stunned into inaction. Blanca turned her face away when the taxi passed the man's car.

Paquita lived in a small but comfortable house now. She sat proudly in her rocking chair on the tiny porch, finally a proprietress of a house that faced the street. It was a definite step upward from the alleys and the lagoon. Paquita agreed to care for Taína. She would provide room and board for both for a weekly sum. Mutual sympathy never existed between Paquita and Taína. They tolerated each other because of Blanca.

The man hid behind bushes to spy on Blanca while she read on the porch or scrubbed the living room floor on Saturday mornings. He followed her to work, and at the end of the work day, she noticed his long green car waiting to follow her back home. If some incautious male co-worker walked out of the office with her, the man waited for Blanca to leave, then approached the victim, threatened bodily harm and demanded that he no longer seek the company of his wife. One afternoon, Blanca left work accompanied to the parking lot by her boss, who, after suffering the threats of the man, fired her the next day.

Blanca straggled from job to job. Even after the divorce, he continued harassing, removing one by one any rival who might approach her. Because if she was not his, he claimed, she would not be anyone's.

One night, when Taína and Paquita were already asleep, Blanca washed her face and applied some facial cream. Uncomfortable with her own reflection, she turned away from her bedroom mirror quickly. Ready to take her bathrobe off, she sniffed the scent of masculine cologne in the bedroom. Her heart sank when she recognized it. She poked her head under the bed and discerned a big dark figure. She jumped up, turned the light off quickly so the neighbors could not look in, and ordered him to come out.

"How did you get in here?"

"I have my methods. You know how it is, baby."

"Don't baby me. What do you want?"

"I want you. Just because we're divorced doesn't mean me and you can't get together once in a while, you know. Remember how we did it in the other house while the old woman was asleep?"

She glowered at the silhouette that grew more distinct with the dull light coming in from the street lamp. Her temples throbbed. But she was no longer a vulnerable adolescent.

"Get out of here!" she said in a low voice edged with frost. "If you don't get out of here right this minute, I'm going to scream so loudly my grandmother's not the only one who'll hear me. The entire neighborhood will. Then I'll call the police. The police will come, the neighbors will come, even the stray dogs will come after all the screaming I'm going to do. So get out now. I can't stand the sight of you. Get out, I said. Are you deaf?"

The man hesitated, uncertain about calling her bluff.

"I'm going to start screaming right now, I warn you," the words hissed tightly.

He left that night, but continued the onslaught. Now, regardless of whether he saw her with a boss or not, at every one of her jobs he approached her supervisors menacingly, accusing them of having an illicit relationship with his wife. Since the bosses were invariably married, he threatened to reveal this information to their wives. Fired again and again, Blanca considered her alternatives. She could fly to New York and lose herself among the masses. He could never find her there, although she was not entirely sure. She examined the possibility of immigration to Australia. She had read somewhere that the Australian government was encouraging the immigration of women with skills because of the high male-to-female ratio. No, it seemed impossible. Australians had racist immigration policies. Whichever the alternative considered, they all required substantial sums of money, and now she was not even employed.

As though through the pure desperation of her wanting it, an ad appeared in the help-wanted section of *El Mundo*. The Department of Justice advertised the opening of a secretarial position. She realized what this position meant. She knew that working in the Department of Justice would grant her freedom from the man's ceaseless persecution. She knew his weaknesses well. He would never risk a confrontation with lawyers, especially prosecutors. In the end, he was a coward. No, he would never dare.

Predictably, when Blanca was appointed to the job she sought, the man stopped following her for a few days. Blanca received a few phone calls at the office. Only static was heard on the other side. Confirmatory calls.

She thought the man had abandoned his mission. Then one morning while driving into Old San Juan, she glanced at her rear view mirror and noticed the green car behind her. Without hesitation, she pulled up to a young policeman on patrol at Muñoz Rivera Park. She showed him her ID card.

"Good afternoon, officer. I work at the Department of Justice and I need your help. You see that green car parked there?" she pointed a finger.

"Yes, señorita."

"That man has been following me, and I'm afraid he's going to hurt me. Could you talk to him and tell him that if he doesn't stop bothering me, I'll file a complaint against him at the Department of Justice?"

"Of course, señorita. I'll speak to him right away."

"Thank you so much, officer. I really appreciate your help."

"At your service."

He never followed her again. As soon as he felt threatened, he forgot Blanca and Taína. They became a cloudy dream, insubstantial, intangible.

# 22

Jorge bowed his head and with an elegant "at your feet, señorita," conquered Blanca with the gestures of a gallant gentleman of a past century. He had the fine, expressive hands of a pianist. It was obvious that he had handled nothing heavier than papers. Tucked in his pocket was a gold watch, attached to a belt loop by a gold chain. Tall, slender, handsome, and bold as the moon, he gleamed like a prince. Blanca could not believe someone like him existed. He belonged in the pages of the fairy tales she had read in childhood. When he spoke in his soft, steady voice, she felt comforted, safe. She imagined him in court prosecuting cases, sending all the evil people to jail with his intelligent arguments.

After four-thirty, when the office was empty of witnesses, they talked. He offered vistas of the world of a cultivated, educated, courteous gentleman well-versed in social amenities, vistas Blanca had never known before. When he engaged in philosophical, humorous, or literary conversations, she felt lost in the vastness of his knowledge. She listened to him raptly and picked up his heady scent of blossoms and roots and the smoke of fogs.

He was married with two children, so she banished thoughts of possibilities in her insomnia-ridden nights. Everyone slept then except Blanca and a neighbor who had been hit by lightning and suffered incurable burns. He was discharged from the public hospital to die at home. One night, he had attempted to throw himself from his second-story home. Lying with eyes open like the bottoms of empty cups, Blanca drowned the moans of the dying man with the thought of Jorge's name.

On Secretary Day, she woke up giddy with excitement. She wondered what had gotten into her when she knocked on his door. He looked up from his papers and smiled.

"Are you going to the party this afternoon?" she asked.

"Sure I will. A little late, though. I have to finish a deposition, but I'll be there."

"Will you dance with me once?" she blushed fiercely.

"Of course, Blanca. It'll be a great honor. In fact, I'll dance with you more than once."

At the party, Jorge approached her in his gray tailor-made suit. He extended a hand and said, "May I?" They danced *merengues* and *guarachas*. He swept her on the dance floor effortlessly, gracefully. Night fell. The orchestra mellowed, and they danced to the strains of old romantic *boleros*. Jorge closed his eyes, breathing deeply. He squeezed her hand, interrogating. She responded with a slight affirmative pressure on his. They danced to the door and walked quickly to his car. Twilight flickered on their backs.

Love struck suddenly once she no longer denied its possibility. She surrendered like a feather in the wind. He kissed her sweat-drenched face and pressed hungrily against her. Their naked bodies shone in the dark hotel room sparkling as they tumbled into bed. The ascent drove him breathlessly to the top. His culmination came quickly, too quickly. They lay still, a tangle of arms and legs. He pushed wet strands of hair away from her face and kissed her slowly and deeply, unhampered now by his desperate longing. Blanca, who only longed to be held, was finally content.

Nostalgic for something vague, something she had never experienced but believed existed, Blanca tried to understand her yearning for what lay dormant, undiscovered. Paquita mocked Blanca when she revealed her plan. How could she possibly work, go to the university, and tend to her daughter at the same time? It was sheer stupidity. Another crazy idea. If she studied and worked, when would she have any time to spend with her and take her places?

"You'll never amount to anything" was Paquita's final pronouncement. "You've already messed up your life. It's too late now."

When Blanca stayed up after ten to study for her university night courses, the usual hour at which the old woman retired, Paquita shut her light off, growling that she was wasting expensive electricity. Blanca bought a flashlight, hid under the sheets, and studied until late into the night. She rose early to work, her eyes stinging and ideas swirling in her mind.

In the Spanish Literature class, she pondered the problem of language as a natural or social phenomenon. She learned the meanings of philology, alexandrine, syllepsis, and *carpe diem*. She discovered that Unamuno was not an African protagonist of colonial history, and that to die like Icarus was preferable to living without attempting to fly. In Humanities 101, she learned that humanities does not signify a plurality of people, but the awakened consciousness of human beings and their situation, the formation of the human culture, the analysis of humans as historical beings. Through essays, *The Iliad*, lectures, and *El Mío Cid*, she became conscious of her condition. The world of ideas gleamed in her mind.

In a year, she entered the university as a full-time student, working part-time as a legal secretary and delivering newspapers at dawn every morning before going to work. The lingering suspicions and diatribes of her grandmother continued, as did her constant badgering about people who read too much becoming blind or crazy. To preserve her sanity and the ability to realize her goal, Blanca rented a tiny apartment where she could enjoy some privacy and peace. When she moved out, Paquita suffered fits of apoplectic rage and accused Blanca of being a wretched ingrate. She predicted that no decent man would ever marry her, a divorced woman living alone. Elena came to the rescue and agreed to care for Taína after school.

The romance survived Jorge's absence every night, on weekends, and holidays. His visits were limited to work days and after-office hours. Blanca's small apartment became a refuge disconnected from their daily routines. There, the lovers forgot the engagements and responsibilities of everyday living. At times they dreamed the impossible.

"One day we'll be together always, I promise, my love."

"When?" she asked full of hope.

"I don't know, but I adore you, and I want to be by your side always."

Crestfallen, she said nothing.

Taína refused to eat ants even when her best friend Ivette offered them fresh from the moist soil of her garden. Taína was born with an innate ability to explode an emphatic "no," adamant and unequivocal, when she did not want to participate in proposed adventures. She feared no one: not her mother, not Paquita, not Elena. Paquita once asked her to go to the store to buy a pound of bread while Taína was watching cartoons. Taína swung around impatiently and yelled, "Take it out of your nose!"

On the infrequent occasions when Paquita ran after her with a belt to teach her a lesson for some mischief, Taína escaped like a gazelle. The old woman chased the child until she was so tired that she had to sit down, halfheartedly promising a beating as soon as she rested. By that time,

Paquita invariably forgot the mischief and her threat. When Paquita took her siesta, Taína, who never slept during the day, got bored with herself, went up to the bed, pried one of Paquita's eyes open, and asked, "Are you awake, Grandma?" When Taína got angry, she yelled, "Bad words, bad words," believing it a terrible epithet. She was surprised that her outbursts did not earn her a spanking. She was always searching for some interesting mischief which would keep her occupied while she waited for her mother to pick her up at Elena's.

After years of mourning Margarita, Elena and Lito acquired a sedate mongrel who would not even bark at thieves. His laziness had its limits, though. At times when sleeping on the tiled floor, he sniffed danger in the air, opened a weary eye, and caught sight of Taína bouncing into the room. Whenever he saw her, he ran, tail between his legs, to hide under the dining room table. Undaunted, Taína crawled under the table and stuck toothpicks in his ears, hung paper clips to his whiskers, or forced his long tail into his mouth. For the sake of variety, she covered his head with a burlap sack, and when the dog stumbled blindly about, she shouted merrily, "Look, it's José Feliciano!" She bent over laughing, her voice ringing as she celebrated her own antics.

On her first day of school, Taina was required to take a timed test. In the test booklet there were drawings of fruit: lemons, bananas, apples. A teacher wielding a stopwatch instructed her to select which was largest and which the smallest. Taina cried, "But my favorite fruit is mango and there's no mangoes here!" She fumbled through the whole booklet crying, "Where are the mangoes?" until her time was up. She never finished the test.

In the second grade she became subdued with the burden of academic responsibility, which was becoming more onerous each day. When she emerged from Gautier Benítez Elementary School at dismissal time, she climbed up the hill of

Eduardo Conde Avenue, the afternoon sun burning the crown of her head. She carted a heavy canvas book bag, and at the top of the hill, streaming with sweat, she stopped to rest for a few minutes across from the cemetery. There, Don Francisco, the tombstone maker, offered her a glass of fresh water. She quaffed it gratefully and waved goodbye to the small old man who lived on the memories of his frustrated marriage.

Don Francisco was the protagonist of a legend that circulated throughout the barrio. Many years before, when he was a young man with thick black hair, he married a fifteen-year old girl from Cantera. The girl was innocent of the facts of life. Young Francisco, on the other hand, had the reputation of an ardent stallion, not because of the plurality of his romantic conquests, but because his member was of such magnitude he could barely hide it under the leg of his trousers. Wags maliciously countered that he had to tie it to his thigh, it was that long and fat. The young couple married, and after the wedding festivities, retired to a wooden one-room house with a four-poster bed, a white mosquito net above it, and several wooden crates to sit on. Timidly, the young girl lay in bed under the mosquito net in her white cotton slip. A candle was still lit on a crate, and she glanced nervously at the young man as he removed his pants. When she saw the size of his erect member, with her eyes round and wide like chamber pots, she leaped out of bed and climbed through a window. She surfaced out of breath and scared to death at the door of her parental home, where she swore, quaking with fear and disgust, that she would never go back. The reputation of Francisco's member assumed epic proportions, and it was said that thereafter no woman ever dared venture into his bed.

Too young to have heard this tale, Taína drank the glass of water offered by Don Francisco every afternoon, wiped her mouth with the back of her hand, and walked down Fajardo Street to Elena's mirador.

# 23

Blanca and Rosa met in a course on Cartesian metaphysics. They met David there, too. The three friends sat under the tropical palm trees to discourse upon the ultimate substance and attempt to solve problems of global scale. Three brains against a world, a triple conscience poised against an unconscious mass. David and Blanca proposed a socialist society. Rosa laughed at their naivete. Capitalism will never die, she said. Nor will social injustice, violence, or the degradation of man by man. Hobbes said it. "That's the nature of human beings. Every man is an island," she asserted.

David was a Baptist minister, an atheist, and a communist. He perceived his ministry as a way of achieving his social objectives. All he wanted was to help the poor from his humble church in La Playita. He married a young widow with three children. It was an act of social responsibility. He was propelled into marriage by the compassion he felt for her plight and his overwhelming desire to do good.

He had finished his seminary work, but still uncertain about the depth of the atheism that resulted from his studies for the ministry, he took philosophy courses at the university. Once convinced that his doubts had become his faith, he considered leaving the ministry. How could he perform his job without religious belief? He feared his flock would see right through him, that his nakedness would be revealed. If he did not believe in a god, what could he possibly say or do? Where could he find solace?

"Listen, David," Blanca advised him when she listened to the agonizing debates he carried on with himself. "Your life is tied to your parishioners, your political beliefs, your social commitment. Whether you believe in a god is irrelevant because your love for humanity, the consolation you give everyone, and your commitment to a better society is religious and certainly Christian. You accomplish a lot of good doing what you do. Maybe that's what god really is: an act, an act of unselfish love, commitment, giving."

David nodded and looked up at the palm fronds rustling in the breeze. "I may be condemned to doubt all my life," he said sadly. "You're right, I might as well stay in the ministry where I can do some good."

Rosa was in the throes of a tumultuous affair with a wealthy lawyer. Juan Carlos was the love of her life, she liked to say. An only child, he had "married" his widowed mother and proudly escorted her to the opera and ballet while Rosa languished in an apartment he rented for her in Río Piedras. He tried to compensate for his absence with lavish gifts of beautiful jewelry and designer outfits from the most elegant boutiques in San Juan. Rosa continually threatened to deprive him of her affection forever. Right this minute, she swore she would leave him unless he spent more time with her. He promised, thousands of times, but never fulfilled his pledges. Rosa railed against him in irate episodes. Juan Carlos escaped nimbly from the apartment before a shoe, a lamp, or whatever weapon Rosa had thrown, clobbered him as he beat a hasty retreat.

Blanca and Rosa immediately understood the congruency of their lives. Born in the Polvorín Barrio of Naranjito, Rosa was also attempting to wrench herself from her destiny. They studied together and talked about their men, the similarities of their lonely lives. Encouraged by the luck of having stumbled into each other, they read Plutarch's *Parallel Lives* and marveled at the ways their own lives had woven intricate paths, so different, yet the same, and how they pursued the same dreams. The joy they dreamed about, though, had an indefinite, elusive quality. No matter how hard they tried, they could not envision the colors of happiness.

The two friends agreed to ensure that Taína would become a strong, liberated, independent woman. But they never articulated how they would achieve this goal, and Taína was only exposed to the experience of two women who suffered the constant bitterness of their lovers' absences.

When they needed some recreation on Saturday nights, Blanca and Rosa drove down Ashford Avenue in El Condado while Taína slept in the back seat. They looked away uncomfortably when they saw prostitutes with skimpy dresses and faces painted for urban warfare accosting tourists. On Sundays, they would take Taína to the beach across from El Capitolio. The three waded into the warm waters of the Atlantic Ocean where the waves knocked them down, bottoms first, and drowned their laughter. When the mighty waves receded, they scrambled up, spitting sand, and rinsed their breasts in the shallow waters of the shore. Then they sat on a grassy knoll and looked out at the shimmering waters, whitecaps rippling across sandbars, until the sun set.

The two friends shared the sadness of daily desertion, living on the margins of their lovers' lives. Often they met at the university library with the best intentions of studying together, but inadvertently and invariably they were distracted by whispered dialogues about contraceptives, the persistent yeast infections that attacked them periodically, and their dissection of the mystery that is the masculine psyche.

"Men are incomprehensible," Rosa often said. "They're so different. There's no way the two sexes will ever understand each other. I think it's hormonal. If I were Juan Carlos, I would have married me by now. But he won't leave his mother alone in the manor, he says. And look at Jorge. He's incapable of divorcing his wife and marrying you despite his feelings for you. You know, sometimes I think that men are nobler than we are."

"Or more cowardly," Blanca sighed, believing herself capable of any sacrifice for her loved one. "I believe Jorge loves me, but he can only love me so much. He has no more to give."

"Oh, Bopa!" Rosa hunched her shoulders. She always called her friend Bopa when she was nostalgic or sad, conditions she suffered frequently. "How long are we going to put up with everything men put us through? It's not fair that we're here by ourselves, on a Saturday afternoon for goodness sake, waiting for them to have some spare time to see us. Sometimes I'm tired of being the one who always waits, the one who gives all, tolerates all. Since Juan Carlos' mother couldn't bear the fact that he's fallen in love with a woman without pedigree from a barrio in Naranjito, he's never told his family about me. So we can't share anything with his family or friends. He always takes me places where he's sure he won't run into people he knows. And all because he wants to spare his mother from anguish. You'd think I'm a lady of the night or something. But she would consider me a plebeian, which amounts to the same. I'm telling you, Bopa, every society has its caste system, and we belong to the lowest. We're the Puerto Rican untouchables.

"Have you calculated how much time we spend waiting for the phone to ring? Is that all we deserve? You'll see, we'll be old women, alone, without anyone, sustained by memories of the crumbs they threw in our direction once in a while. I hope that at least we'll have each other. I feel more certain of the possibility that you and I will end up living together than any promises Juan Carlos may make."

Blanca drew the words inwardly. She felt sad and angry, the two emotions that Jorge inspired most frequently.

"I've been waiting for years," Blanca said, "for a decision, a gesture, a slight nod of the head. I'm the woman he keeps on the side, the one who can't call him when she's sick in the middle of the night. I don't even know his home telephone number or where he lives. I've never asked and he never volunteers information about his personal life. I know that on weekends he goes horseback riding at his father's ranch. He likes to talk about that. I also know he's a chronic insomniac and rarely takes a vacation. But his daily habits are mysteries to me. So many ordinary things I don't know about him. What does he have for breakfast, what are his kids like, how does he spend a rainy Sunday? Jorge hasn't even met Taína. Isn't it incredible that the two people I love most don't even know each other? I love him deeply, but his silence in my nights really gets to me. We have a working-hour romance. It's a crippled and crippling relationship. It lacks the essential intimacy and details of daily living that truly unite a couple. Sometimes I ask myself whether I could live with him some day, there is so much about him I don't know. And a year ago, he had a vasectomy. That was a clear message I've refused to acknowledge."

They sat very still, thinking about the many subtle messages their lovers transmitted. Then they became aware of their surroundings. A very young woman was sitting diagonally across the library table. Having listened to their stunning conversation, she stared at them wide-eyed. Blanca and Rosa looked at the young woman's stricken face and, attempting to control their hilarity, rushed out.

"Imagine," said Rosa laughing, "what that girl must think of us. She's probably a virgin and has never heard anything like that. We're like characters in a soap opera."

"I'm going home. There's no way I can study with you around," Blanca said.

"All right, all right." Rosa ran to her compact car, a gift from Juan Carlos. "Call me when you're done," she yelled.

Blanca picked up Taína at Elena's house and called on her grandmother on the way home. Paquita had calmed down a bit after Blanca moved out, but she demanded a daily visit. "Whether it rains or thunders, it's your responsibility," she would say. Blanca pacified her with daily visits, running errands for her and, on occasional Sundays, taking her on drives to the country or the beach. Because for Blanca, Paquita's visit to her apartment would constitute a desecration of her sanctuary, she had never allowed her grandmother to cross her threshold, regardless of her many attempts to invite herself. In her minor rebellions, Blanca was rewarded by small victories.

The telephone rang when Blanca walked into her apartment. She knew it would not be Jorge. It was Saturday and late in the afternoon.

"Where were you, Bopa?"

"You know, the required visit to my grandmother."

"I'm so relieved my family lives quite far away and I have a good excuse not to visit frequently. Sometimes I miss Mami, but my father, he's another story. The less I see him the better. The moment I walk through the door, he starts his harangue against *independentistas*. He makes me real nervous, and you know I'm not a patient woman. At the blink of an eyelid, we're at each others' throats. My father's a rabid *Muñocista*. One day he slapped me because I accused his revered Muñoz of betraying the Puerto Rican people, delivering the island to Washington. Well, it's more accurate to say he sold it. Listen, that reminds me. Are you going to the FUPI demonstration on Monday?"

"Can't. I have work in the morning and then classes all afternoon. I signed the student petition though, but I can't miss classes. Are you going?"

"No, same problem. Got a killer History of Art exam on Tuesday. I'll spend the day memorizing slides. Well, call me tomorrow. Ciao."

Taína was watching a TV program on the endangered Bengali tiger when Blanca hung up. She should make something to eat and then work on the monograph on Franz Fanon's theory of violence that was due in a week. Suddenly, she felt a cold stab deep in the right side of her head. Images and dots drowned in a strident light that almost blinded her. She groped at the walls as she ran to the bathroom, retching. The pain worsened. She filled a glass with water and stumbled into her bedroom searching for some Fiorinal.

"What's the matter, Mamita?" Taína asked.

"Migraine again. Make yourself a sandwich and have milk with it, not soda."

She crawled into bed clutching her head. Taína, used to her mother's migraine attacks, drew the curtains and found some Fiorinal to give her. At times the overwhelming pain eclipsed all stimuli. But at other times, any stimulus—sound, light, smell—assaulted Blanca's senses. She covered her head with a pillow and cowered in her pain like a fly in a spider web, still, very still, until she fell into a black dream.

The mailman brought a manila envelope. It was big and heavy. Her heart missed a beat. A small envelope contained certain rejection, but this big envelope...No, she couldn't bring herself to hope. She ran up the stairs. In her apartment, she sat on the rocking chair and rocked slowly as she read the return address on the envelope. She hefted its weight on spread palms. She placed it on her lap and read her name. Yes, it was definitely for her. She rubbed her thumbs against the coarse paper. Harvard University it said. She realized she had been holding her breath and exhaled abruptly. She wedged the envelope under an arm and had a glass of water. It was a big envelope. There was hope. She tore the flap open, attacked by sudden impatience. She scanned the cover letter quickly, her eyes fluttered like feathered wings in flight.

Congratulations, it read. Accepted. Scholarship. She cracked an incredulous smile and kissed the letter many times. She had to tell Taína. Would she understand the significance of this? She must call Jorge and Rosa. There were forms to fill out, questions to answer. Was it possible, was it all possible? Or was it a dream? Or worse, a morbid joke?

Those who said she would never succeed swallowed their mocking words. Years had melted away, hundreds of books digested, dozens of monographs composed by the lamp on her solitary desk, abstruse lectures, seminars, vigorous dialogue, delivery of newspapers, typing legal documents, migraines, quarrels with her grandmother, a Magna Cum Laude degree. She had lived in a whirlwind during those four years. Finally, she was reaping a tangible reward. She paused before calling anyone. Frightened by the punishment exacted for her every joy, she folded her uncertainties in her heart and waited.

At midnight Rosa, drunk with pain, knocked on Blanca's door. She looked haggard, her eyes puffy and red. Juan Carlos took her to dinner to celebrate her graduation. During dinner, Rosa reminded him of his most important promise. Once she graduated, they would marry. Juan Carlos, still married to his mother, said the final words, the last words Rosa wanted to hear. It wasn't possible, he said. Not yet. Not ever, Rosa responded. She drove aimlessly through the solitary streets trying to reclaim her dignity and marshal some strength.

The two friends hugged under the clear sky. A sliver of a moon hung over them.

# 24

Winter crows pecked at bits of snow. A man trudges down the street in the wind-swept snow, his head humbled by the icy wind. The elm rocks its arthritic claws. It is warm in the common room, and though ill at ease in the room, I am glad not to be out in the cold. I turn away from the window and sit down to read.

I read *Caballo de Palo*. Absorbed in the long poem, I did not hear the muffled steps of a nurse approach. The nurse speaks to me in English. Since I am reading in Spanish, I think in Spanish and look up at the nurse's face. I cannot recognize what the woman has said. Several seconds tick by, and still I remain in a linguistic limbo. Then the nurse's words gather somewhere in my brain where they are recognized. I respond to the nurse's question, turn my eyes toward the frosted window, and suddenly feel very tired.

Snow makes me melancholy. It is laden with reflections of death. It brings back images of my arrival in this stark land, farther north than I had ever been, where something inside me has died.

Clasping Taína's hand and a letter of acceptance, Blanca arrived in Cambridge, Massachusetts, in what is called by many the Continental United States. The August afternoon was sweaty with thick humid air. Clouds tumbled over clouds. Through the taxi's window, Blanca and Taína scanned the new world that began at Logan Airport and spanned bridges, highways, and a river so long it showed them the way. Glassy buildings fired reflections of the sun. The air smelled different. Bitter, acrid. Blanca sneezed repeatedly.

They took in the tall buildings cut against the sky, feeling the smoky air on their faces. Sitting on Blanca's lap, Taína needed to touch her mother's skin and see the strange city through the same window. That way she was sure they would both see the same scenes, the same tones, the same people. They confirmed each vision with the perception of the other.

Taína's hair curled tightly in the hot breeze. On Brattle Street, a multitude of young people in T-shirts and shorts crossed the congested road or stood peering into the window displays of colorful boutiques. Restaurants and cafes enticed with their air conditioners. Reflections of water on the pavement reminded Blanca inexplicably of Jorge. He had taken them to the airport and met Taína for the first and last time. Jorge said he had a lump in his throat. He would miss her. He promised to find a way to visit her. Blanca kissed him, spun around, and rushed to the gate, weeping bitterly. She knew they would never meet again.

Night swooped down too soon. Blanca hardly slept, and at eight, she woke Taína. They washed in the common bathroom on the landing of the rooming house and settled in a cafeteria to have their breakfast. By the third day, when things either fail or are realized, the university housing office assigned them a studio apartment in a housing complex for married students.

When Taína returned from her first day at school, she brought home a schoolmate who only spoke English. Since Taína only spoke Spanish, Blanca was puzzled by the odd attraction that existed between the two which did not require the mediation of language. The friendship did not last long, as Blanca had anticipated. After the initial novelty of speaking in signs, the effort of making constant grimaces and gestures without achieving understanding became too much of a chore. To explain a simple idea was as difficult as explaining colors to the blind.

Taína began school in the jumble of enigmatic English sounds that found no dwelling in any receptive nook of her brain. She listened to her teachers and classmates whose speech was like a symphony of dissonance she was sure had been produced by a mad composer. The language battered against her understanding and only succeeded in giving her headaches. As the days and weeks and months passed, isolated sounds began to cling to her. Her newly-acquired awareness gathered the sounds in gradual recognition, and she hoarded them until her word-treasure burgeoned and each word became fused to a concept, a sound, and was finally learned. House, two, it's time for lunch, good morning, José can you see.

Her native language helped. She listened to a word and applied the rules she had created in her mastery of Spanish to the learning of English. She dove deeply into her experience of acquiring her native tongue. Entire phrases made sense, whole sentences understood. Then, after a period of silence and occasional futile warbling, she achieved the miracle of speaking in a different language.

At the Graduate School of Education, Blanca eased into the library stacks to read books on reserve and compose her papers. Her first class was in a large auditorium. It had something to do with education and social policy, though she was not at all sure what that meant. Although Blanca understood almost everything the professor said, she really understood nothing. She understood words and phrases. She knew what a sentence meant in its isolated grammatical context, but she did not understand the deeper meaning of his words.

It shocked her to hear students calling the bald, bearded professor by his first name. Certainly that lack of respect was due to his not wearing a tie. He also wore funny shoes that tipped forward. And then, adding shock to shock, the professor referred to a student as "the woman sitting in the third row!" How dare he call a lady "a woman?" Why was she not insulted?

Who were these men and women, professors and scholars, who held forth on educational equality, racial integration in the schools, qualitative and economic disparities of whites and blacks in public schools? What were they talking about? Blanca wondered. In her experience, public schools were equally mediocre. After all, only the poor go there. Or so she thought.

She dug into books, into professional and scholarly journals, into her own experience. She dug into newspapers and conversations of students and professors. She dug into the history of North American education and discovered an injustice so terrible she could not believe what her intellect told her. She dug deeper in the news media, in the conversations of people on the subway, and she was terrified by the turbulence, the chaos, the convulsion that existed in the city.

It was 1974, and a Federal judge had ordered the racial integration of schools. What kind of society required justice to be mandated? There were schools for blacks in black neighborhoods, schools for whites in white neighborhoods, and schools for Hispanics. In some schools boundaries gradually faded, and there might exist a mixture of races, though this was rare. Since segregated schools constituted educational inequality, the judge ordered Black and Hispanic students bused to white school districts and white students bused to so-called minority districts. No one was completely pleased with the court order. Not whites, not blacks, not Hispanics. White racists opposed racial integration with venom. In the streets of Boston, shots were heard and bloody battles were fought. It was a revolution. Racist insults brought on an unending uproar, vitriolic attacks, the crime of intolerance.

War was unleashed in streets and schools. Windows and heads were stoned, houses burned. Men and women, girls and boys, adolescents and teachers stumbled into the streets and shouted insults. Every crack of the city in chaos reeked of hatred and fear. Blacks were killed. Whites were killed.

Blanca and Taína were plunged into the murky world of minorities. They were considered less than white. They lacked something they never managed to define adequately. Was it whiteness, a Boston accent, Protestant or Irish surnames? What was it that earned them so much contempt? Why was their honor and dignity denied because they were foreigners and brown? Why were people color-coded? Blanca struggled to maintain her identity intact, not to fall into the madness of not being who she was. She refused to assimilate into a foreign entity, although the cultural invasion bludgeoned her mercilessly. Blanca felt imprisoned in a chunk of marble, and she clawed at the hard folds of her skin.

One morning, when she returned to her apartment to pick up a forgotten book, she found Taína sprawled on the sofa watching television.

"Why aren't you in school, Taína?"

The startled child, finding nothing to do or say, burst into tears, postponing, she hoped, her confession.

"Taína, has something happened? Tell me, child, you know you can talk to me. Say something," and she pulled a tissue from her handbag. "Come here." Blanca wiped her face, kissed her on both cheeks and rocked her daughter in her arms.

"Ay, Mamita, I'm so unhappy!" Taína bawled. Reluctantly she confessed her offense. She had been truant from school for two consecutive days.

Taína had gotten off the school bus on Monday afternoon. A gang of schoolmates waited until the bus pulled away. The burliest boy grabbed Taína's collar, shoved her on the sidewalk, and the gang punched her mercilessly. They called her Puerto Rican garbage, filthy spic, and other epithets she refused to repeat because they were so shocking. On Tuesday, the gang pummeled Taína again. They yelled words of loathing and cruelty. They accused her of dirtying their school with her spic stink. As she ran away, they chanted, "Taína's a dirty spic, Taína's a dirty spic."

Blanca hugged her. "Tomorrow we'll go to school together, and I'll talk to the principal. They can't let these things happen. Don't worry, everything will be all right. Isn't it true that Mamita always solves our problems?"

Taína nodded, though unconvinced that her troubles would soon be over.

Chins thrust forward, Blanca and Taína called on the principal. He promised to take care of the matter. During the rest of the week, he said, he would accompany Taína on the school bus. No incident occurred and the week seemed to end unremarkably. Then, on Sunday evening at nine, the phone rang.

"Is Taína there?" a young boy's voice was at the other end of the line.

"Who wants to speak to her?" Blanca asked suspiciously.

"Tell 'er if she goes back to school, me and my friends are gonna kill 'er."

Blanca called the police. They could do nothing except intercept the phone in case the boy called again. They could only interfere if someone hurt the child.

"All right, Taína, this is it. You're not returning to that school. Tomorrow I'll try to enroll you in the alternative school at Central Square. It's a public school with a limited number of students. They offer a humanistic education. Is that okay?"

Blanca spoke to the principal of the Cambridge Alternative School and met with teachers and parents who volunteered at the school. Everything seemed to be in order and the student-teacher ratio was such that someone would keep an eye on Taína. But Taína remained unconvinced that her woes would end soon. Taína was the only Puerto Rican in school. She had one friend, Rita, an Indian girl who lived in her building. Whites rejected her because she was dark, and blacks rejected her because she was not dark enough. Taína curled into herself the day she returned to the apartment and found a message smeared on the wall with red spray paint. The ugly words were, "Spics, get out. Puerto Rican pigs."

Blanca left school late because of detention duty and stopped at the library to check out the copy of *Don Quixote* she needed in order to tutor Moisés. It was snowing, but she had the morbid impulse to walk through the Brighton cemetery. It was a cold day. Austere pines and melancholy cypresses shrouded the slabs of inscribed stone in a sullen mist. Blanca trod slowly through this icy world where the wind swirled in a macabre dance. An absolute silence dug into her brain like a prolonged shrill. She held her breath, fearing that any movement might demolish the frosty calm that existed there. She thought of the cadavers lying under her feet, their flesh shrivelled, fulfilling a fateful cycle. She wondered what it would be like to open a casket and examine the dregs of life. Would she be able to find an answer there? Would she know, finally, what existence is, or more importantly, what it is not? The neat tombs looked pathetic in the midst of an incongruent order and cleanliness. The odor of dead flowers, snow, and marble took on a new dimension. It was the odor of decadence. Blanca shuddered. Her fear of death reflected her deepest wish.

Terrified of the danger that a sinister hand might shove her onto the subway tracks, Blanca kept her distance from the platform. Death could not be crueler. To die crushed, emptied, her eyes hollowed in purple cavities, members amputated by an iron machine. She was grieved by thoughts of death. She envisioned death as a truculent specter hovering over her head like a honed and impatient hatchet. Sometimes she woke up in the middle of the night with the horrible certainty that she would die. Death to Blanca was a brutal cut of the delicate thread of consciousness, coarse shears that snipped the link when least expected. If birth had been violent and absurd, death seemed even more undecipherable.

Entertaining thoughts of a horrid death, Blanca stared at the steel rails uneasily. A tall thin man, with half-closed eyelids as if in a trance, seemed very suspicious. She inched toward an apparently inoffensive older lady who possessively held a transparent plastic shopping bag full of trifles. On the opposite rails, a tunnel swallowed the trains in flight. Her train approached. She entered the clanging iron snake.

It was always annoying when there were no vacant seats. Holding on to an overhead strap, she slid her handbag under an arm and held on to her book with the other. The bodies were so crowded together, she could barely breathe. A young man smiled at her. She was too shocked to respond.

She felt disconnected from the packed bodies and crawled into a cocoon of alienation. She recognized none of the faces parading before her. These were faces drawn by alien experiences. Indifferent faces, ambitious faces, faces blemished by bitterness. When Blanca stumbled on a smile in this marsh of strangers, she was paralyzed by confusion realizing it was she who was foreign, alien, different.

She swayed back and forth holding the strap tightly. She had not mastered the game called living. She had lost her anchor in this disconcerting environment. She had no key to let her enter into a world of definite identities. She only had a map and she clutched it, searching through a cloud of uncertainties for a destiny that would fill her void. She suffered a searing split, not knowing who she would become. She observed her own movements indifferently, looking at herself from the distance of light. She stared at herself and saw a stranger.

The train stopped at Kendall Square, and the smiling stranger stepped out. The wheels squealed once more like a skinned cat. The train was still packed as it approached the last stop at Harvard Square. A little blond boy sat with his young mother. His sneakered feet dangled from the seat and he scissored them back and forth. Blanca thought of her own Taína. Years of maternity weighed her down. When she basked in Taína's delicate face, soft in its peaceful innocence, she shook her head to banish the visions of the tears that her daughter would inevitably shed, the baffling changes of puberty, the desecration of her unpolluted flesh during her first sexual experience, the brutal violence of maternity. Then, year upon year would bring deeper crevices. Furrows in her brow, lines gripping her honey-colored skin with a vengeance. Her breasts drooping with her buttocks and her hopes. And what would be waiting for her at the end of the way? Total disintegration.

Blanca examined her face in the dusty window and turned away. The train stopped and the urban hordes filed out. She mounted the dirty station stairs which led her to the dirty streets of the city. The grime brought back memories of the streets of her childhood where she explored the run-down shops of the South Bronx, her mouth watering at the sight of appetizing sweets exhibited in the shop windows. Her grandmother had often forced her into the cold darkness of winter to run errands which had consisted of furtively handing money and lists to the numbers' runner, shopping, doing the laundry, or taking warm food to her Uncle Tomás at the hospital. She had shivered under her threadbare coat, the cold wind piercing like a blade. To distract her fear of the dark and erase the eerie night noises, she had hummed the same tune over and over, head bent, hands shoved in her pockets, until she returned home. She had lived a forlorn life, lonely with disruptions and farewells. She wished she could divert this destiny from Taína. But sometimes she felt powerless to move under the weight of her pain. Maybe Taína would be better off without her.

That very night, with Don Quixote by her side, instead of deciding to teach Moisés the big words, she decided to die.

# 25

Miguel's shoeless shadow approaches, then recedes. His bare feet slap on the cold tile floor as he roams through the common room and hall. After his escape attempt, his shoes were never returned to him. Negative reinforcement they call it. Silvia and Castule, eyes riveted on the TV, follow the latest mindless entanglements of doctors and nurses in a soap opera. I look around. I try to concentrate on a book, but can't make any sense of the words. There isn't enough silence. I feel entombed in the rabble of routine and schedules. Nothing else seems to matter here, and I feel outside of myself like a lock without a door. The eyes of others look me over without recognition. I try to remember the *buenos días* the island had instilled in me, but I have no use for it here. Transparent as a piece of furniture, I recall my grandmother's words. She always called me a useless piece of furniture, and now, in the midst of beings who cannot see me, that's what I have become.

We sit for dinner and Celia listlessly picks at her food. I worry about her depression, her destructive thoughts not tempered by a will to live. I wonder whether her sense of defeat is fuelled by her treatment at the hospital. I look at her, bent over her plate, drowned in lethargy, and I am stirred by a sense of self-preservation. No one has suggested shock treatment for me, but I dread it. I am at the brink, at any moment, of having my freedom to decide taken from me. All Dr. Hackson would have to do is declare me mentally incompetent. I couldn't let that happen. Not when I'm so close to leaving this place. I must continue the lies and the deceit to get out.

Before we know it, the meal which constitutes the culminating part of the day is over. The evening ritual augers an illusory rest. More patients crowd around the TV. Daffy, toothy mouths spew promises of happiness from the screen if the sink is scrubbed with Brand X powder. Marital bliss is guaranteed by removal of ring-around-the-collar. The purchase of a slinky car secures a scantily dressed blond. Hemorrhoids can be shrunk, the mouths grin, and I remember how poor women in Puerto Rico applied hemorrhoidal cream to their faces to tighten their skin and make them look younger. The poor woman's cosmetic surgery. The toothy grins flash in sheer delight. See, they say, you can be as happy as we are. As long as you follow the rules and buy buy buy bye bye.

I walk away from the loud-mouthed peddlers, preferring to read or listen to the buzz in my head. Miguel smokes and wanders around the room, unable to sustain his attention on anything, and distracts me from my thoughts. His bare big toes look like light bulbs.

Visiting hours begin, and Nina's son comes into the room to fulfill his obligations to his braying mother. She is unusually quiet this evening. Other patients converse with family members and friends. But Nina's son stares at the patients uneasily, sitting at the edge of his chair, squeezing his fingers. He behaves like a captive ready to climb the scaffold. I am examining the man's expressive hands from my chair when the hall phone rings. It rings three times, like that night when my grandmother called me long distance.

"Hello, hello. Do you know who it is?"

"Of course. Give me your blessing."

"May God be with you."

"How are you?"

"So so, as usual. I bet you don't know where I'm calling from."

"From Puerto Rico?"

"No, my child, I'm in Ramón's place."

"You're in New York?"

"I came last night and gave my sons the surprise of their lives. Heh, heh, heh."

"I can imagine. What are you doing in New York?"

"I want to investigate things to come live over here."

"With my father?"

"No, of course not. You know that boy lives alone in an apartment that's so small even the cockroaches have trouble moving around. And Salvador, he doesn't want to hear anything about my staying here. Says he won't allow me to sell the house in Puerto Rico. But, like I told him, I have a power of attorney he himself signed years ago, and I can do whatever I feel like with that house."

"Tell me, who will you be staying with in New York?"

"No, no, my child, I'm not staying here. I'm going to live with you."

"With me?"

"Yes, yes, of course. All my sons tell me the same thing. I'm too old and sick all the time, and I should be with someone who can take care of me. They say that, since you're the only girl in the family, it's your duty because they're men, and they don't know anything about these things. So I'm getting ready to move in with you."

"Listen, this can't be decided so easily. You don't know what my situation is like here. I'm studying and working very hard now. For goodness sake, I have to start working on my thesis soon. I have a lot of pressures, both at work and at school. You just can't live with me right now. I'm sorry, but you should have discussed this with me first before making up your mind."

"What? What are you saying, you wretched ingrate? After I gave you your life, after I gave you your very being, you abandon me in my old age. After I saved you from a certain death which is what would have happened had you stayed undernourished in that barrio of Arecibo. That's how you repay me, right? You turd. I should've known you'd treat me this way, abandoning me now that you're doing well over there. You're too good for me now, is that it? Now that I'm old and sick I'm of no use to you, right? Now that you're going to a fancy university, you don't want anything to do with me. You shit. May God listen to me and may your daughter make you suffer as much as you've made me suffer, because he who kills by the sword, dies by the sword. May you meet a bad end!"

Click.

I shake my head and refuse to remember. Not now. My many layers of skin slough off painfully, one by one. I become the coarse texture of dreams, the clay amphora brimming with grievances, thick as lard. I am myself and I am another. I can as easily look into myself as step out and examine my own skin from afar. Yet I cannot define what I see, and in that inability rests the tragedy of my inexistence. In the clatter of cultures and languages that clash outside, I drown in anomy. I dig constantly within, to peel my layers of pain. My pain and my past are one.

Nina's son sweeps by, having fulfilled his fifteen-minute visit. He glances over his hunched shoulders to make sure he does not suffer a surprise attack from a patient. He beats a path to the door. Taína and Rosa won't visit tonight. I miss them, especially my daughter. Taína always arrives smiling, exaggerating the boring lectures of her teachers with grimaces, inflections and gestures, just to make me laugh.

Celia talks to her husband Juan, who gestures angrily. In a world defined by walls and slow-moving clocks, Celia is a link to myself. Sometimes we talk about Puerto Rico, afraid of poisoning our memories with words injudiciously spilled inside the imperious walls of the hospital. Concerned that a nurse might hear and order us to speak English because "You're in America now," as though Puerto Rico were in Australia, we whisper in Spanish, the language of music and stars, when the lights are switched off and before the sleeping pills drag us into our relentless nightmares.

Celia's husband leaves the common room with long strides. For a second, he sucks the light from the hall with his corpulence. When he crosses the threshold, Celia comes over and sits next to me.

"How's Juan?" I ask.

"He's very well."

"What's the matter, Celia? Are you all right?"

"I don't know, I don't know," she holds her head in both hands. "I can't think. I feel so empty inside. It's a painful emptiness. I don't know how to explain it."

Celia wrings her hands. She is on the verge of tears. "Juan just told me that he hired a very nice girl to care for the children and do the housework. She lives at home now, so he found a substitute for me. I'm sure she's young and pretty. He says I shouldn't see my children for the moment because they're adjusting to all the changes. And the psychiatrist agreed with him. It's not therapeutic, especially now that they've increased my shock therapy sessions."

"Oh, no, Celia, that's awful. How many more treatments do you have?"

"I don't know. The psychiatrist, what's his name, I forget, told me, but I forgot that, too."

"Don't give up, Celia. I'm sure you'll feel better soon. You never know."

"That's right, I don't know, what's-his-name doesn't know, no one knows. All I do know is that I've lost everything, even my dignity. What dignity can there be in a mind like mine? There's no dignity in a body convulsed by electric shock. I lost all that's important to me. I lost control over my own life, my own destiny. There's nothing left."

"Listen, Celia, don't give up now. You have so much to offer. You'll get well and live the life you want to live, with your children supporting you all the way. Your life is so precious."

Celia looked at me, eyes brimming with sorrow. "It takes a lot of courage to live with this pain. I don't think I'm that brave."

"Yes, you are. You have to be. Maybe someday you won't feel the pain any longer and can enjoy being alive."

"How about you? Don't you want to die, too? You tried to kill yourself, that's why you're here."

"That's true, I do think about dying. All the time. But you know, sometimes I ask myself, why, if I want to die, have I struggled so hard to live? That's a mystery to me. There must be a part of me that refuses to give in. Despite the pain."

"You have the courage to live with the pain. I don't," Celia says and gets up. She has a distant look. "What can I do, Blanca? No, don't say anything." She waves her hands in front of her. "No one can tell me what I should do because I have no will to do anything. I've lost even that." She turns away and heads toward her room.

I want to comfort her. Knowing there is no possible consolation, I try anyway. Celia is in bed staring at the ceiling. The lights are off. I sit next to her and hold her hand. I look at the darkness beyond the window bars and think about the world out there for a moment. People. Shelter for people. Cars for people. Stores for people. Parks and movies for people. People come and go like fish swimming in dark waters. In the room,

Celia and I defy the ocean out there. But in doing so, we are smothered while the people outside can swim.

The nurse comes at nine.

"What're you two doing here in the dark?" she asks, and switches the light on.

"Just talking." I wrinkle my forehead and squint at the stark light.

"Time for your medication. Then you'll rest quietly all night and not bother anyone."

I understand perfectly well the nurse's concern. I swallow the pill with a gulp of water. Celia takes hers and turns to the wall. At ten on the dot the lights go out. The nurses check each room, making sure that everyone sleeps.

"Good night," I say, but Celia doesn't respond.

"Are you okay?" I persist.

"I'm just trying to sleep. Don't worry."

"If you need anything, just call me. All right?"

"I will. Good night, Blanca."

I plunge into my dreams quickly. I stand in a room so brilliantly colorful it hurts just to look at it. I crash to the floor when fragments of red walls float by and wispy faces appear plastered to the ceiling, laughing. On the floor, I roll my eyes up and admire the reds, blues, greens, all primary colors of happy brilliance. The floor quakes and the walls float with the furniture stuck on them like decals. Then naked terror saturates me, and I can find no escape. I try to scream, but an invisible force encircles my throat and squeezes hard. Like a tornado, the force lifts my legs and crashes me into the ceiling, flattening my chest against an iron blackness. Entangled in my nightmare, I listen to my own voice urging me to wake up, wake up, but the steely fangs of the force dig into me. My face wet with tears and perspiration, I escape the terror somehow. I land on my feet in the middle of the room, heart beating like a loose board in a hurricane. I turn around taking in my surroundings. I see a dresser and look at it in confusion. Where am I? Where have I seen this? It looks familiar. But what is it? I notice the chair next to the bed and a fold in my brain recognizes it as a chair, a chair I have seen somewhere. But where? Where am I? Where am I?

A delicate light comes like a mist into the room. Garrulous birds welcome the dawn. I don't know how long I've been standing next to my bed studying the chair, the dresser, the window, sinking into the emptiness of my memory for some indication which would help me recognize my surroundings. My eyes dart uncontrollably from one side of the room to the other. Then I tip my head gingerly toward Celia's bed. The blanket is the color of wet sand. Under it, I see Celia's slight figure. A black stain darkens the blanket. The stain drapes to the floor. Daylight enshrouds me now, and the chirping birds are quiet. Silence resonates through the room. Terror clings to my throat like thorns. I try to wrench myself from my own body and fly like a frightened butterfly toward the elm. My eyes are struck with fear. My lips peel back. I scream and fall in the puddle of blood that lies so very still.

Secured with leather straps to the bed, I see them take her body away. I fight to stay awake despite the injected tranquilizer. I will not surrender. I must stay awake and drink in the blood that clings with its mordant smell to my skin and seeps into my pores. The caked blood on my face and hands feels heavy, like a burn. Celia's blood demands life and becomes my own.

Thinking I am asleep, the nurses talk about Celia openly. She had filched a glass from the dining room and hid it under the pillow until the nurse distributed the sleeping pills. She pretended to take the pill, but didn't. When she was certain the nurse was gone and I was asleep, she wrapped the glass in a towel and cracked it against the wall. I must have been in the midst of my own hellish nightmare not to have heard anything.

I can imagine how she does it. I know too well how it feels. The sense of inevitability, the impotence of even one's own children to prevent it. The relief. I can see her executing her self-immolation.

Her heart beats like a drum when she pulls the covers to her waist. She gropes for her wrist. She holds her breath and slashes the veins of one wrist. Quickly, before her strength wanes, she passes the bloody shard to her other hand and slashes deeply again. She draws the blanket over her head with blood-drenched hands. Under her shroud, she feels the throbbing pain of her wrists and her heart stammers wearily. An icy chill encases her and she is blind, swimming quietly in a cloud of ice. Her brain attempts a mutiny, but tires of raising unheeded warnings. She slips into darkness and sleeps.

They remove the straps, and I am free to amble aimlessly in the common room. I look out the window at a patch of blue sky. I lose myself in it, imagining the contours of freedom. Is Celia free now that she's dead? Free from the wounds, free from the shackles of hurt?

I wonder if I have the courage to live with the pain.

# 26

Winter, recalcitrant as an old man refusing to die, lingers on for unending chapters. Tulips blossom late, but finally spring explodes with color and warmth. During my confinement, winter has melted into spring. The sudden warmth comforts me, although the hibiscus in my room refuses to flower and *coquis*, tiny as cowry shells, remain alive only in my memory. Nurses bristle with professional efficiency. I watch them and wonder whether it is possible to be human in a uniform.

Patients in the common room are agitated this afternoon. Everyone says it's spring fever. They all want to go out and breathe the gentle air. Nurses are hard-pressed to keep the patients under control. Everyone is jittery, unsettled. Except me. I feel peaceful. Odd. My time is up, and I'll leave the hospital tomorrow morning as soon as Dr. Hackson signs the liberating documents. His last act of power over me.

Dr. Stevens, the resident psychiatrist, offers his congratulations, but not before launching into a tedious lecture with specific instructions for appropriate behavior in the outside world. As though I were a child. Or had been in here for decades. Dr. Hackson wants to see me in his private practice in Boston. He shouldn't hold his breath, for I never want to see him again. All I want is to return to my apartment with its dusty books and the odor of old cooking that clings to the walls. I want to hug Taína, absorb her aroma of loved child. We will take long walks in the park holding hands, recapturing laughter.

I hope that someday she will understand what has happened. I hope she will have the strength to overcome her own anger and relinquish the guilt that anger engenders. So that she may forgive and live on, unencumbered by the inevitability of patterns, the tyranny of chains.

My odd sense of serenity vanishes, and I feel edgy. In the bathroom I undress and carefully fold my clothing on a wooden bench, tucking my underwear under the skirt. The hot shower pounds my neck and shoulders. I relax a bit. I dress quickly and start packing. Standing by Celia's bed, which is still unoccupied by a new patient, I smooth the naked pillow. I can still smell Celia's blood.

I lie on her bed and cover myself with the blanket that soaked up her sorrow. I breath in the remnant of Celia's humor and, in a sudden mood shift, plunge into a deep despair. Anger washes over me. I am dismayed that some patterns in life persist: Cruelty, betrayal, loss, madness, death. Always there, incarnated in people all around us. Always the struggle to destroy what would destroy us. Destruction against destruction. The only way to survive. And to live, for what? For the struggle? It's so much easier to die. Too easy.

At five I sit at the dining table. Miguel washes down his food with long gulps of water. Silvia listens to Castule, who whispers urgently in her ear. Nina does not remember that she had not eaten yet, and she walks away to the common room expecting her son's visit. A nurse leads her back and sits her at the head of the table. By now Nina has already forgotten she had thought she had already dined that evening.

An undercurrent of excitement animates the table when the other patients join us. Everyone chats energetically during dinner; even Silvia contributes hoarsely to the din. I can barely eat. At seven Taína arrives. Like two conspirators, we bunch into a corner to plan my departure.

"If you want, I'll skip school tomorrow and pick you up."

"No, it's not necessary. I want to leave here on my own two feet, without leaning on anyone. I came here humiliated, but I intend to leave with some dignity."

"Oh, Mamita, but I don't want to go to school tomorrow. I'll be so nervous. The day will seem like a century, waiting to go home and see you there."

"Well, I have a suggestion then. In the morning, instead of going to school, go home and wait for me there. Then we'll have the whole day to celebrate. All right?"

"Yeah, we can eat at the Chinese restaurant and I'll give you the present I made for you in carpentry class. Oh, Mamita, I'm so happy you're coming home. I hate this place."

"It's almost over. You have the key to the apartment, don't you?"

"Yes, it's at Rosa's. I'll ask her for it tonight."

"Visiting hours are over. Be careful on the subway. See you tomorrow."

*"Hasta mañana, Mamita."*

I smile before falling asleep, drifting gently into a deep black hole. I smell the scent of clay, thick and wet with dew. Gradually I am enveloped by enormous petals, smooth as midnight. The snow is gone, and I cleanse my skin of harshness. In my nudity, I no longer dream.

I have only coffee for breakfast, to keep me alert. I pick up my suitcase, full of books, drawings, and unsent letters. I sit at the edge of the bed and wait for Dr. Hackson to sign the release papers. Dr. Stevens drops in to say goodbye.

The nurse walks me to the door. I step out of the psychiatric wing and the massive door clangs behind me. I walk down the long, waxed corridor. I pause a few seconds in front of the outside door, the final door, the door that will open all doors. I push it open and feel the warm air on my face.